MW01139754

ELITE:
MOSTLY
HARMLESS

by

Kate Russell

Published by Fantastic Books Publishing
Cover design by Heather Murphy

ISBN: 978-1-522822-75-2

Based on the space trading game
Elite: Dangerous by Frontier Developments.

I dedicate this story to 811 strangers from the internet.
I wrote it with the sole purpose of entertaining you.
I hope it does.

Credits

These credits are broken down into various levels of support, for each of which I am truly grateful.

Revenge killing:
These charming souls pledged the most out of all my backers, for the pleasure of naming a character whose fate was to die a grisly death.
Dave Vint
Glen
Sullivan
The myTalky team Neil, Woz, Tor and Dan

Nosy Parkers:
This wonderful crew have been by my side every step of the way with advice and support in my Google Plus 'Nosy Parkers' forum. As well as offering support and encouragement they have helped me massively with certain creative points too. Thank you, all of you.
Marc Goldman
Matthew
Benson Paul
Lewis Anthony
M. Olver
André Michael
Czausov Stewart
Forgie
Phil
Clarke
Simon
Maher
Stephen
Usher
Robin "SubWolf"

Beckett Kevin

Gilmartin

John Urquhart

Ferguson Simon

McBride Commander

Sharky

Creatively challenged super fan:
This group completely blew me away with their generosity in pledging to Elite: Mostly Harmless for no other input than just a mention in the credits… so here it is – and by the way you rock!

Mika Peltola

Darren Bowles

Barry Wright

Steve "Konimai" Morgan

Programify Ltd

Richard Allen

Nick 'Cyber Pig' Roberts

Marcel Schön

Gareth Lewis

Digital Divas:
These backers named a character and gave me some personality traits to include. It was a lot of fun developing these characters and weaving them in to the plot.

Alex Guha

Andrew

Wright

Richard Ansell

Julian Crisp

Commander Kevin Jameson

Random input backers:
Bill Irving wanted me to include a 'special electric guitar'

Roland J. Veen suggested a venue: 'Anna & Roland's Zen Garden' Terry Walton asked for a mention for his 'Wayout Walton Westies'
Commander Hieronymus Drake threw me a massive curve ball with a request for 'a stuffed meerkat'
Andrew Sayers wanted nothing more than to see Angel spend time in a bar in Slough – and who am I to argue with that?

Creatively challenged enthusiasts:

With no more spots for random input these brilliant people still decided to pledge at the level for just a thank you in the credits. So, THANK YOU!
Stefan
(NightFlyerMD) M
Michael Segal
Lee Jordan
Graham
Jones

All my generous backers:

The great unwashed readership of Elite: Mostly Harmless. I thank you all for your support and hope you enjoy this book that you helped create.

A. Mellor, Kurt J Klemm, Keith Sanderson, Roman Mironenko, Arne Lofthus, Hakan Svahn, Konstantin Goreley, Ilkka Ahola, Sigbjørn Kjetland, Chris Luke, Jim Collins, Aidan Thomson, Jeffrey A Bristow, Jonty Campbell, Wayne Nicoll, Terence John Walker, Michael Cooper, Paul Maunders, Richard Thomas Harrison, Stuart Godbolt, John Abel, Chris Lepley, Francis Whitehead, Victor Tombs, Christopher Blair, Paul Hart, Paul Reynolds, Nicholas Bucksey, Steffan Westcott, Steph Wyeth, Alexander Saunders, Andrew Davis, Lee Musgrave, Dan Green, Stoo Collins, Spike, Gabriel Green, Bill Heron, Frank (the old-timer), Shane Gleeson, WotNoName, Ian Miles, Tink Graham Tinkler, Hobdonia, Dave Brooks, Michael Brookes, Muttley, Jeremy Curtis, Emteec, Andy K, Spacial Katana, Chris Benson, Barry Neville, Elliott MacQuien, Pog Crawf, Dave Clarke, Rob Lowe, Chris Jordan, Carl Agnew, David Widdick, Mike Large, Peter Govan, DJ Fozza, Edward Farglebiter, David Scott Gaipa, Ari Abraham, Liam Rafferty,

Ned Ludd, Jimbo Jones, Justin Bowdidge, Anthony Scicluna Valentino, Knight Drei, Robert Pearce, Mark Harper, Kenric Hamerstein, Deusx_ophc, Chand Svare Ghei, Simpsoid, Adam J Purcell, JPS IT Ltd, Mike Clarke, Get Running, Martin Theiß, Andrew Jay Nicholls, Lars Nørregaard, Joel Edvardsson, Michael Warsop, StarkMischief, Damien Letham, Arve Haugland, Frank Tifino, Brian Logsdon, Kaji, Kenneth Johansson, SCL411, Michael Rozdoba, Robin Barnard, Michael Gresswell, Juan Rial, James Clark, Marianne Bormann, Andreas Meyer, Tal, Martin Gear, Mr Bryan Mark, Wilde, Kimberly Seo McAfee, Kash Farooq, Charlie Michael Jonsson, Giles, Peter Augustin, Matthew Abel, Jack Anderson, Royston Craig, Derrick, Jelle Veraa, McVillan, Alec Stevens, Majogu, Gordon Macleod, Eamonn Coffey, Bifford the Youngest, Detective William Hilditch, Gromit, Tycho, Jedra, Darren Lloyd Webber, Louis Michael Digby, Russ Brack, Andy Piper, SocialSafe, Alexander Tutass, Gareth Knipe, Andy Long, Peter Young, Rasmus Sindberg, londondesigner, Marcus James Adams, Joanna Sefton, Gavin Smith, Allen Bell, Waffoo, Stud Hillshire, Becky Scott, Iain Davidson, Staffan "Mad Swede" Tj, Iain C Docherty, Richard Morris, Steven Lockett, StuDo, Mick Freed, Matthew Ash, Colin Andrew Dunwoody, Duncan Irvine, Brother Dave (Keeper of the Holy Data Book), Tim Hawkins, David Berquist, Gavin Udall, Lee Andrew Hardy, Philip Harris, Brent 'bos' Sinclair, Zar Peter, Bruno, Hammer, Devil "Rienkar" Moscatelli, Luc Bernardin, Richard Hicks, Paul Murphy, Mark Cowan, Paul Collins, Stoker, Andrew J Clark, Guy Adams, Anthony Stiller, Michelle Zimmerman, Toby Bates, Stephen Varey, Sloma, Ian Collings, JabbleWok, Beth Rushton-Woods, Colin Barker, Shao, Zoe Peters, Jix, Dalkev, FlapperGirl, SchlapStar, Commander Rowan Wagstaff-Weston, Steve McGarrity, Kram-Tomat, Jeremy Cerda, Spooksta, David W. Weaver, Frank Haussmann, Lucas Crocombe, Barnaby Madgett, Robin Wemmenlöv, Basnom, Guy Thomas, Daniéll, Gareth Kennerley, Dan Keating, Exobyte, Dr Phillipe Roden, redhotrobbo, Kimondo, Klaas van Gend, Patrick Breen, Laura Shearing, Flat Rabbit, Becci Rainbird, Amxitsa, Laura Kaye Tomlinson, asteroid Ogier, Christopher Mueller, Richard Parkes, Andrew Carter, David Aldridge, Joel Francois, Nick Homes, Hadley Robert Denton, Mark Wilkes, Harry Hausenogger, Swinders, Jon Lean, Perriard, Jay Watson, Peter Gerrard, Pete Bramley, Drew Wagar, Jurriaan "Voyager_NL"

Wittenberg, Craig Gormley, Simon Green, Simon McLucas, Cloudwork, Sean Houlihane, John Lambert, John Whitehouse, Michael Lefevre, Darren Rees, Tim Palmer, Jon Baker, Luke Parsons, John Osmond, Shadow Stalker, Hugh Cowhead, Gregg Chamberlain, Richard Deniz, Joerg Ritter, Jakob Aabel Østergaard, Nick The Geek, Rupert Wood, Matthew (Mad Dog) Barker, Hans Christoffer Sandnes, Stefan Plagemann, Robin Layfield, Lieutenant Commander Rouse, Gunnar Högberg, Drew Griffiths, Tom Meades, Morten Nyrup, Abey Campbell, Michael Bree, MogMartin, Simon White, Cmdr Jynx, Jim Kirk, AnthonyV, Jan Gehrer, Kaynary and Zannalov, Karl Goodloe, Andreas Gustafsson, Styggron, Stephan Ditz, Jeff Petre, Phil Taprogge, Aiden Montgomery, Peter Barrett, Andy "Codfish" Harker, Anthony De Souza, Kam Ho, Simon Foley, Karim Kronfli, Sten Lindgren, Nevikson, Will Lowe, Jonathan S. Chance, John "polymorp" Spence, NumptyDo, Kaserei, Thomas Kolbe, Tim Elwell, Holger Peters, Accalia de Elementia, Jürgen Schmidt, Fusion, Tom Ryder, Sonya Fireclaw, Dave Castle, Kevin Reilly, Rob (Wrongway) Lister, Leif B. Nielsen, Don "Rico" Purdy, Andrew Clucas, Jeff Moore, John Morgan, Andrew Holmes and Duncan Gray.

Author's Note:

I was once cornered by a disciple of the Church of Scientology in a shopping centre in Slough. It was a rainy, Tuesday afternoon and his strategy to tempt me into the fold of the religion was to make me realise how rubbish and unfulfilled my life was. The short interview with the weasel-faced man, conducted under the shelter of a Greggs Bakery doorway with the smell of fresh sausage rolls wafting around my face made me realise two things: I have a pretty awesome life, and I never want to go back to Slough.

The Slough of Despond in John Bunyan's allegory The Pilgrim's Progress (1678):

'This miry slough is such a place as cannot be mended; it is the descent whither the scum and filth that attends conviction for sin doth continually run, and therefore is it called "the slough of despond": for still as the sinner is awakened about his lost condition, there ariseth in his soul many fears, and doubts, and discouraging apprehensions, which all of them get together, and settle in this place; and this is the reason of the badness of this ground.'

Chapter 1

Angel rebooted the nav-panel as she watched the riveted maw of the space station hurtling towards her through the heads-up display.

'Hope, don't fail me now,' she said through gritted teeth as she grappled with the roll and yaw levers, scissoring them apart at the same time as pumping on alternate thrusters to jiggle her rear end into line.

Hope. That was a laugh, thought Angel with about as much humour as a hologram in a power cut. Her mother had named the Cobra *Hope Falls* after the district she grew up in back on New Saturn, forty light years away. It often seemed like more of a narrative to Angel than a ship's name.

'You need to straighten up Commander, and you're coming in too fast.'

Angel could hear the rising tension in the controller's voice as she thumped the power supply, cursing at it through tight lips. It crackled indignantly and the nav-panel finally winked on again, the holographic view of her approach wiring itself back together on the dash right in front of her eyes.

'I know. Calm down Rachel. I just lost my eyes for a sec. Everything's under control.'

Angel used her left foot to toe the thrusters into reverse. Engines roared and the outer hull moaned. 'Don't expect me to dock from this angle without hammering the shields,' it seemed to be saying.

'Shit!'

Angel stamped harder on the thruster and leant into the starboard roll. The irony was if she could get the damn thing into port any time soon without busting up her equipment she might be able to afford a new docking computer; her last one had been knocked out in the backwash of a kinetic blast when she'd jumped out of hyperspace right in the middle of a raging battle between an Imperial Cruiser and a band of heavily armed pirates.

'Err … Commander Rose …'

She could see the engineer's face through the control deck window now, bleached out by halogen lamps and worry. Neon ad-hoardings outside the window screamed at Angel to "GET RUNNING LEAN WITH JPS EMTEEC-

EXOBYTE SCL411 SPIKES TODAY!", or "INSIST ON ANTHONY COLIN'S TAL-TIES FOR UNBEATABLE DENTAL FUSION!" They flushed the pale face in the control window on and off with vivid red as her dark eyes flipped back and forth between the desk and the rapidly approaching vessel. Her equally red lips made an 'o' that looked like it was expecting trouble.

Angel checked her velocity.

'Yeah, you'd better nip into the airlock Rachel, just in case.'

Resigned now to at least some structural damage she flipped a couple of switches and reached for her EVA helmet, twisting it into place around her neck. It was old and grubby but if push came to shove and she breached the hull at least she wouldn't waste a remlok survival mask too; those things were painful expensive to recharge. The helmet hissed and her ears popped as the bay controller retreated behind several feet of solid lead. She was on her own now as she hurtled towards the cavernous docking hangar.

Her arm muscles burned, the atrophy of three months in space making it much harder to stay in control as she fought to keep the ship's rotation in absolute sync with the station. As little as two-degrees off and you're vapour; even deploying an escape pod would be pointless as it would just ricochet off the edge of the letterbox entrance to the spaceport, cracking open like an egg as the rest of the ship exploded about your ears.

She flicked her eyes to the console. She was half a degree off, tops. The worst, the absolute worst she could do was fracture the hull. But she hoped her ship was tougher than that.

It usually was.

The entrance screamed towards her through the HUD but she held her course and switched her thruster foot to the top of the pedal, ready to tap it into neutral. She was coming in hard and fast and burning way too much fuel but she'd landed worse approaches than this. You might say it was her speciality.

She flipped the engines to neutral and immediately stomped on the wing flaps with both feet. There was a loud groaning sound as her ship scraped through the slotted entrance of the dock. A fuse on her console popped with a spray of electricity and the portside aft-shield indicator sunk to fourteen percent. Her heart sunk with it. *There goes a stack of creds*, she thought. But then the scraping sound turned into a ripping sound she wasn't so familiar with. She craned her neck to the left just in time to see a data-band aerial go flying off into the vacuum of space, trailing behind it a decimated maintenance pod and what looked like a box of chicken drumsticks. She swallowed, hoping there wasn't an engineer in that pod, and then the left wing clunked one last time and her ship shuddered violently as one of the portside landing lights joined the escape party into oblivion.

Angel's body was wrenched painfully forwards as the station's berthing computer took control of the situation, lighting up her flight console with the emergency break pattern at the exact same moment as the artificial gravity in the loading bay kicked in. It wasn't much – about half-a-gee as this made loading and unloading heavy cargo bins much easier – but it was enough to make sure she ended up with an uncomfortable amount of kevlar webbing wedged somewhere unmentionable.

'Ouch.'

She yanked the harness out from between her thighs, watching as the shield indicator continued its downward journey all the way to zero before going completely dark.

'Inter-bloody-galactic,' she said, feeling anything but.

She punched the harness release in the centre of her chest and hauled her body, uncharacteristically heavy after so long in zero-g, towards the hatch. The airlock on the control deck opened up and Engineer Rachel Hanandroo peered out, checking the state of her latest arrival.

'Nice work Commander,' she said, words crackling with sarcasm through the comms link inside her helmet.

'Okay genius, it's only a flesh wound. I didn't even breach the hull.'

Angel turned and leant into the rack of life support tanks by the door, snapping one into place on her back – she might be back in limited gravity but there was still no atmos in the spaceport hangar, not until the loading airlock was fixed around the cargo bay doors and the chamber had been purged. The air around her head hissed again as her flight suit pressurised and she popped the Cobra's hatch, ignoring the extending foot ladder and leaping gently down onto the landing pad below. Once she was clear the engineer started the loading tunnel mechanism which clamped into place on the side of the Cobra. The engines farted rapidly cooling gas as the chamber filled with air.

Once the cargo bay area was secure the lower airlock hissed and Rachel ducked through the circular hole it left, tapping on her tablet. Angel had already extracted her head from the helmet and was raking fingers across her dirty blonde fuzz of hair, cropped tight against her scalp to avoid any silliness with equipment entanglements working in zero gravity.

'Well it's an improvement I guess. You're lucky Frank Kenric was taking a piss or you'd be out there fishing for a dead broadcast technician too. I am going to have to bill you for the aerial though – do you know how much those things cost?'

Angel looked at the engineer with open despair.

'What? Oh come on. It wasn't my fault. The cargo hold is practically empty and I forgot to recalculate my mass. It's an easy enough mistake.'

Rachel sighed, ready for a string of unconvincing excuses.

'And why, pray tell, when you left here with half-a-ton of iridium and enough marble to make a small moon, would you be returning with a practically empty hold?'

Angel went back to extracting herself from her heavy space gear.

'Bastard economy is what. Caelinus III is at the tail end of a vicious drought and there is a lot of demand for consumables in Caelinus right now. Plus Mervon sent in a fleet of Anacondas two days before I arrived and all they had left was a few bolts of rare silk and a weekend pass to Pog Hobdonia.'

The engineer looked up from her inventory tab. 'Pog Hobdonia?'

Angel nodded absently, absorbed now in systematically unclipping her flight suit.

'You went to Pog Hobdonia?'

Angel stopped and looked at the engineer whose cheeks flushed pink. 'It doesn't live up to the hype, you know?'

'I know.'

The engineer blushed harder and went back to her digiwork. She pulled the lever that unwinds the cargo bay ramp and peered inside.

'Nice. Pink.' She grimaced, scanning the bolt of silk cloth before closing the hatch back up. 'Value?'

'Twelve thousand credits.'

The engineer raised her eyebrows into a sceptical "m". Angel nodded.

'It happens to be very rare, and until I sell it I can't pay for any repairs,' she tilted her head towards her damaged wing before mumbling almost inaudibly, 'and any extras like data band aerials.'

Rachel bit her bottom lip, which was trying to protrude like it used to when they were cadets.

'Fine, so I'll take the heat again. You just do what you want Angel. You usually do … and who I am I to argue? Your dad equals my boss. I get the dynamic.'

'Hey!' Angel stopped for real this time and caught the engineer by the elbow. 'Look, I'm sorry, okay? I've had a rubbish trip. Three months in space and all I have to show for it is four hundred metres of pink material and a fading UV-tan. I'm told the cloth is worth enough to fill my hold with iridium twice over, as long as I can find the right buyer, here in Slough. Where life is about digging metal out of rock and serving heavy time; neither of which you want to do dressed in baby-pink silk, for many reasons.'

Rachel glared at her uncharacteristically. 'I'll mark the cloth as pending.'

Angel let go of her elbow and started packing up her bag.

'Well, whatever. If I manage to make a good trade I'll buy you another aerial, Rachel. But right now I have no clue where I am going to find a buyer, so I am going to find a drink instead.'

'Oh well, you'll be on familiar territory there at least,' Rachel said swiping the lighting grid on her tablet before heading out of the airlock, leaving Angel to finish packing up in dark.

* * *

Half an hour later Angel was entrenched in her favourite booth at Anna and Roland's Zen Garden, a half-finished Glasgow Hullstripper in front of her. She gazed out at Slough through the observation panels lining the upper wall. The big planet turned lazily through her view. It looked rather beautiful from this distance; a glazed and hazy purple that belied the true nature of the barren, poisonous atmosphere on the surface. Angel took another slug of the poison sitting in front of her and grimaced as it burnt a path down to her empty stomach. What her body really needed right now was a spin and a large bowl of carbs, but her head was in control and it was planning to get as obliterated as possible so that it could forget how screwed she was. She watched as a hyper-gravity pod spun its merry way towards the purple hunk of a planet below. She grimaced again. The passengers would be strapped into their bio-bays contemplating eight hours of torture as they headed down into the Stokes two kilometres below. Down there the gravity was 1.5-g. It was punishing. Hard and heavy, surrounded by rock and metal and the constant banging and clanking of diggers and cutters. To prepare their bodies visitors were spun at 2.5-g all the way down in those pods. Angel shuddered. It was like riding a spinning teacup with an elephant sitting on your chest for eight hours straight.

She swallowed the last of her Hullstripper and slid the empty glass onto the refill matt. The NFC terminal by the condiment holder beeped and flashed a depressingly low number at her in amber.

'Yeah, I know.'

She was closer to broke than she'd ever been … she didn't need a machine to tell her that. A couple of minutes later Anna bustled up to the booth and smoothly replaced her empty with a full.

'That was quick. Are you going to eat?'

Angel pulled the full glass towards her and stuck a grease-stained finger into it, jangling the ice cubes.

'At your prices? 'Fraid not.'

She took her dripping finger out of the glass and sucked it noisily.

Anna frowned in a very un-Zen-like way and wiped off the droplets of alcohol Angel had spilled on the shiny table.

'Nice. Elegant. No wonder you're still single.' Angel made an uncomplimentary noise.

'Just don't get too drunk. I don't want to have to get Roland to pull you out of the meditation pool again.'

'That wasn't because I was drunk …' Angel raised her damp finger to object but Anna was already on her way to serve the next customer, uninterested in feeble excuses. She lifted the deep red liquid to her lips, this time transporting it by glass rather than finger, and sucked peevishly at the rim. She was already starting to feel the buzz of the liquor and this was only her second drink. That was one of the good things about living in zero-g for so long; your bones and cells got weak and fragile but you were a very cheap date for a few weeks when you got home. Nonetheless she resolved to book in for a spin in the morning and went back to sucking on the rim of her glass.

* * *

Several hours and at least three too many Hullstrippers later Angel made her way back to the spaceport, ricocheting off the walls as she tried to remember which hatch opened onto her ship's airlock. Most of the berths were full now so there was hardly anyone around. Still on duty though, Rachel was working on a sketch of the Imperial Cutter in bay three when Angel stumbled onto the control deck, tripping over the first aid crate and tumbling into the room like a Moscatelli dust devil in the reduced gravity. She came to rest eventually in an angular heap at the controller's feet.

'Mission accomplished then?'

Rachel put aside her tablet and reached across to the coffee machine to punch in the code for 'sober up'.

Angel took a moment to figure out which way was up – it was funny how gravity could play tricks on you when it had been absent for a while – then untangled her arms and legs and struggled to her feet

'Your mother has been here looking for you.'

Angel grimaced at both the thought of her mother and the strong black coffee Rachel handed to her.

'How sche know where I'm am?'

'Your Spacebook status I guess. You know when you post stuff there it can be seen by everyone, across the galaxy? Location co-ordinates and everything?'

'Ahh sheet, Shpaybook.'

Gravity finally won the argument with Angel's legs and she stumbled backwards into a swivel chair, spinning around gracelessly while spilling coffee everywhere.

'Yeah, well you might be in luck. She said she had a buyer for your cloth.

She had me open the hold for one of her men.'

This news sobered Angel up like a slap round the face. 'You did what?'

'I opened your hold and she had one of her men take the cloth...'

Angel sat there goldfishing at her friend, trying to make sense of things through the fog of booze.

'Rachel ... my mother ... why would you?'

Rachel's brow pulled down into a cross-looking 'v'; her face appeared to be working its way through the alphabet today.

'Let me think about that for a moment ... oh yeah. She's scarier than a radioactive bra and, by the way, happens to be my *boss's wife*! What did you think I was going to do?'

'I can't believe ... this is ... my rep ...' Angel's words trailed off as she considered the consequences of dropping two reputation levels in one hit as well as being flat broke. 'I have to find her before she sells it,' she said as she lurched to her feet and stumbled clumsily back towards the interior of the space station leaving the empty chair spinning in her wake.

Chapter 2

The first thing she became aware of was her tongue. It felt alien and dry; too big for her mouth. She sucked on it noisily and pried her eyes open, squinting into the dark trying to figure out where she was.

'Lights on,' she croaked, somewhat relieved when her timid eyes were assaulted by violent fluorescence. At least she had made it to somewhere that recognised her voice before collapsing last night.

'Lights fifty percent,' she groaned and the room dimmed to a less-challenging ambience. She raised herself gingerly into a seated position and went back to prying her eyes open.

Her subsidised pilot's lodgings were compact and functional, for which she felt extremely grateful as she swung her feet over the side of her narrow gel bunk and popped the lid of the cold box with an outstretched toe. She reached down, wincing as her forehead throbbed, then pulled out a pouch of water and twisted off the cap. Drinking deeply her tongue tingled as her brain continued to thump behind her eyebrows. She sank back onto the narrow bunk moaning. She tried to piece together the details of last night. She had gone to her parents' quarters; she remembered getting there and helping herself to a large drink as Andrew the compartment boy went to fetch her mother.

Nothing after that.

She scanned the room with hopeful eyes just in case she'd managed to rescue her cloth. All she saw were the sparse essentials and stacked lockers typical of subsidised living. Most pilots were away so much they didn't need extravagant quarters and were used to living in cramped conditions on their vessels anyway. She stretched back over her head and felt for the ID panel, planting her palm across it. The computer beeped.

'You have four messages.' 'Play messages.' The first was from The Slough Observers Wellbeing Centre, welcoming her back and offering a discounted rate on their range of anti-atrophy spa packages. The next was from her mother, presumably not long after she'd docked as her voice was bright and breezy, inviting Angel over for supper and reminding her about the reception the following night.

Angel winced. An Imperial delegation was visiting the space station and she was expected to roll out and play the dutiful daughter, to be sneered at by puffed up politicians and pompous plutocrats. Then there was Captain Riley, who would be doing more leering than sneering. The thought made her skin curl up at the edges.

The third message was Roland; apparently she'd made it back to the Zen Garden last night and owed him twenty creds for a shelf full of glasses smashed during an animated game of Flat Rabbit. Finally, there was another message from her mother; earlier this morning, this one brief and humourless: 'I hope you're enjoying your hangover and that you will leave it in the waste pipes with your stinking attitude for tonight's reception. Andrew is bringing a dress over for you this afternoon. You'd better be wearing it. Seven o'clock at The Overlook. DON'T be late ...' there was a meaningful pause, '... or drunk.'

'End of messages.'

* * *

Angel slipped onto the huge observation deck and skirted the edge of the growing throng; wealthy patrons, feds and investors, all dressed in their finest and positively glowing to be seen at such an exclusive affair in one of the system's most decadent venues. She'd taken a shuttle pod over from the space station a couple of hours earlier rather than get caught up in the gravy train of executive shuttles organised for the guests. It had given her the chance to have a swim in one of the spas to wash off the dust and grime of the space station before stiffening her resolve with a Hullstripper or three in the Spinner's Arms.

Even though such an ostentatious display of wealth went against Angel's principles she had to admit the view from the Overlook's main deck was impressive. The clear-vision panels in the outer hull were huge; at least two hundred metres across and running the entire circumference of the vast ringed-chamber so that the planet could be seen throughout a complete rotation of the coriolis. It coasted gracefully around and around along with everything else in space giving the impression that this vast luxury hangar was at the very centre of the universe. The Overlook occupied the upper ring of the Observer I's main hub; the most exclusive of the three renovated generation ships that had brought their ancestors all the way from earth over a thousand years ago. The ships were beyond vast – you could fit a Federation Battle Cruiser into the central eco-dome and still have room to manoeuvre it above the vegetation that made up the living, biological heart of these deep-space civilisation boats. The dome spun with centripetal force to create the illusion of gravity that the plants needed to flourish, but fully adjustable depending on requirements. For tonight's exclusive event the gravity in The Overlook was set at a refreshing 0.8-g, which caused sagging jowls to lift flatteringly and made dancing in heels a lot more comfortable.

A huge Imperial Cruiser coasted across Angel's view trailing a swarm of angry-looking Vipers as passenger class cruisers queued to drop off more guests for the party. A serve-bot glided past bearing a tray of glasses full of bubbly golden liquid Angel took to be alcohol. She swiped two; one for her, and one for later, then started scanning the room for friendlies.

The guests were mostly Orbitals and visitors; predominantly Imperials by the look of the gaudy attire, though she recognised a few muted Federal colours in there as well. There was a spattering of token Spinners too, easily picked out by their short stocky frames; broad shoulders and thick foreheads evolved through several centuries of biological tailoring living down inside the planet. Far from being second-class citizens, Spinners had always been revered and highly valued; so-named because of the barbaric way their ancestors had been trained to survive Slough's oppressive 1.5-g atmosphere. Today they still held a lot of sway, both politically and in business, but you didn't often see them at a posh Orbital event like this on account of their reaction to booze – which invariably made things messy quite quickly as their over-achieving circulatory systems deployed the intoxication of alcohol with ruthless efficiency. It was one of the reasons that the clubs and bars on the less exclusive Observer III were so popular with stag parties from down in the Stokes.

Angel spotted Stewart Forgie waving at her from over by the canapé belt. He was the press officer for Stoke Poges Industries – a lean and nervous looking man in his forties, with kind eyes and a slight stoop – and despite what you'd expect from his profession probably among the more genuine people here tonight. Angel raised a hand of acknowledgment as he flagged her frantically from across the room. She started weaving her way towards him.

Suddenly her momentum was halted by an arm thrust out from the throng to bar her way. She stopped abruptly and felt hot breath on her cheek.

'Well, hello my Angel …'

The words slithered up the back of her neck and around her throat causing her breath to catch and her skin to try and crawl away from them. Captain Riley. She spun to face him as he captured her hips from behind, pressing through the crowd pelvis-first in an effort to get closer to her.

'Good evening, Captain …' Angel's face burned under his scrutiny as she pressed her body away from his, hands flat against the crisp lapels of his naval uniform. She always felt like she'd forgotten to wear clothes when he looked at her.

'You're in a hurry. Stop and have a drink with me.'

He slid his hands from her hips and closed them about her wrists, squeezing a fraction too tight as she edged away from him towards the canapés.

'Ah, sorry no can do,' she said awkwardly, wishing she hadn't agreed to wear a dress tonight as his eyes roamed down towards her cleavage, 'need to catch up with PR; very important night, politically. Well, you don't need me to tell you that of course.'

She nodded towards Stewart, who was making his way towards her with a look of concern etched onto his face. The navy man glanced dubiously at the lanky spin doctor, narrowing his eyes with suspicious annoyance. But he loosened his grip anyway and Angel slipped free.

'I will see you later then,' he said clicking his heels together and bowing formally as she was swallowed up by the crowd.

* * *

'What was that about?' Stewart asked once she had reached the safety of the canapé belt.

Angel eyed the little crystal boats filled with savoury treats as they trundled past down the ever-moving canal of canapés, the glistening liquid beneath the boats gently pulsing through the colours of the rainbow with the rhythm of soft music permeating the room. She had no idea what most of the dishes were, and was unnerved by a couple with eyes that seemed to glare at her as they glided past. But she hadn't eaten anything since this morning and with the warm glow of alcohol already clouding her senses she felt she'd better at least make a token gesture.

'Smarm-ahoy, nothing I can't handle,' Angel said, snatching up a snack that seemed least likely to try and bite her back. It looked a bit like a sausage but tasted disconcertingly of fish when she popped it in her mouth. 'For some reason Captain Riley still thinks I should be impressed by his money and power – but who would want to be rich if you have to eat crap like this?'

Stewart winced.

'Do you have to swear? There are some important people here tonight and just because power and influence don't impress you personally, they are still a very significant part of your father's work.'

Angel looked confused. 'Was I swearing?'

He cocked a hand to his cheek and mouthed '*crap*' at her theatrically, checking left and right to see that no one was watching.

'Oh please. Are you serious? That's a *fact* not a swear. It comes out of *all* our arses and some people's mouths every day. If you want to hear swearing just get me a couple more drinks and ask me how my life is going.'

'Yes, well I already heard from your mother how good you are at that, following your late-night excursion to her chambers last night.'

Angel was about to ask if he could fill in any of the blanks for her on that account when a flash of baby-pink in her peripheral vision caught her attention. She snapped her head around to see a line of eight obnoxious-looking children snaking around behind the chocolate fountain on the east terrace; all blonde, little girls of varying ages between toddler and teen. They were all dressed in a distinctive baby-pink; jumpsuits and tabards all cut from the same flowing cloth. *Her* flowing cloth; her whole livelihood now transformed into Von Trap-style playwear for a flounce of spoilt Imperial princesses.

Chapter 3

'No more alcohol,' her mother hissed into Angel's left ear at the banqueting table later that night.

She'd done a pretty good job of avoiding her parents so far, but once the sit-down meal had commenced there was no escape. Her mother rained false smiles down upon her gracious subjects as she reprimanded her daughter through the corner of her mouth. Her face was tight, but that was as likely to be the latest age-defying spa treatment as the tension of her relationship with her daughter.

Angel just sighed and took another sip of her drink. 'Last one mother. I promise.'

Her mother glanced back to the conversation happening between her father and Arve Neville-Tutass, the pompous Imperial patron for whom all this extravagance had been organised. Evidently satisfied it was still on track she turned her attention back to Angel, who was trying very hard not to engage in conversation with Captain Riley, seated on her other side.

'You look nice in that dress, doesn't she Captain?'

The captain dabbed the corner of his mouth with a crisp white napkin as his gaze crawled over her like hungry spiders. She wanted to sink through her chair and slither off under the table as he placed the cloth slowly in his lap, licking his lips salaciously and pressing it down into his groin with inappropriate firmness.

'Oh yes, my Lady Maugvahnna, she looks very fine indeed.'

Angel's mother frowned then, reaching out to touch her clipped head as if to brush an imaginary lock of flowing golden hair tenderly back from her face. Angel twitched away.

'I wish you'd let your hair grow though. Or wear a wig at least – the Agnew-weave actually knits itself to your own follicles you know? So it looks completely natural, even for someone with hair as tragic as yours.'

Angel made a face and started looking furtively about for the closest serve-bot. Her mother was obsessed with physical beauty and the illusion of youth and had had so much work done she looked the same age as Angel – or at least that's what her dermal physician kept telling her. With sculpted blonde hair and skin pulled shiny-tight across her forehead and cheeks, she spent more time in the zero-g spas and hyper-gravity-cleansing booths than she did in her own quarters in a desperate attempt to defy time's relentless assault on her complexion. Angel didn't understand the superficiality of it all, and with her shaved head and make up-free face was quite obviously a constant disappointment to the 'Lady of the Station' as Maugvahnna's adoring minions liked to call her.

'So,' her mother continued after an awkward moment of silence, 'what's next for you? Are we to see you around the station a bit more for a while? Or are you running straight off to sell rocks in space again?'

Angel's mood darkened and she scowled at her mother from under her eyebrows.

'Well thanks to you giving my livelihood away to be made into pink romper-suits for chubby little monsters, I'm not entirely sure what I'm going to do.'

Her mother looked nervously back at the business discussion beside her, gripping her daughter's knee under the table and squeezing a vicious warning.

'Ow!'

'Lady Kimondo Hausenogger is a very important patron and her children are little cherubs,' Maugvahnna said beaming at no one in particular in case they had been overheard. 'You would do well to remember the importance of collecting friends in high places young lady.'

'Meanwhile, I don't have any creds to buy new stock, so how exactly is that supposed to help me?'

This time her father did notice the raised voices and her mother pressed another clawed warning into her knee under the table. But Angel was on a roll now, the fire in her belly stoked nicely by the alcohol.

'And by the way, since you're so concerned about rank, you might be interested to learn they are going to drop me two reputation levels when they find out what that cloth went for. I'll probably have to sell myself into slavery – I'm sure one of your lovely Imperial friends needs a floor scrubber?'

Her mother sighed dramatically, now so drawn into the conflict with her daughter that she forgot to maintain her composure.

'Let's all worry about your *trade* reputation,' she said, her voice dripping with sarcasm. The word 'trade' slid out of her mouth through a sneer, as if she found it distasteful on her lips. 'It was your choice to become a common hawker – don't blame me because you're a failure at it. Goodness knows I've given up enough for you. We've offered you the galaxy on a platter, your father and I; you could have married into any one of the most powerful courts in the Empire, or be sitting beside an officer at the heart of the Federation right now. But you have thrown every opportunity back in my face.'

The "Lady of the Station" put on her best tragic martyr expression and Angel felt her fight seeping away through the cracks of her hopeless situation. Her mother would never understand her need for independence; to stand on her own two feet so that she could happily look her reflection in the eye each morning. How could she, when her own journey to adulthood had been entirely about finding a rich and powerful man to support her? Angel sank back into her chair and reached despondently for another drink that was about to go gliding by courtesy of a serve-bot. Her mother tutted loudly, but sensing a degree of victory let it pass.

'Anyway,' she said after several more minutes of uneasy silence, 'I might have the solution for you. Not that you'll be grateful enough to acknowledge my help, but there is an investor who might be interested in backing you.'

Angel's eye's narrowed suspiciously. Her mother's 'introductions' typically concluded in an awkwardly declined proposal or an ill-advised attempt to cop a grope; which had once ended in a black eye and a narrowly avoided diplomatic incident.

'Actually it is Captain Riley's contact. He knows someone looking to finance a gold-run to LHS 3439 and when I told him about your financial predicament he said he could get you a place on the fleet. It's a wonderful opportunity, isn't it Michael?' She nodded at the captain across the back of Angel's chair, urging him to step in with more details.

Angel quivered with revulsion as she felt him rest his hand on the skin between her shoulder blades.

'Yes, my Lady, of course. A *huge* opportunity. Three clear reputation levels in one shipment and enough credits to keep you for at least a year.' He leant in close and Angel could feel his hot breath puffing against the back of her neck. 'Since you do insist on keeping yourself rather than letting me keep you.'

Angel felt like she was being circled by Thargoid warships as her mother giggled coquettishly.

'You know I don't do high risk mother,' Angel said, draining her glass again and scouting around for an escape route; desserts were being served now so it wouldn't be long before she could make her excuses and leave.

'Oh, this is hardly high risk,' oozed the captain as Angel continued trying to squirm away from the touch of his hand on her back. 'The plan is to fill three courier vessels with precious metal and send them off with a fleet of heavily armed Vipers. We are talking a *lot* of gold here and the investor is no idiot. He would hardly send you out across bandit controlled space with a belly full of his credits and no protection, would he?'

Angel's mother and the captain laughed again, a little too loud she thought.

'So, you'll go and meet the investor in the morning Angel? Angel?'

'I can't go in the morning. I'm booked in for a spin.'

'Oh Angel, do you have to? You know it will make your boobs sag, even more than they are already? All that horrid hyper-gravity pulling at your wobbly bits.'

Angel blushed furiously as Riley ogled her cleavage again and a young couple further along the table pretended not to hear.

'Mother, with respect,' she said through gritted teeth, 'the one thing I do *not* need is for you to discuss the efficacy of my breasts in a public forum.' Angel's voice was tight and her mother sighed loudly again.

'Well, it's not good for a girl that's all I'm saying. We're made more delicately than that. I can already see it pulling at your jowls, even in this flattering gravity ... At this rate you'll never find a husband. Who wants to marry a saggy old hag? I'm sure even Captain Riley will be put off eventually, won't you captain?'

'Oh, I don't know about that,' Mike Riley oozed something close to confidence, only a lot slimier, and continued focussing on Angel's cleavage. 'Some things have a lasting appeal, even flawed.'

Chapter 4

'Relax,' Bowsen said. 'Don't hold your breath. You know it will only make you sick if you fight it.'

Angel loosened her grip on the handles and tried to relax. She hated the centrifuge. It was like being stuck under a container load of slag pouring off the back of a construction freighter. But it was the fastest way to get back into shape after an extended period in space so she just had to grin and bear it – quite literally once the g-force started piling up. As the heavy pendulum gained momentum the chair she was strapped in tilted back to horizontal, keeping her spine aligned with the prevailing gravitational force.

She tried not to imagine what it must have felt like as a child, strapped into a similar device, the weight of reality crushing down on you before you were old enough to understand why. The Spinners of old – the original miners who'd carved the first chambers and caverns out of the planet's interior – had started their hyper-gravity training as toddlers. Just three years old and they were subjected to forces of one-and-a-half-g; two-and-a-half-g; three-and-a-half-g and up; by the time they were teenagers spinning for sustained periods at a gut-mashing twelve-and-a-half-g. It made their bodies tough, thickening up their cytoskeletons so that their cells didn't collapse and their bones crack under the pressure of working the mines down in Slough.

To Angel it seemed like a brutal thing to do to your child, but the financial rewards must have been persuasive. Only the strongest babies were selected; their parents handsomely paid. Many of the early settlers had started self-selecting into genetic pairings that gave them the best chance of birthing a candidate. Over the decades this practise saw the divide between Spinners and Orbitals grow wider, both physically as well as in status. Nerves of steel and an iron constitution were required to work in the planet below. *But, Angel thought, for a three-year-old strapped into a cradle at the end of a huge pendulum as it started to glide faster and faster around the circumference of a bleached out laboratory, it must be a frightening experience.*

Forty-five seconds into the spin and she was at four-g. Her body now weighed around seven hundred and twenty pounds. Her mother would have apoplexy, although luckily the weight wasn't going only on her hips. It was in her guts, on her chest; even her eyeballs felt like they had been replaced with lead ball-bearings.

She watched the red dots on the light-bar marching relentlessly inwards; clicking the thumb button each time they reached the centre of her vision. At four-and-a-half-g she released the lever in her left hand and the machinery clunked as the massive swinging pendulum locked in to a set pace.

'Four-and-a-half? Well, that's pretty pathetic.'

Harry Bowsen's voice carried to her through the speakers in her headrest. Sound was weird at this speed. The words undulated and twanged, like someone was swinging them from the end of a bunch of guitar strings. Four-and-a-half-g was pretty pathetic. She would normally spin at around six but having spent the last three months in space her tolerance was low. Another night of heavy drinking hadn't improved her motivation either. The last thing she needed was to go g-LOC and have to be stretchered out to a recovery bay unconscious. No. Four-and-a-half-g was plenty for today.

Angel concentrated on her breathing and settled in to the hypnotic march of the red dots as Bowsen locked down the centrifuge controls. Spin-speed set he'd be monitoring her vitals for the next thirty minutes – which meant he could catch up on Spacebook, maybe find something entertaining for them to do later? The technician leant back in his chair, propping his feet up on the softly beeping electrocardiogram machine as he flipped the medical readout screen over to the uniweb channel and fired up a browser.

* * *

'Okay, commander, you've done your time.'

Angel blinked, propping herself up on unsteady elbows. The pendulum had ground to a halt but she still felt like she was moving.

'Already? But I was having so much fun.'

Harry smiled as he tapped biometric readings into his tablet. 'I can't tempt you with a hot float?'

Angel shuddered, pushing herself all the way up to sitting. 'You're quite right, you can't.'

She couldn't think of anything worse than taking a float around a steam-filled chamber with a bunch of sweaty rich people. There was a whole stack of delights like this available in the spa centres on Observers I and II, where rings layered inside the central dome could be turned on and off to null or increase the ambient gravity, whatever the treatment required. From deep pore cleansing in hyper-gravity to a steamy float through zero-g. She stood shakily and the young technician stepped in front of her, shining a light into each of her eyes, observing her carefully. Angel looked straight ahead. They were both on autopilot now.

'A drink then? My shift finishes in about an hour,' Harry poked something medical into Angel's mouth to hold her tongue down and peered inside as he spoke. 'There's rumour of a Jonty table over on Observer III later if you're interested?'

'Uhh-thay …' she nodded, looking him directly in his sparkling blue eyes.

They seemed to be smiling without any help from his mouth.

'Good. Meet you at the Spinner's Arms at two? Liquido burrito; you look like you could do with cheering up.'

Angel took a moment to consider whether a liquid lunch right before a meeting with Captain Riley's investor was the best idea in the galaxy. She shook her head as if to rattle the thought right out of it through her ears. The trouble was, she mused, Harry Bowsen had eyes that you just couldn't say no to.

Two hours later she was still trying to find the word 'no' in her vocabulary when Harry lifted up a fresh Glasgow Hullstripper and saluted the table, a big grin on his face. They'd picked up a couple of his old friends from med school – Iain Irvine and Gareth Coffey – and after a brief but convincing drinking session in the Spinner's Arms had all jumped on a shuttle from Observer II to catch the card game. Now she was in for a dove she didn't really have and extremely late for her meeting. Harry Bowsen, the annoying little shit with the irresistible eyes, had been winning rather convincingly all afternoon. The dealer glanced at his hand and decided to dive. He threw his cards face down on the table, folding his arms in disgust.

'Jonty,' said Harry, grinning at Angel like a fuel scooper.

Angel bit her bottom lip, feeding him false tells as her heart fluttered in her chest. She had a strong hand – there were only two possible hands that could beat her in fact – so she was feeling more than confident. But if she was going to sucker-punch this gloating git into giving her back the four credits he had already taken her for, she was going to have to play it cool. Draw him in.

'Jonty-up,' she said, doing her best to look shifty and uncertain as she pressed her thumb on the credit panel in front of her. Her sleeve vibrated as somewhere under her jacket the NFC chip flashed crossly with an ever-increasing red number. Red was not good, especially when related to your net economic worth. She had a limited overdraft but this game was eating through it faster than a corpse in an acid bath.

Two more hands at the table took a dive but two stayed in, both locals. They looked like grubbers; engineers who spent their days crawling the maintenance tunnels of the Observers, keeping these ancient generation ships ticking along. Their overalls were grease-stained and their hands calloused. If the tatty badges pinned to their chests were to be believed their names were Gavin McAfee and Lee Hamerstein. They glanced to one another and then across the table at Harry and Angel. She felt the mood in the room take a definite turn. Harry was annoying enough when he was drunk but he was an appalling winner too. These grubs looked like they were starting to take it personally.

The final card was turned by a sulky dealer and everyone who was still in studied their hands seriously. Except Harry, who broke into a broad grin and started whistling the theme tune to 'i-Galaxy'. It was so obvious he had a great hand it just had to be a bluff. But maybe that's what he wanted them to think? The double-bluff. Or was it? A double-double-bluff? Angel shook her head to banish the infinite circle of maybes. He might have a nice hand, but her hand was better. She was pretty sure of that.

'Jonty,' she said, clutching her cards to her chest and holding her breath. Leading the last round she was in the perfect position to control the game.

Her raise had just taken the bet to one hundred and if Harry or any of the others took the bait and raised to two hundred she could kick it one last Jonty to four hundred, which would be a tidy little pot for the winning hand.

McAfee eyed her, trying to get a read on her tells. Angel smirked inwardly whilst exuding what she hoped was foolish bravado.

'Pledge,' he said eventually, thumbing his own panel to match Angel's bet. 'Jonty-up,' Hamerstein surprised everyone with this raise, pressing his thumb into the console a little too fiercely.

All eyes turned to Harry, who was busy eyeing up a leggy brunette leaning across the JabbleWok table next door.

'Oh? My go?' He flashed a boyish grin and planted his thumb on the glass panel in front of him. 'Jonty-UP!'

Angel's heart was now yammering inside her chest; ohmygosh-ohmygosh-ohmygosh it pumped. She hadn't expected them both to raise. The bet was at four hundred with three hands in; did she really dare to raise it to eight hundred? She did a quick mental tot-up. It would completely clean her out; credits maxed out against the security of her ship with not a single other possession left to her name. She glanced again at her cards; four queens against her chest and a fifth on the table. It was the third strongest out of a possible five hundred or so combinations of hands, and with the cards now on display – a King, two Knaves, her Queen and a four – there was only one achievable hand that could beat her. She was laughing all the way to the chip scanner. Surely?

'Jonty … Up,' she said deliberately, this time keen for them to clock her confidence to avoid being priced out of the game – unlikely though as eight hundred creds was an insane amount for a game at this level.

McAfee growled menacingly. He was only in for one hundred so far and clearly decided it wasn't worth seven hundred to see her so he threw his stack down on the table and said, 'I dive.'

Hamerstein had more at stake and resentful eyes settled on her as he thumbed his bet in to the console.

'Pledge.'

Angel's chest tightened. If Harry went in too she would clear almost three K in one pot, putting her back on track with enough credits to get her shield fixed and fill the hold with a shipment of shale – not exactly the glamorous end of the market but there was good profit to be made short-running construction material. She checked her cards again; just to make sure those four beautiful Queens hadn't run off with a passing Knave, and then noticed Harry looking at her mischievously.

'Nice hand then? Must be, to go in for almost an eagle.'

Harry lifted the corner of his cards, which were fanned out across the table in front of him. He tilted his head sideways so he could peek at their faces – though from the theatrical way he performed the action it was clear he knew perfectly well what he was holding.

'But what if mine is better?'

Angel shrugged, trying to look nonchalant as she drained the last of her drink and placed it on the refill pad. The chip around her wrist vibrated violently and her heart leapt up into her mouth. Before she had time to connect her brain to her limbs and snatch the glass back off the pad, the display embedded in the centre of the table bleeped crossly and flashed up the message *"Transaction denied. Nil credit"*.

Angel blushed furiously as Harry and several of the other players sitting round the table sniggered. That was it. They knew she was broke. All Harry had to do was raise her one last time; she would have no choice but to take the dive because the bet console wouldn't accept any more wagers from her. She was an idiot and she'd just thrown everything away.

'Well, well,' Harry beamed. 'You appear to be in a bit of a predicament.'

He leant across in front of Angel and picked up her empty glass, replacing it gently on the refill pad as he stared at her, inches away from her nose. She pressed her cards defensively to her chest, not that it mattered if he saw now anyway. The NFC reader flashed the drink up to Harry's account and he sat back in his seat still watching her with dancing eyes.

Eventually the one remaining player still in the game broke the silence. 'Okay you two, get a room. But first can we finish this hand? We have a communications grid to service tonight.'

Harry looked across the table at the impatient player.

'You're right!' he declared suddenly. 'I call pledge! Let's see what everyone's got.'

He thumbed the console and the whole table drew in a sharp breath, looking at him with open mouths. Leading the slack-jawed parade was Angel herself. He hadn't Jontied? They were all in for eight hundred and the round was over; the game was over, and Angel was sitting on a practically unbeatable hand against a threeK pot. Harry sat grinning back at the table, some of whom were beginning to look very cross.

'Are you some kind of jack-flapper? Why wouldn't you raise? You know she can't follow. You just threw away the chance to force her dive!'

Lee Hamerstein had slammed his cards face-down on the table and was leaning forward aggressively.

'You got some kind of 'thing' going on here have you?'

Harry sat back, looking relaxed. He had the air of someone who was enjoying this a little too much.

'A 'thing'? A *thing*? Let me see… Do I have a *thing* about buying my friend a drink just before I take all of her, and your credits? Well yes, yes I think I do! Do I have a *thing* about seeing her suffer the indignity of taking a dive because she ran out of credits? No.'

'And if her hand beats yours?'

The engineer glared at Harry who smiled back benignly. 'It won't. Have you seen her luck lately?'

Angel cleared her throat and the two men looked at her, waiting to see her cards. She was so bowled over by the lifeline she'd been thrown that she forgot to be wary of the growing tension on the other side of the table.

'You might want to check your egos on a landing pad boys,' she said nodding thanks to the waiter who switched her empty glass for a full one from the trolley hovering in front of him. She fanned out her cards on the table, revealing one, two, three and then pausing dramatically before showing her fourth Queen. Everyone's eyes flicked across the cards, a murmur breaking out as they clocked the additional Queen in the Jonty.

'Oh,' said Harry sinking back into his seat with an air of defeat.

'You IDIOT!'

The locals were getting angry now. Hamerstein flipped his hand over revealing four Aces. Amazing cards; but without an Ace in the Jonty hand it didn't beat Angel's Queens. All eyes turned to Harry. Angel's heart was practically exploding, blood rushing loud in her ears.

'You let her win!'

Three of the grease-stained labourers on the other side of the table had leapt to their feet now and Angel stood too, body tense. It looked like these grease-crawlers weren't going to take the defeat lying down and Angel wasn't entirely sure how many of the people from her side of the table would stand beside if it came to a fight.

'Steady on fellas, he didn't let me win. The cards are good. If I hadn't accidentally put my glass on the refill pad we wouldn't even be having this conversation.'

Two more of the locals stood to join the growing lynch mob facing her across the table and Angel started to feel very exposed. Then Harry and his med school friends all scraped their chairs back from the table and stood beside her, bringing the numbers to four on five; these were odds that gave Angel a little more hope of getting out alive. Maybe.

'She's right,' Harry said.

Angel was momentarily surprised by how reasonable he sounded considering he was about to lose eight hundred creds.

'I didn't let her win.'

He threw his cards down on the table from behind her. Three landed face-up – all Kings – and one fell face-down. All eyes flew to the Jonty to confirm the King they had all known was in there. So far Harry's hand put him in third place, but there was one card still to be revealed. Angel's heart stopped trying to burst and decided to turn to stone instead. She jumped as Harry touched her shoulder lightly to move her aside, reaching to flip the last card over on the table.

'Excuse me,' his voice was tight and seemed teetering on the edge of laughter.

Flip.

A King.

Angel had a brief moment to savour the crushing weight of defeat as it fell on her from a very great height before she was fighting for her life in a mad scramble of greasy overalls and flying fists.

Chapter 5

'Rose.'

Angel looked up; the guard beckoned her over to the holding cell door, gesturing for her to place her hand on the bio-scanner so he could punch in the release code. The pad went green and she was able to step through the glowing barrier with no more resistance than a slight tingle. Harry had followed her to the entrance and was hovering hopefully by the scanner.

'I guess it pays to be the station commander's brat. I don't fancy pretty boy's chances of getting out so quick though,' the guard sneered through the force-field at Harry whose face fell with the realisation he was to be abandoned.

'Can you call my mum for me, Angel?' he shouted after her.

She felt a bit bad leaving him on his own but there wasn't much she could do. His med school mates had fled the scene when it became clear that station enforcement would be called out to clean up the mess. Angel and Harry had been buried deep in a mob of angry grubbers at the time so were unable to execute such a prudent strategy.

She hobbled after the guard on one bootless foot.

'Well, don't you look a sight?'

It was Stewart Forgie, making good use of the station's PR hush-budget to bail her out.

'Where is your boot?'

Angel looked down at her mismatched feet and shrugged. As well as having a black eye and a fat lip she was starting to sober up; the beast of all three-day hangovers threatening to settle in if she didn't get a drink inside her to take the edge off.

'Well, you can't go anywhere like this,' he started shepherding her out of the detention centre where each weekend hundreds of over-exuberant revellers would be processed; fined and rudely sobered up. It smelt of bleach. The staff looked weary and disinterested as Stewart hurried Angel past under cover of an oversized hoodie. The detention centre was strategically located to rapidly evict hung-over revellers off the Observer, so it wasn't long before they arrived at the shuttle bays. Angel slid down a chute into an executive pod with her father's decal on the upholstery. She immediately began hunting for a drink.

Stewart slid in behind her and started buckling himself into a seat.

'Forget it, this pod is dry. Just get into your harness because I told the pilot not to hang around.'

At that exact moment the boosters fired and the shuttle was blasted out of the launch tube into space. Angel was sent bouncing about the shuttle's interior like a pong ball as gravity lifted abruptly.

'Ow,' she tried to shield her battered face as she ricocheted off the comms panel.

'Yes sir?'

It was the pilot answering the buzz of her forehead connecting with the talk button.

'Carry on Commander Sefton; we're all good back here.'

Stewart muted the cabin mic and caught hold of the back of Angel's jacket, yanking her down towards a seat until she was able to get one arm hooked into a harness and bring the rest of her limbs under control. The press officer looked at her, shaking his head.

'What am I supposed to do with you? You look like a Diso cage-fighter, not the young lady of the station.'

Angel scratched her fuzzy scalp. *Incoming lecture; set neural pathways to ignore,* she thought darkly and tried to assess the damage of her recent bar-fight by her reflection in the shuttle window. Through the mirage of her pounded face she could see dozens of ships of various flavours zipping around in orbit. Frigates, couriers, transporters and cutters – some with the distinctive avian features of Imperial vessels, but mostly independents or the flat and muted designs of the Federation; traders and tycoons here to do business or take some R-and-R at one of the luxury Observer resorts. Her thoughts turned to getting back out on the interstellar highway as quickly as possible. But then something her addled mind had been doing its best to forget popped up; a memory from the card game earlier that day – or had it been yesterday? It didn't really matter anyway because she was flat broke, maxed out on negative creds with a busted shield and no stock to sell. When her credit for next week's berthing fee got rejected in six days her ship would be evicted, shield or no, and without any stock in her hold her reputation would fall sharply just for taking off. That would mean kissing goodbye to her pilot's digs too. She was more than screwed; she was methane-vapour at a fire pit.

'Angel?'

As she had wallowed in despair Stewart Forgie had continued speaking, mapping out his plan to get her back on the straight and narrow with the minimum negative publicity.

'Sorry, missed that. What?'

'I said you are lucky Captain Riley thinks so much of you as the investor has decided to go ahead based on his recommendation alone, despite the fact you missed your appointment yesterday afternoon and are in no fit state to go anywhere today.'

Yesterday afternoon? So, she had been in the detention centre overnight. She lifted up an arm to sniff her pit. She wrinkled her nose and Stewart sighed. 'Yes, you smell like a stink-gland. We'll get you back to your father's chambers and you can take a shower and get some lunch. I'll make sure no guests are invited into the family rooms until we've got you and your cage-fighter face out of the way.'

He pulled a tablet out of the arm of his chair and tapped the screen, passing the terminal over to Angel when he was done.

'Your generous benefactor has offered to pay for your repairs, so please tap in to authorise them. Tomorrow morning we'll get your cargo bay filled up and ship you out of Vesper-M4 before anyone can see you. The thuggery plastered all over your pretty face should be gone by the time you get back.'

Angel was about to argue; she wasn't a piece of meat – although right now to be fair she did feel a little like tenderised beef. But metaphorically she certainly wasn't and she hadn't agreed to this high risk mission for some faceless capitalist.

But that nagging thought from earlier returned and insisted on laying her cards down on the table. It didn't take long as she didn't really have any. She either had to take the job, or sell what was left of her ship and move back in with her parents. No competition. Her mother was far more terrifying than crossing pirate infested space with a belly full of gold.

Chapter 6

As Angel marched through the passages and platforms of the space station heading towards the port she felt a bit weird. She was fully sober for the first time in three days; not even the trace of a hangover. Stewart and her mother had conspired to purge the family quarters of anything even remotely resembling alcohol the night before and she had been too battered and exhausted to head out in search of contraband. At one point her headache had got so bad she'd been tempted to try a sip of the large bottle of Amxitsa cologne left out on her dresser, but instead she'd showered and eaten a huge meal, then slept for fifteen hours straight. Her eye was still puffy and starting to turn yellow at the edges but the swollen lip was almost back to normal size with just a decorative scab over a blossoming rosy split. After a very cold shower to de-fuzz her brain Angel felt alert and, dare she say it, was beginning to feel an edge of positivity creeping back in.

Maybe she could turn this all around?

It was mid-morning and the bulk of the hubbub that marked the start of the day was over. Her boots clanked against the metal walkway as she strode through the corridor, holographic advertising boards oscillating in her peripheral vision left and right. They peddled the usual familiar promos; haulage spares from Logsdon Bruno, export accounting from Ian and Elliott Simpsoid and legal services courtesy of Giles, Purcell, Letham, Meyer and Watson. There was even a long running commercial for Hilditch Investigations, although the smiling portrait of the good detective Alec Hilditch made him look more like he was advertising toothpaste than private investigation services. Angel had always thought anyone with teeth that white couldn't work under cover.

As space stations went, the Slough Orbital was fairly basic. It was an industrial outpost; the riveted plates and grills lining the chambers and tunnels gradually scabbing over with centuries of oily crud and smut. The flickering 3D commercials espoused the virtues of the latest hardpoint mining laser or heavy-duty cargo extender. Graphite dust accumulated in every corner, rounding off the sharp edges of metallic construction with a greasy crust. There was little point in trying to fight the grime when your entire economy was based on the filthy business of hauling metal and rock.

But rock wasn't what she would be hauling today. Her hold would be packed with a dangerous load of precious metal that she would be dragging right through the heart of LHS 3443. This made her very nervous.

Still, she thought, *at least I'll be part of a convoy accompanied by heavily fortified fighters.* After making four good jumps she could deliver the payload and collect her creds, and after a few more repairs and some long overdue upgrades she might even have enough left over to keep going for a couple of jumps; just pick a direction and flit a couple more light years further out, see where her sensors took her.

'You're looking very pleased with yourself.'

It was Jeremy Kram, leaning on the control room hatch puffing on an atom-pipe.

Angel wrinkled her nose.

'Haven't you managed to quit that ridiculous habit yet? You must be the only person this side of Lave still sucking on one of those things.'

He sucked on it a couple more times, blowing a puff of the odourless vapour it produced in her direction. Angel recoiled, disgusted.

'Don't you care about your health?'

'Apparently it's not as bad for your health as an afternoon with you.' Angel was confused for a moment and then remembered her battered face.

'Yeah, well I haven't got time for your crapola today; I have a job. Excuse me.'

The cocky pilot in the doorway barely moved as she went to squeeze past him. He smelt of cheap aftershave and garlic.

'Well you'd better make time for me. I'm your escort.'

Angel stopped dead. There were two things about that statement she didn't like.

Number one, Jeremy Kram? He was a nice enough guy; boyish charm; inappropriate sense of humour; really stupid vapour-habit. He was even quite a zippy pilot when he could hold on to the tail end. They had graduated from the academy together – Angel, Jeremy and Rachel – three years ago. Not a bad flyer, but as far as weapons control went he couldn't hit a space dredger with a dumbfire at twenty paces.

The second thing about the statement that bothered her was more fundamental though.

'Escort?'

Angel was glaring at him from just six inches away in the doorway. 'What do you mean, *escort*?'

Kram smirked.

'You see, that's what alcohol and bar fights do to your brain? Have you already forgotten what an escort is?'

Angel pushed all the way past, brushing him off.

'I know full-well what an escort is. What I *don't* know is when my cargo train and heavily armed convoy turned into an idiot with a pulse shooter.'

She burst into the control room to find Rachel Hanandroo on duty. She was busy tapping away on the vast console spread across the desk to bring a Fer-de-Lance back up on the launch deck. Angel glanced out into the expanse of the spaceport through the control room window. She saw her own Cobra sitting out on the platform with a couple of maintenance droids busying themselves around her portside wing.

As well as the 'Lance there was a beaten up looking Anaconda still smoking from battle, and a single blunt-nosed Federation-style Eagle berthed up beside her. She shook her head, running her eyes over its less than impressive armaments. A couple of beam lasers, two medium hardpoint cannons and a missile launcher. If they came across anything even vaguely prepared to do battle they were toast.

'Rachel, where is my convoy?'

'Convoy?' The engineer ran her finger across the manifest on her tablet. 'I have you and Tailspin heading off for Mervon in LHS 3439 in two hours; Paul Martin is running a short haul of granite slag to the dump yard at three, and there's a stag party organised by Guy Clark Adventures going out on some souped up Shao-shuttles when they've sobered up enough to find the spaceport. Nothing else due in or out today.' She looked at Angel, confused. 'What are you carrying?'

At that moment the comms board beeped demandingly and Rachel flicked the channel open.

'Consignment for Commander Rose,' the voice crackled through the intercom.

'Oh, never mind. I'll see for myself.'

She thumbed a button to let the delivery runner into the loading tunnel clamped on to the Cobra's belly and initiated the scanners. A red meshwork graphic scribed the composition of the container load across the flat screen in front of her. Rachel's eyes widened.

'Gold?'

'Exactly. Hence my interest in a convoy. Do you really expect me to jump into the middle of LHS 3443 with a bellyful of gold and this space-cake beside me?'

Rachel swiped at her tablet a couple of times, worry creeping across her face.

'Angel, the convoy for Mervon left yesterday afternoon. You're more than 18 hours late. Today I only have you and the space-cake leaving Vespa-M4.'

'Erm, I am actually here you know? With feelings and everything,' Kram said in a sulky voice from the doorway.

'Well, there is no way,' Angel stated bluntly, ignoring him. 'You can tell them to take their gold back to Mr Corporate Affairs and he can shove it up his nebula.'

Rachel frowned down at her tablet again.

'How are you going to pay for the repairs? Did you sell the silk?' Angel winced.

'Not exactly. Mother gave it away.' Rachel's face went white.

'Oh Angel, nothing? Your rank,' she looked back at her tab and started tapping away furiously. 'I'm going to have to bump you two levels. You'll be right back to square one. You won't even qualify for your bunk.'

'Thank you for your frank and observant appraisal. Ship's morale officer you are not.'

'Looks like you're stuck with me,' Kram had sidled up behind her. 'Aww, come on, we'll be fine. The convoy will have dredged the area just ahead of us and you know I can fly my little princess in rings around any chancers that do stumble upon us. Four quick jumps and we both pick up one of the best pay-creds we've ever earned.'

Angel looked at Rachel who was still staring at her with dismay.

'You know what will happen if you can't settle for the repairs. I have no control over private contractors; those bots are merciless in recovering bad debt.'

Just when Angel thought it couldn't get any worse, Captain Riley came striding into the control room.

'Everything alright, ladies?'

'Err, what about me?' Kram said.

The naval officer looked him up and down with open disdain before turning back to leer at Angel and Rachel.

'Like I said, everything alright, ladies?'

Angel felt like she was being circled by Vipers. Her whole body screamed that this was a bad situation she should have nothing to do with, but what choice did she have? Without the credits to pay for the repairs her ship would be pulled apart by corporate salvage bots before being impounded for not being space-worthy when she failed to pay next week's berthing fees. But worse than that she would have to collect her gear from her Pilot's Federation quarters and move back in with her parents. She bit her lip and made a very hard but unavoidable decision.

'Everything is just spacey, thanks. Loading up the hold now and then lady Tailspin and myself will get moving.'

'Good, good,' he unclipped a small tablet from his belt and handed it to her. 'I need your thumb on the contract; it's pretty standard.'

Angel took the pad and glanced over the tiny scrolling text, not reading it at all.

'Fine,' she said, utterly defeated as she placed her thumb in the sig-box.

'Great!' The captain pulled what looked like a thin metal manacle out from his inside pocket. 'Wrist please.' Angel looked at him. 'Sorry?'

'I need your wrist.'

'Err, why?' She was backing away from him holding her wrist defensively to her chest.

'Don't worry, it's just insurance. You did read the contract you just signed, didn't you?' His smirk told Angel he was fully aware that she had done no such thing.

Angel's eyes flicked to the bangle. 'What does it do?'

'Oh, this thing? It's mainly a location sensor. It links you to a little programme that keeps an eye on what's happening around you. It's a brand new system just out of R&D so you're actually very privileged. Its job is to protect the interests of the investor and since you are carrying a large chunk of the investor's interests that means, by de facto, it will be protecting you.'

Angel remained dubious. 'How?'

The naval captain sighed and started to look impatient.

'Look it really doesn't matter. You signed the contract and spent the repair creds, so unless you want to talk about *another* way you might be able to settle your debts...' his comment was loaded with innuendo and Angel shuddered, forcing her right arm to extend so that he could clip the bangle around her wrist. 'Good girl,' he crooned.

He closed the metal band and it clicked decisively shut. Then she heard a whirring sound from outside and a hover-bot glided in, propellers buzzing. It was about the size of a family selection biscuit tin and hovered at head height. Seeing it arrive the captain reached inside his breast pocket and pulled out a small control pad. He punched in a code and the lights on Angel's wrist clamp flashed red. The lights on a small panel mounted in the robot's chest were blinking in a similar way. It hovered a little closer and then the LEDs on both panels flashed in sequence together before all turning green.

'All set,' the captain looked at her directly. 'Meet your new best friend and business partner. DORIS here is programmed to keep an eye on you, stop you from making any stupid mistakes that might put your shipment at risk.'

Angel looked from the hovering biscuit tin to her wrist. 'DORIS?'

'Detail Oriented Remote Investment Surveillance bot. It's chipped with a database of sound financial decisions and programmed to make suggestions about the best course of action based on your current status.'

'Best from whose perspective?' Angel was highly suspicious of the whirring computational tin. She'd heard a whisper about this kind of development on the uniweb. Some people had dubbed the technology 'conscience bots'.

'Why, from the investor's perspective of course.'

'I suppose this is a geo-tag?' Angel asked, twisting the clamp around her wrist.

'Clever girl, and don't even think about tampering with it as I have a personal link to the output and will come after you so hard it will feel like being run over by a meteor. Likewise if you try and leave the bot behind; if it gets more than fifty metres away I come looking for you, and I won't be amused. Understood?'

This day just gets better and better, Angel thought, before brushing past both the captain and her escort to get suited up.

'What do you think?'

The small propellers holding the hover-bot aloft whirred a little faster and it followed her out of the door.

* * *

Angel pulled the keyboard out of its storage slot and tucked it under the flight-desk clamp in front of her, leaning back in the command chair as she checked the ship's forward display. She looked down at the "H" key, worn to sheen and no longer actually showing the letter "H" at all. Most people used voice-control these days but she'd never fancied that upgrade, even though it wasn't expensive. She preferred to be in physical control of her ship, punching in the co-ordinates she wanted to travel to directly rather than asking it politely to take her somewhere.

'That mode of interface is outdated and ineffective.'

Angel nearly jumped out of her flight suit at the voice that came out of the whirring bot that had entered the cockpit behind her.

'So you speak? You scared the living space out of me!'

'I am fitted with a voice synthesiser and speech recognition circuits to better deliver my analysis and recommendations.'

'Your analysis?'

'Based on comparisons from a database of over fifty billion possible scenarios sampled from a cross-section of mainstream trade negotiations and professions, crowd-sourced from across the galaxy since 2566. I am a personal drone programmed to continually analyse your decisions and suggest a better course of action when the data reveals one.'

'Perfect. So I am saddled with an electronic know-it-all as well as a suicide mission?'

DORIS whirred momentarily.

'I found no record of a suicide instruction in the contract details. Your interface is obsolete though.'

'What?'

'That keyboard contraption that looks like it belongs in a museum. Why have you not upgraded to voice-control?'

Angel glanced at the plastic relic on her dashboard, accumulating dust and grime from years of hauling minerals and rock. There was a certain beautiful irony in the fact that this question was being posed by what seemed likely to be the most annoying collection of computer circuits attached to a voice synthesiser ever invented.

'No comment.'

The drone whirred as the lights in its processor core flashed.

'I calculate an eighty-five percent increase in productivity if you upgrade to voice assisted controls. This is an unprecedented amount.'

'Matched by an equal drop in mental acuity,' Angel started punching numbers into the keyboard, gritting her teeth.

The drone's circuits flashed busily.

'Your assessment of the data does not compute.'

'I didn't assess any data. I made an observation; formed an opinion. It's what we do, us humans. It's why we are superior to machines,' Angel turned to the hovering bot and looked at it meaningfully, 'like you.'

DORIS whirred with an air of indignation.

'My circuits are capable of processing more than fifty petaflops of instructions. Compare that with the average human brain, which can only handle around one hundred and fifty trillion computations and I think it's clear to everyone who is superior.'

'Computational volume does not equate to intelligence. And if you keep up the logic-based chat it's going to drive me mad enough to do something stupid, which is exactly why I didn't upgrade to voice controls. So you can stick that in your data-sets and compute it, you silicon shithead.'

Lights flashed and the drone's helicopter blades whirred earnestly.

'Your analysis is flawed,' it said eventually, 'and your language is appalling.'

'Commander Rose, you are cleared for orbit,' Rachel's voice crackled through the comms panel, breaking the tension.

Angel pulled her harness tight and flicked a switch to hand the controls over to the station's berthing computer, which lifted her ship deftly up off the landing pad before spitting it out into orbit. Immediately they left the slowly rotating maw of the spaceport, zero-g kicked in and everything felt a bit lighter. Now redundant the rotary blades above the bot stopped whirring and retracted back inside its body as it switch to magnetic pulse control. *It was a relief to get rid of the buzzing noise*, thought Angel.

She looked out at the ships flying this way and that around the station as her moderately armed Eagle escort slipped in behind her. It reminded her again what a foolish errand she was about to run; strange how DORIS didn't have anything helpful to say about that.

She checked the sector-view map on the side display panel then tapped some co-ordinates into the keyboard. Her vision blurred with the reverberation of the cockpit as the engines roared and the Cobra shifted lanes, accelerating through the traffic to get ready for the jump. The soothing robotic voice of SysCon kicked in as they approached the slipstream to jump-orbit.

'Good morning Commander Rose, please state your destination.'

'LHS 3439.'

There was a slight pause before her navigation panel lit up with her clearance code.

'Thank you Commander, you are cleared to jump. Travel safely.'

'Are you on my back, Tailspin?'

The comms panel crackled again and it was Kram, sounding wounded.

'I am ready to piggyback the jump yes, and I wish you wouldn't call me that.'

'Yeah, well you know what wishes got?'

'What?'

Angel flicked the comms link off, leaving him to wonder while she finished preparations for their first jump. She just hoped they would make it unmolested through the next fifteen light years as they had to refuel in a pretty hot sector. She didn't like making herself such a juicy target for any stray bandit with a taste for gold.

'And you'd better buckle up too, DORIS, because antique interface or not this puppy's about to jump into hyperspace and your moral compass won't look quite so clever bent around the air vents.'

Angel smirked at the effect this had on the robot, which hummed darkly as it activated its magnetic safety strip and was summarily stuck to the cabin door. Angel turned back to the front HUD.

'Let's get this space-train moving then,' she said to herself as she leaned forward and tapped an incredibly worn out 'H' key.

Chapter 7

Angel nudged the nose of the Cobra into perfect alignment with the jump corridor etching itself out in a thin matrix across the HUD. As the ship locked on to the trajectory she sank back into her command chair, the g-force of rapid acceleration pressing against her whole body like a hungry lover. They'd done this many times before, her ship and her, but she still felt the thrill of it when the hyperspace drive kicked in. The engines throbbed, vibrating the air around her and making her teeth rattle as the ship screamed towards a crack of impossible brightness that was blossoming on the black canvas of the non-horizon; a rip in space and time that she could slip into for a shortcut through reality. Hyperspace; she didn't really get the science behind it so remained in awe of the magic even after thousands of jumps. In an instant the space in front of her roared with incandescent energy and they were sucked between dimensions. For a heartbeat it was like all reality went white – perfectly, completely and quite unremarkably white. Even sound turned white in that instant, then almost before it began it was all over again, hyperspace spitting her out light years from where she had started; regurgitated back into normal space like a cosmic furball.

Time's up ... energy spent. Time to fuel up before jumping again ... 'Hop, hop, hop, like a space bunny trying not run into a fox.'

'I beg your pardon?'

DORIS whirred, detaching itself from the wall and hovering over to look at the HUD readouts.

'Are you still here?'

Angel looked to her right to see Kram's ship spat out just behind her. Good. He was managing to get that right at least. She sat there, cold; ship's systems on minimum, shields down, waiting for the sector to be drawn up on the holo-dash in front of her. She gazed at the red dwarf they were here to visit; to scoop up a bit of fuel before making the last two jumps to payday. The fading sun glowed a pinkish red through her windscreen, crystallising ice creeping in from the corners framing it in twinkly light. *So beautiful; like candlelight at a romantic table*, she mused, and then mentally thumped herself several times in the face for having such a ridiculously sentimental thought.

'Okay, set a course for a quick scoop and let's get on our way. This area is reading very hot for piracy, so let's run as cool as we can; try and stay out of sight. Okay?'

'Sure captain,' the voice over the comms link was snarky. 'If you can't stand the heat, stay cold like a turkey. I gotcha.'

Angel frowned.

'What does that even mean, you freak?'

DORIS started making ticking noises as its processors ramped up.

'I believe your escort has confused his idioms,' it said in a voice so full of scorn it seemed hard to believe it wasn't human. 'Let's hope he's a better pilot than an intellectual because my sensors detect long range scanners from sector G15 are probing us.'

'What?'

Angel grabbed the keyboard out of its slot and started hitting keys, bringing up the scan logs.

'Oh, piss and gravity.'

DORIS was right. There was a ship in range; something big and bad looking.

'We've been spotted, Kram. Sector G15. Someone's definitely showing an interest. I'm going to put up my shields and hope they didn't spot the gold yet, but get ready for company.'

'Right you are.'

She looked out of the side window at Kram. He grinned like a moron and gave her the double thumbs up.

'Just keep your hands on your flight stick Tailspin, and don't let anybody get on my arse.'

Her own scanners now hard at work to assess the danger, she saw the wedge-shape of a Fer-de-Lance sketched out on the dash in front of her. This ship was built with one purpose in mind; destruction. It was bristling with armaments; hard points loaded up with shield crushing cannons and missiles; hull ripping multi-cannons and lasers mounted on gimbals anywhere else there was room. She swallowed hard. They didn't have the fuel to jump out of there and the Fer-de-Lance was coming in fast, like a wolf on the scent of its prey.

'Shit,' she looked at DORIS hovering over by the nav-panel. 'Round about now would be an excellent time for you to come up with something brilliant.'

Its processor chucked and whirred.

'You can't outrun them. Your shields will probably last two hits. My advice is to surrender.'

Angel stared at DORIS.

'That's it? With all your billions of scenarios analysed and assessed? I could have come up with that myself. In fact, it was just what I was thinking.'

'Sometimes the simple answer is the right answer, so even an idiot can be right occasionally.'

'You're a useless heap of silicon chips is what you are,' Angel said, burned by the inference.

DORIS hummed indignantly but didn't add anything else.

Angel looked at the sector map, celestial objects mapped out in wireframe hologram. There was a small asteroid belt a little way off to port. It might offer them some shelter, a chance to dodge the larger ship like cat and mouse in amongst the flying space rock until help could arrive. It was worth a try anyway, and they could still surrender after the first shot was fired; if a first shot ever got fired. She punched the keyboard to open a comms channel to Kram.

'I'm going to make a run for it to that rock garden in G10. With a bit of luck they spent so much on that arsenal they overlooked decent thrusters. If they give chase just keep them off my back. We're not looking to engage, Kram – we're just sticking our toe in the cosmic pool of 'can we get the fuck out of here?' Okay?'

'Sure thing.'

Kram sounded far too happy for Angel's liking, considering what was headed their way.

'And don't get killed,' she added before snapping the comms link off and stepping on the thrusters, pulling the flight stick over hard to port to bank the ship in the direction of the asteroids.

The engines burned fuel, rattling the cockpit and causing her peripheral vision to shudder as she pushed *Hope Falls* to her limit for normal space. She glanced at the course readout for the Fer-de-Lance. Perhaps it was innocently on its way somewhere else and just happened to look like it was making a beeline for them? This optimistic little fantasy was rapidly quashed as the 'Lance changed course to intercept, accelerating hard through the distant space as its crew figured out where they were heading. By the clip they were travelling at it looked like they hadn't skimped on thruster upgrades either.

Damn. Time to panic, thought Angel. 'They're closing in.'

'Okay, taking up a defensive position. Just keep your foot to the floor. I'll try and slow them down.'

'Kram! DON'T get killed, you got me? If they even get one solid hit on you I want you to surrender, because I sure as hell will be.'

Kram's ship fell out of sight as he dropped behind and to starboard, putting himself protectively between the Cobra and the approaching interloper. Her ship's telemetry sketched out a hologram of the Eagle. It looked tiny beside the 'Lance and although she had to grudgingly admire Kram's bravery it didn't exactly make her feel safe. She tweaked a couple of settings and channelled a bit more power to the thrusters, pressing her foot down hard enough to make her thigh muscles quiver.

She watched the green dots at the centre of her display pulse softly as the orange dot heading in from G15 got closer and closer with every sweep of the radar arm. She glanced at the sector map just above it. They weren't going to make the asteroid belt before the 'Lance cut them off.

'Piss and gravity!'

Her chest tight, ears pulsing with adrenaline-fuelled blood, the seconds stretched out into interminable minutes as the radar sketched out the approaching doom. *That's the trouble with space,* thought Angel. It was so damn big everything took forever to arrive, then suddenly it was there and all over in the blink of an eye. It really jangled the nerves.

A couple more radar sweeps and the 'Lance registered close enough for Angel to scan its combat computer. Pretty much every one of those bad old guns was powering up and pointing at her. Her HUD began to flash numbers that made her stomach flip over as the hologram of the Fer-de-Lance lit up along its fuselage with the various guns coming online. Angel watched with grim despair as two tiny dots detached from the ship's missile launchers, rushing towards her and Kram.

'Shit! Incoming!'

She took evasive action, yawing to port to put a little distance between her and the Eagle and priming the heat sink vents. Kram nosed up in front of her protectively and fired off his own pair of missiles towards the incoming dots. The radar showed the distance between the two sets of projectiles closing rapidly. Five clicks; four clicks; three, two, one … a puff of orange blossomed in the distance as opposing missiles met and detonated. All gone, but the attacking vessel was already launching a fresh salvo. Four missiles – from the look of it these were heat seekers. She checked her vents were still primed and ready to dump hot waste if the missiles got past Kram.

'Keep on a course for the rocks. I'm going to draw them away from you.'

'Shit! Tailspin, don't be an arse. You don't have the shields for close combat with that tank!'

Ignoring her, Kram broke away from the Cobra in a high looping arch, swinging the Eagle to starboard at its apex and peeling away as he vented a flood of hot plasma to grab the attention of the heat seekers. It worked; as he banked sharply all four of the missiles adjusted course to match his, locking on to his howling thrusters. Angel checked the readout on her dash.

'Shit! SHIT!'

The missiles might have been tempted by Kram's plasma fart, but the Fer-de-Lance was still closing on her fast. An orange beam arced experimentally through the blackness, but the 'Lance was still too far away for short range weapons to be effective so it was obviously just meant to intimidate. *It worked,* thought Angel as her mind scrambled for ideas in the void of her rising panic. She was definitely very intimidated. She flicked the comms link over to an open broadcast channel.

'Mayday, mayday. All combat capable ships, this is Alliance trade vessel *Hope Falls*. Urgently requesting backup in sector G12. We're under attack! Any combat capable ships in range please respond!'

She glanced around her, trying to spot Kram. He was off to starboard a few clicks, dancing and twisting the Eagle in a mad ballet as he tried to stay one step ahead of another barrage of missiles. As she watched he managed to detonate two harmlessly in a slew of heat sink exhaust, but another two went slamming into his hull and tail, tossing the small ship about like a stuffed toy in the hands of an exuberant toddler.

Angel tapped her keyboard to see how much damage he'd taken but the chatter of machine gun fire yanked her attention back to her own predicament. A spray of tracer fire raked across the windscreen and then pinged a rapid assault along the top of her cockpit. The 'Lance had come up hard and fast, choking her escape route to the asteroid belt with ease.

She banked hard to port. The engines roared gleefully as she opened up the thrusters, the hull groaning under the stress of the tight turn as pipes and panels throughout the ship's interior popped and fizzed. Her ears roared as fiercely as the engines as adrenaline pumped, her body pressed back into the command chair with the g-force of the manoeuvre.

The cabin was suddenly lit up by twin beams of broiling fire as a beam laser cut up the space in front of her. She flung the flight stick from side to side, corkscrewing and rolling left and right to avoid the scorching path of the beams. The whole cabin shuddered and trembled as she threw the Cobra erratically about.

'Mayday, mayday,' she screamed into an open channel as she wrestled with the flight controls. 'All combat capable ships, this is Alliance trade vessel *Hope Falls*. Urgent assistance required, sector G11. Urgent assistance! Please respond!'

She checked the shield monitor as the laser fire raked sizzling gashes across her fuselage. Eighty percent and falling with every hit. Her dash was blinking and flashing with a stunning display of system alarms as the onslaught intensified. If no help responded by the time her shields fell to twenty percent she would run up the white flag. Hand over the gold and hope to get away with the ship undamaged.

'Where are you Kram? I'm getting hammered here!'

There was a brief moment of silence as the tracer fire stopped, then the ship's radar started bleeping ominously as a volley of small dots were released. The radar showed three heading towards Kram who was limping around to her right; the other three were heading straight for Angel. She gulped and wheeled the ship through the chill of space, opening the heat sink vent and spewing a blanket of hot matter in her wake to throw off the missiles. A rapid concussion ripped through the cockpit as the missiles took the bait, cracking open the darkness with blinding light, warheads booming on every side. Angel's head whipped cruelly from side to side as the ship was flung about, hull shrieking. Deep inside the belly of the craft pipes burst open, vomiting angry steam and gas. The glass in the forward windscreen made an ominous pinking sound as the fuselage twisted with the force of the after-blast swallowing the ship. Angel glanced at the shield readout – *twenty percent*. Dear Lady that was a big hit. One more of those and she was toast. She looked out of the side window to see the 'Lance looming up again, close on her port side.

Kram was nowhere in sight. She looked at the console. Her heart sank. His ship's wireframe was deconstructing in front of her eyes, replaced by a series of radiation and heat signature data scattered about. Before she could run a scan to check for an escape pod, a fresh volley of tracer fire demanded her attention. The Cobra's thrusters howled like a wounded dog as she banked hard to the left, causing bullets to chip across her tail rather than ripping through the belly of her hull.

Shields were eighteen percent. She opened up a proximity channel.

'This is Alliance trade vessel *Hope Falls*; attacking ship hold your fire. I am lowering my shields, you can have my cargo.'

She punched a few buttons on the keyboard and dragged the emergency autopilot control into the navigation bin on the dash. The shipped banked straight away as the computer took over the helm, flattening out its flight path and decelerating to a safe speed for emergency measures to be deployed. An SOS beacon started flashing on the dash letting ships in the vicinity know she was standing down, surrendering. Any more gun play would mean a reputation hit for her attackers – this was where the madness ended.

At least, that's the way it usually went.

Sporadic chain gun fire chattered from behind her, plinking across the hull. With the shields lowered one bullet actually chipped a hairline fracture in the windscreen. It started spreading immediately.

'What the—'

Angel grabbed her EVA helmet and slapped the comms panel again to make sure the channel was open. 'Stand down. I SAID STAND DOWN! I've lowered my shields. I surrender. You can have the damn gold. It's not worth my life.'

She watched, breathing hard as her assailants banked in a lazy arc and then levelled up to face her across a few clicks of cold space. Now the frantic pace of battle had calmed she could read the decal on the nose of the 'Lance. Two broken red rings around a yellow disc with a section cut out – like that Pacman character from ancient Earth computer gaming. The ship's name was 'Majogu's Mutt'.

The comms link crackled as they patched into the channel.

'You have thirty seconds to get your arse into a pod and get clear. I have a new dumbfire missile I've been itching to try out and your ship looks just about dumb enough for target practice.'

The voice sounded amused and there were goading cheers in the background.

'Hey! Wait! I am standing down!'

'Twenty nine … twenty eight … twenty seven …'

'Piss!'

Angel hauled herself out of the command chair and propelled herself towards the escape pod hatch. A quick twist and it was open, the pod already powered up.

'What about me?'

It was DORIS. Angel had all but forgotten about the bot. 'Fifteen … fourteen … thirteen …'

Angel was swinging her feet into the pod now, straightening her body so that she could slip into the narrow cylinder.

'I'm afraid you're on your own; only room in here for one.'

The bot was saying something else but Angel already had the hatch pulled closed and was initiating the eject sequence. The tiny chamber hissed with pressurisation.

'Five … four … three …'

She couldn't hear the comms channel any more but she was counting down inside her head, praying the pod would make it out in time. As it popped out into empty space her ears popped too. The temperature fell sharply and reality shrunk down to a pinpoint, the beating of her heart the only sound. Her breath came next, fogging up the EVA helmet in front of her eyes. For a moment inside that misty bubble the oppressive silence of space seemed inescapably eternal. Then suddenly the galaxy was torn apart by the screeching din of a violent siren.

Chapter 8

The Asp's sensors identified the chunks of twisted metal drifting through space as the carcass of a Cobra. The heat signature coming off what was presumably once a thruster suggested the wreckage was only a few hours old. Katherine whistled.

'Someone really did a number on you,' she said, scanners picking over the debris in search of anything worth salvaging.

She tweaked the roll lever, nudging her vessel out of the path of a particularly angry-looking lump of ex-hull and whistled again as a billion tiny fragments spun like stars through the silent space around her. It was unusual to see a cargo mule blasted apart like this. Whoever was responsible would have taken a big reputation hit and would most likely be wearing a healthy bounty on their head for their trouble. Katherine flipped the HUD to long range scanners to check if the attacker was still mooching around. She quite fancied a dogfight if they were evenly matched and a bounty would definitely come in handy. An impressive snake's nest of dreadlocks decorated with clay beads and metal cuffs floated about her face as she stared into the black depths. It got in the way a bit in zero-g, but she was very proud of her hair, which had seen her christened with her pirate name: *Dread Katherine*. Her flight suit was dark, even before a couple of decades of oily soot from life inside the Hollows had done their work. She wore a broad, heavy studded girdle cinching it tight about her waist. Matching gun-metal cuffs around her wrists and neck and a hooked bolt through the septum of her nose completed the look. It was a look that said 'don't screw with me'. People generally took its advice.

The scanner probed with its electro-magnetic fingers. Nothing close – at least nothing operational – but there was another heat-sig registering not far off the scanner's outer range. Another wreck? Hard to tell at this distance. She flipped the HUD back to short range so she could finish up here and go check it out. The radar swept around her in a lazy arc as she eased her vessel carefully through the slowly tumbling chunks and spinning fragments.

BLIP.

Uh-oh. Katherine stared at the green dot on the outer circle of the scanner as it faded away and then pulsed back to full strength when the radar arm approached again.

BLIP.

Life. Most likely the Cobra's pilot floating through space in the claustrophobic shell of an escape pod.

BLIP.

'Oh, piss in a zero-g bucket ...'

The pirate thought briefly about turning around and ignoring it. The wreckage of the old Cobra suggested the body inside the pod was unlikely to be worth much. Picking up floaters from a recent skirmish almost always ended up being a pain in the cargo bay. You never recovered your costs unless there was a salvage reward on offer.

BLIP.

'*Damn IT!*'

There wasn't much else on the scanner so she decided she might as well scoop up the pod. Maybe its occupant would have a decent environment suit to trade for safe passage? She could definitely do with a new one as hers was falling apart at the seams ... and it wasn't like the Cobra's pilot would need a flight suit with their ship in a million pieces all about them.

Katherine twitched the controls and the Asp's tail-end swung around as the engines pulsed, rattling her teeth through the command chair. The vibration made her nose itch so she rubbed it with her grime-stained sleeve then tapped the display panel to lock on to the escape pod. She eased a few clicks of forward propulsion out of the thrusters, using her other hand to prime the salvage scoop.

'Come to momma,' Katherine cooed as her ship approached the drifting metal pod, rolling gently through the vacuum of space like a human-sized flask. She cut the thrusters as she drew alongside it, peering in through the vis-panel to catch a glimpse of her prize.

Inside she could see someone with arms clamped about their head as if in pain. She switched the scanner to biognosis. Everything seemed in order; occupant undamaged, vital signs strong and the pod's environmental readings were all normal. The body was slight, probably a woman then. At that moment she looked up, hands clamped over her ears as her eyes met Katherine's across the short expanse of nothing separating them.

'Help me,' she screamed silently through the vis-panel, clearly in agony. 'Pretty,' Katherine said as she got to work on the controls again, manoeuvring her salvage scoop into position. The anguished face staring up at her was both vulnerable and strong, the rough and practical shaved head adding to the illusion of tough fragility by the delicate bone structure it left exposed.

'Maybe this will be a worthwhile salvage after all.'

* * *

As Katherine approached the large metal cylinder now clamped in her salvage rack she could hear a high whining sound, modulating in pitch from annoying to even more annoying as what would appear to be a siren blared inside the capsule. She pulled herself hand-over-hand along the grab rail lining the tunnels of her ship then planted her feet either side of the pod's hatch before flipping a switch on her magboots to activate them. Her feet stuck to the metal surface of the capsule creating the illusion of gravity so she could reach down to turn the release valve. The metal tube hissed as the pressure inside equalised with the cargo bay. The siren grew louder.

When the hatch was fully unlocked Katherine hauled it open and the capsule's passenger thrust her right arm up through the hole as if trying to get away from it. The arm screamed with the modulating tones of the siren and Katherine tripped the magnetic switch on her boots to off, tumbling backwards away from the offensive noise. Next the shaved head with the delicate bone structure followed the arm out of the hatch and screamed at her.

'Towel!'

'What?'

'A wet towel. To wrap around it!'

By "it" she clearly meant the thing on her wrist, which was the source of the racket. Katherine cast about for something to muffle it. No towels but she did use the vent pipes in here to dry her laundry, what little she did while she was in space, and there were some long socks and a bra tied to the thermal vent. Katherine launched herself off the grab rail across the room and pulled them off the piping. Angel had floated over too and stuck her arm out towards Katherine, who proceeded to wrap the damp socks around the blaring wrist clamp before tying them in place with the bra. The two of them tumbled slowly as one through the null-gravity as she worked.

Angel raised her eyebrows as the bra was tied on. Katherine had the decency to blush a little as the sound of the siren dulled slightly under the layers of clothing.

'Not everyone carries a towel around with them,' she shouted over the top of the still piercing sound of the siren. 'How do we make that stop?'

'My bot! Did you see it on the scanner?'

Katherine shook her head.

'Proximity alarm. We need to be within fifty metres!'

'Sit tight, I'll take a look.'

Angel nodded and shoved her bundled up wrist between her thighs to deaden the blare a little more.

'Please hurry. My brain is about to explode.'

Katherine had a moment to feel envious of the screaming wrist band, clamped as it was between those strong-looking thighs, all wrapped up in a damp bra. She smiled wickedly at the thought before pulling herself back into the ship, twisting the airlock tight behind her, leaving Angel alone with the din of the siren.

* * *

Just when Angel thought she could stand it no more the alarm suddenly stopped, leaving in its wake an equally deafening silence ringing with tinnitus bells. The airlock opened and the girl with the dreadlocks came back in. Her skin was pale, like most people of western Earth heritage who spent their life in space, but smeared with grey streaks of oil and grime – again another sign of a solitary pilot's life in a floating tin can in constant need of repair.

'Better?'

Angel felt vaguely uncomfortable under the girl's scowling scrutiny. 'Yes, much better. Thanks.'

'How long have you been like that?'

Angel winced. She'd been floating in that torturous capsule with the alarm blaring for what seemed like days, but it had probably only been ninety minutes or so.

'Too long.'

'It's just outside,' Katherine nodded towards the salvage hatch. 'We need to get you into the ship before I open the hatch up. Unless you fancy a spacewalk without your pod?'

Angel followed, pulling herself along the grab rail through the corridor linking the cargo bay with the rest of the ship. Up on the flight deck Katherine regarded Angel carefully as she instructed the salvage arm to bring the bot inside.

'I'm Angel,' Angel said, reaching her hand out in greeting.

'Nice suit,' Katherine said ignoring the hand. 'Shame about your ship.' Angel looked out at the remains of her Cobra and sighed.

'Yeah, well that seems to be my luck right now. I had a hold full of gold too, which I'm sure my client will miss a lot more.'

Katherine's ears perked up.

'You were out here alone with a belly full of yellow?'

She tapped the scanner display to start sweeping again. A nice little load of gold bricks would go down a treat right about now.

'Not alone, no, there was an Eagle with me.'

'Ah, the other wreck on my long range sensor?'

'My escort. We were ambushed by a heavily armed Fer-de-Lance. Take no prisoners kind of mentality; decal was broken red circles around a yellow disc with a section cut out – like a cheese. Did you see any other pods?'

Katherine shook her head. 'Sounds like the Cypher Punks from the decal. I'm surprised they blasted you into so many pieces though. Not their style at all and they'll be paying for it in rep levels. I suppose they got all your gold?'

'I guess so. Hard to tell really when you've jettisoned yourself in a metal tube and your eardrums are being split open by an air raid siren.'

'How about this bot?'

'What about it?'

'Worth much?'

Angel sighed. 'Oh yes, that's right. I'm just a meal ticket to you?'

Katherine shrugged. 'It's just business sweet cheeks. Don't get all thermal. I could have left you floating through space to become fertiliser.'

'The bot is a surveillance unit. The client attached it to me to make sure his booty was safe.'

'That worked out well then, didn't it?' Katherine said as she finished the pressurisation sequence in the salvage hold and made her way back down the ladder to check out the new cargo.

Angel followed.

'I doubt it would fetch much in material salvage. Whether the data has any value will probably depend on how into pie-charts you are. But you'll need to find a way of deactivating the proximity alarm before I let you take it any further than fifty metres from this wristband again.'

Angel's face darkened slightly as a thought occurred to her. 'Unless you're planning to sell me with it?'

'Tempting, but you can relax. I'm not a slaver – and there isn't enough meat on you for livestock.'

Katherine laughed at the look on Angel's face then twisted the airlock open and pulled herself through the hatch to check out the bot.

* * *

DORIS was floating in the middle of the cargo bay humming indignantly. When Katherine approached the bot ran a quick scan and started buzzing crossly. 'Oh perfect. Not only have you lost all of our cargo but now we are in the clutches of a pirate. Well done, Commander Rose.'

Angel hung beside the dreadlocked pilot defiantly. 'It's not as if I had a choice you stupid robot. If you recall I was drifting through space in an escape pod with your proximity alarm perforating my eardrums. We're lucky to be anywhere at all.'

'If you had followed my instructions and stood down immediately instead of trying to be a hero we wouldn't be in this mess, any of it.'

'No offence DORIS, but I don't take instructions from a glorified calculator, especially not when it is telling me to roll over and play puppy dog.'

'Oh really? And yet here we are; captive of a pirate, no ship, no cargo and a dead escort. That's pretty much playing puppy dog tied up in a sack ready to be tossed into the river. So congratulations on executing a terminally flawed plan.'

Angel bristled. 'Listen you heap of over critical circuit boards, I didn't want to take this job to start with. I told Kram not to get killed, but he took on that tank anyway. And besides, how do you know this woman ...' Angel realised she still didn't know her name and turned expectantly.

'Katherine ...'

'Thank you,' she turned back to the bot. 'You don't know *Katherine* is a pirate.'

'Oh purlease,' the bot's circuitry radiated sarcasm in a way no other type of electronics could. 'Filthy, shabby flight suit; grubby face and hands; jewellery that looks like it could knock satellites out of orbit and a twelve inch blade strapped to her belt? Not to mention one of the smelliest-looking mess of rat's tails on her head I've ever seen. Then there is the small matter of the skull and cross-cannons decal on this rust-bucket of an Asp that scooped us up. How many clues do you need? You can't really be so naïve as to think anything else can you?'

Angel was fuming now. Katherine just looked dumbfounded at the verbal onslaught from the whirring box of electronics hovering in front of her.

'Erm, I can hear how rude you're being.'

DORIS turned its flashing sensors on Katherine. 'And this should concern me for what reason?'

Now it was Katherine's turn to bristle. 'Well, I could chuck you back out into the vacuum of space for starters. So you be polite about me and my lovely Mischief's Pearl,' she stroked the metal panelled interior of the cargo bay affectionately, 'and we might let you stay aboard.'

DORIS's circuits hummed as they calculated the odds. 'Unlikely,' the bot stated plainly. 'My sensors detect I'm about the most valuable thing on this floating garbage can, and the only chance you have of recouping your fuel costs is by returning myself and Commander Rose here safely to the Slough Orbital space station, which is owned by her father.'

Katherine eyed Angel even more appreciatively than before.

'Oh great,' Angel stormed, more annoyed by the association of status than the fact the bot had just handed over every card she was holding. She turned to glare at Katherine, arms crossed defensively.

'Well?'

Katherine raised an eyebrow in reply.

'*Are* you a pirate?'

Katherine tossed her hair back over her shoulders and stood tall and proud. 'Arrrrr …' she mocked in a theatrically piratical accent before finally holding out her hand in greeting. 'Dread Katherine, at yerrr service ma'am.'

She hooted with laughter at the look on Angel's face before twisting her body around and hauling herself back through the airlock towards the flight deck.

Chapter 9

'I'm afraid the best I can offer you is a mag-harness on the tank rack, unless you want to slip into a stasis tube? I wasn't exactly expecting passengers.'

Angel frowned. 'And risk waking up on the *unpleasant* side of a pleasure clipper at Pog Hobdonia? I'd rather float thanks.'

DORIS bleeped gently as its processors processed. 'According to my databank you're at greater risk of being sold as medical supplies.'

Katherine snorted with laughter. 'I don't know about that,' she said running an appreciative eye over Angel's rump as it floated past. 'I'd pay for a dance.'

Angel seized the grab rail and spun herself around to glare at Katherine, cheeks flaring red. 'Do you mind? I might just be a piece of meat to you but I'd appreciate a little respect.'

'Your bot has a sense of humour – the electronic one I mean,' she smirked, eyes flicking back to Angel's rear end as she struggled to keep her body under control in the gravity free environment. 'That's pretty unusual for a machine.'

Angel's mood was getting darker by the minute. 'Well, I'm glad you think it's funny. I've only had to put up with this acidic heap of circuits and switches for twenty-four hours and I've already lost my sense of humour.'

'Okay, well there's clearly nothing left of your ship worth picking up so let's go check out what's left of your escort.'

Katherine tugged herself over to the command chair and strapped in, leaving her cabin guests to sort themselves out. She wasn't going to be travelling very fast; there was too much flying debris around to risk running into anything that could punch a hole in the hull, but even at low speeds a passenger who wasn't strapped in could get spun around in a very disorienting way.

The robot's gyroscope would keep it steady relative to the surrounding environment with magnetic pulses, but Angel would have a much more nauseating ride if she didn't attach herself to something solid. She pushed off the back of the command chair towards the rack of tanks over by the hatch, each one filled with enough compressed air to support an EVA suit for about ten hours. Grabbing hold of the rack with both hands she twisted her body around and pushed her back on to a tank, clipping her suit in and thumping the harness lock on her chest to secure it. Ordinarily she would now reach behind her left hip and pull the lever that popped the tank off the rack so she could exit the vessel with it on her back. But instead she remained bolted in place, feeling more like a piece of meat than ever before, hanging helplessly on a butchers hook awaiting her fate.

The hull rattled as Katherine tapped her foot on the forward thrusters at the same time as tilting the flight stick over to the right. The holographic display on the forward dash swung around in tandem with the ship's movement and Angel could just about make out the blinking pieces of Kram's ship scattered across the radar.

DORIS beeped softly as processors went to work reading and analysing the data streaming out of the dials and graphs. The bot moved a little closer to the dash and Katherine watched suspiciously out of the corner of one eye.

'My calculations suggest there will be nothing worth salvaging from such a fragmented blast site. You are wasting your time and the risk of being discovered by additional criminal elements is growing exponentially with every moment we remain in this sector.'

Katherine sniffed, ignoring the bot as she straightened up the Asp's tail and nudged the thrusters, sending it scudding through the twisted wreckage of Angel's ship towards the obliterated Eagle. 'The risk to reward ratio is off the scale – off the *bad* side of the scale – so you might as well just plot a course for Slough and open a jump from here.' Katherine continued scanning the region.

'I'm assuming of course that this heap of half-assed welding is equipped with hyperjump technology?'

'DORIS, shut up!' It was Angel, fuming from over by the hatch.

'You don't know for sure about Kram. We at least owe it to him to scan for a pod.'

'My datasets reveal this is a high traffic area for bandits and looters. Despite the *dread* pirate's aggressive demeanour,' the robot's voice was dripping with sarcasm, 'her ship is not as rapaciously equipped as she is. This area is hot for piracy and we're sitting right on top of the only decent fuel source in sector G. It's not even a probability, it's a matter of time.'

Katherine did look up this time, raising a sceptical eyebrow. 'Rapaciously?' The robot merely hummed.

'Anyway, you both need to shut up. There is a jump point opening up and I don't think it's the bad guys we have to worry about – mainly on account of the fact that I am one of them. Or had you forgotten?'

Both Angel and DORIS turned to look out of the front window where the sweeping sensors on the dash were indicating a build-up of energy not far ahead of them; a build-up of energy that was the tell-tale sign of an incoming hyperspace arrival. Katherine flicked her foot over to the reverse side of the thruster and toed the ship to a standstill. She touched a few switches and activated the weapons array, just in case, then checked her own hyper-jump readout. It was still too hot to use again so whatever was coming through, they couldn't run from it. The atmosphere clenched its cosmic buttocks as they waited to see what would emerge.

A few seconds later the space in front of them split open with a blast of almost-blinding light and a crack you could feel rather than hear. The gash bulged and widened. It seemed to be screaming out of the velvety black space. Energy pulsed around the split, little bursts of plasma-like gas escaping as if the hole itself were panting with the agony of whatever was about to be pushed through it; pushed out of one dimension into another.

In twenty seconds the gash had become big enough to qualify as a rift and without further ado coughed a sleek, midnight blue Corvette into the space before them. It course corrected to intercept, as if it had known exactly what it would find when it jumped out of hyperspace at these coordinates. They watched as the ship approached, smooth and purposeful like a stalking panther, and then slipped silently past them so they could see the regimental decal emblazoned along its flank followed by the name *Retribution's Fist*.

'Damn it!'

Katherine was suddenly a blur of activity, slapping buttons and stamping on pedals, looking around frantically at the control panels spitting out a steady stream of information.

'Navy!'

'Navy.'

Angel and Katherine said this in unison, though their tones of voice couldn't have been more different. For Katherine it was fearful anger, frustrated at being caught off guard by an enemy she had no hope of defeating. Angel on the other hand just sounded depressed. She knew she would now have to deal with the insufferable smugness of Captain Riley having saved her from the clutches of an evil pirate. She glanced at Katherine, noting the deathly pallor of her fear.

'Oh, don't worry pirate. I know this ship – and you just saved yourself a trip to Slough. The captain is a bit of a creep but he'll give you no trouble. Open a comms link and let me do the speaking.'

The Corvette oozed menace as it swung back around to face them, coming nose to nose with the Asp. Katherine could just make out a face through the windscreen of the cockpit. It was too far away for any detail but somehow she knew it wasn't smiling. She looked uncertainly at Angel, who nodded towards the dash. 'Open a link.'

Katherine still looked dubious but tapped on the comms panel to open a channel, hailing the ship with a neutral signal pattern so its captain knew she wanted no trouble; in particular none of the kind of trouble that involved being shot at.

'Stand down your weapons and prepare to be boarded, pirate.'

The voice coming to them through the comms link was dry, almost bored, as if he could hardly be bothered with the conversation to facilitate their surrender.

'Captain Riley, it's me. Commander Rose,' she winced as she listened to the static of the comms link, waiting for a reaction. None came. She looked to Katherine. 'Can he hear me?'

Katherine looked back perplexed. 'That *is* how an open comms channel works, yes. Problem?'

Angel turned once more to look at the Corvette, which was now rotating slowly, manoeuvring to pull up beside the Asp.

'My sensors register a fully functioning comms link,' DORIS said. 'Analysis of the facts suggests the only course of action is to stand down your weapons and prepared to be boarded.'

'I repeat, stand down your weapons, pirate, I'm coming aboard.'

'Riley, it's me. Angel Rose. This vessel came to my aid when my own ship was ambushed and destroyed. Kram …' she swallowed hard, 'Kram's ship was also destroyed. I'm afraid he didn't make it.'

'Pirate, you have twenty seconds to stand down your weapons and deactivate your shields before I deactivate them for you. And Commander Rose?' there was a meaningful pause. 'You can deactivate your flapping lips and start thinking about how you can put them to good use making up for the lack of gold in your possession.'

Angel was shocked. Captain Riley was a sleaze ball but he'd never been outright rude to her. 'Captain, in case you hadn't noticed, I no longer have a ship. We were ambushed by pirates. If you recall I didn't want to run this trade in the first place for this VERY REASON!'

'Ten seconds …'

Katherine slammed her palm on the comms panel to mute it and spun the command chair around to face Angel. 'Screw this. Who is that arsehole?'

'Come along now girls, play nicely and I might let you have a go on my joystick later…' the voice over the comms link goaded.

'He's an arsehole that ultimately has to answer to my father. You might as well do as he says and we can sort this out once he's boarded.'

'Five seconds ladies … don't make me get out my big cannon and fire it at you …'

Katherine growled, actually growled, then swung back around and thumbed the channel open. 'Okay dick-wipe, enough of the smart comments. You're so obsessed with size it makes me wonder if you're compensating.'

'Keep your weapons grid online and you'll find out.'

A spray of tracer fire suddenly erupted from a gun mounted underneath the Corvette's nose, peppering the Asp's left wing before raking across the windscreen.

'Okay! Okay! Put your pods back in your pants. I know when I'm out gunned.' Katherine slapped a hand on the weapons control panel. There was an electronic sigh as the circuits powering her missiles and autocannon wound down. 'Shields too, and no funny business,' the captain said, voice loaded with contempt. 'I'm coupling up and coming aboard.'

Chapter 10

'Well, well, well,' Captain Riley was hanging off the drag frame that cut through the centre of the Asp's cockpit admiring his handiwork. 'Two little birds trussed up and ready for roasting. I have to say I've rather outdone myself.'

Angel twisted against the zip-lock band securing her hands behind her. She was still hooked like a side of meat on the life support tank rack. It was possibly the least dignified position she'd ever been in.

'Look, Riley, I don't know what you think you're playing at. You might have my mother in your pocket but you can't just tie us up like this without any charge. I know my rights.'

Riley let go of the drag frame, leaving Katherine secured to the command chair, and pushed himself towards Angel. When he arrived he gripped the front of her flight suit with both hands, pulling her face in to his smug leer until they were nose to nose.

'You relinquished any flimsy rights you might have once had when you put your thumb to that contract, little bird.'

Angel cringed back as far as her bondage would allow, feeling molested by his hot breath as it puffed against her lips with every word.

'Besides, I've spent years dreaming about having you tied up and ready for roasting. You're not going to snatch that pleasure away from me so soon are you?'

DORIS bleeped, startling them both. 'There is nothing in my client's contract which gives the navy additional jurisdiction over property or personnel. Commander Rose is correct. She is within her rights to know the charges being brought against her or you must release the bonds.'

'Ah yes, DORIS, the little homing pigeon flying with the birds. You've served your purpose and for that I am grateful. But the gold is gone … I'd say it's time to terminate your programme.'

He reached inside his breast pocket and pulled out the control pad he'd used to activate the bot and the bangle. He punched in a code and a pattern of orange then red LEDs flashed across the biscuit-tin sized machine's chest panel. 'There. Now you can go be a calculator or toast muffins or something. Programme terminated. Your mission was a failure.' He returned his attention to Angel, sliding one hand around the back of her neck and pulling her face more forcibly to his. 'Now. Where were we? Oh yes – you tied up and me imagining all the terrible ways I am going to pleasure myself now that I finally have your attention.' He squeezed just below the base of her skull and pressed his body against hers. 'Your mother is right. You are definitely going to have to grow your hair back – I need something to hold on to.'

Angel shuddered, turning her face away and swallowing hard. Her mind raced in useless circles around the situation, looking for an escape plan. It didn't find one.

'On the contrary.' DORIS whirred and moved closer to the captain. 'We were ambushed and the gold was taken. True. But my programming requires that I protect my client's assets. The gold may be gone but until such time as she has replenished its value, Commander Rose is the only asset at my disposal.'

Riley's eyes roamed down Angel's throat and came to rest on her breasts. Despite the fact they were covered in several layers of flame-retardant cloth and webbed straps, his gaze made her feel as naked as usual. 'I think you'll find the commander's assets are at my disposal right now.' He used the hand that wasn't clasping the back of her neck to pinch the fleshy lumps of her breasts, grinning at the way it made her squirm.

'Get off me you goid-loving shit-kicker!' she hissed through gritted teeth.

'Well, that kind of language will have to stop. From now on you'll be ladylike and compliant, like a good little woman ought to be – seen and not heard. Don't worry; I have the perfect supply of narcs to make that happen, just as soon as I get you on my ship.'

'Definitely compensating.'

Katherine's heckle made Riley stop clawing at Angel's body and turn slowly. He glared.

'Any man who needs to tie up a woman and drug her in order to get his pods off may as well wear a sign saying "I have a tiny dick" and have done with it.'

'Oh yes. I had almost forgotten about you, pirate.' He turned and gave Angel's left boob one last grabby squeeze. 'You are a long term project my dear, and will have to wait I'm afraid. Sorry to disappoint, just when we were finally getting somewhere.'

Letting go of Angel he kicked off the tank rack, pitching himself towards where Katherine was secured to the back of the command chair. Reaching her at some speed in zero gravity he grabbed a fistful of dreadlocks to anchor himself. She gasped as her head was snatched backwards to cease his momentum, exposing a soft, vulnerable throat.

'You, on the other hand,' he slammed his hips up against hers, pressing his lips to her ear as he yanked her head painfully to the side by her dreads, 'are disposable. Like garbage.'

He licked her cheek suddenly; tasting her with animal intent. Katherine squirmed as a slick of his spittle dribbled down the side of her exposed neck.

'Like I said, so long as you keep me tied up like this I have to assume you're compensating for having a tiny dick. You were probably bullied about it at cadet school – I know how boys get in the wash room, obsessed with each others' cocks and all that. If you really want to play like a man why don't you release me? Let me lick you back? I bet you'd pre-jack before you could even get your pods out of your pants.'

The air was driven violently out of her lungs as Riley's fist connected with her belly, hard and without warning. She bent as double as her bindings would allow, a moan escaping her lips. He let her groan for a moment and then raked her head back again, dreads still balled in his fist.

'Sensitive topic huh?' Katherine said voice strained as she fought to suck some air back inside her lungs and overcome the wrenching pain in her gut. 'You probably struggle to get it up at all, even in zero-g, never mind unloading in your pants. Right? Can you only do it if a little boy is sucking it? Is that your trouble sugar?'

This time he struck her across the face with his balled fist. It connected like an asteroid wrecker at full pelt, splitting the skin across her cheekbone and making her teeth rattle. His face was a beetroot picture of rage as he reached between her legs, forcing his thick fingers into the Kevlar covered warmth there. His lips pulled back in a vicious sneer as he tweaked savagely at her crotch. He couldn't feel her through the rough webbing of her flight suit but it was clear by the way she wriggled that she could feel him.

'Oh, I can get it up all right you dirty little whore, and it is plenty big enough to get your attention. You won't be wondering about that for long I can assure you.'

Katherine pushed her hips forwards against his hand, causing his rough exploration to falter.

'That's more like it soldier,' she crooned, pressing urgently against his grabbing hand.

He pulled back a little to look in her face, trying to judge whether she was leading him on or not. She watched him with hooded eyes, a trickle of blood tracing the contour of her face from the fresh split he'd made below her left eye. He pressed his hand more deeply into the warmth between her legs and gave a savage squeeze. Her hips arched to meet him and she moaned, this time in pleasure.

'Now you're acting like a real man. Show me what you've got then soldier. Let's see if your cock lives up to your cock-sure.'

Captain Riley looked at her carefully. He was used to taking what he wanted, but never having it offered willingly. He was still unsure whether she was for real, but he wasn't going to untie her so what did it matter? Let her play her games. It was turning him on something wicked. His eyes wandered the length of her body. Her clothes and jewellery looked heavy and aggressive, but without them she would just be another woman; fleshy body, warm and yielding. He was getting hard at the prospect and stepped in close, placing one leg either side of hers. He kept her head pulled back with a fistful of hair and gave her left breast a squeeze with the other hand.

'Oh my cock lives alright,' he said as he ground his pelvis into her hip so she could feel the growing presence of his arousal.

'I guess there might be something useful between your legs after all. But do you know what to do with it?'

Across the cabin Angel's cheeks flushed and she looked away, embarrassed. From the little she knew of Katherine so far she was fairly sure this porn movie scene was some kind of ruse to facilitate an escape. But right now pretty much nothing would surprise her and watching it play out was excruciatingly awkward.

Katherine leant back against the command chair, lifting one leg and curling it about Riley's hip, then repeating the exercise with the other so that she was hooked around his groin, pressing herself hard against his growing bulge.

'Bite me, captain. Can you do that?' She bit her own lip to demonstrate what she wanted from him, leaving a pink impression as she dragged her teeth across it.

Breathing hard, Riley leant in to do as he was told. He'd never experienced a dominant woman before. He loved the feeling of power; having total control over lesser beings as they squirmed beneath his hands. It had been the same since his first bootleg consignment of slaves shortly after graduating from officer training; not exactly navy approved cargo, or behaviour, but hard to resist when they screamed so deliciously. It was incredible what a person could be coerced to do when they were terrified enough for their life.

But this?

His senses buzzed with the sensuality of such a strong woman bending to his will.

This experience was going to be hard to beat.

She squeezed her legs around his buttocks, tugging him in towards her, holding him tight. With one hand still twisted into the dreads at the nape of her neck and the other bracing his body against the back of the command chair he pressed his face into the side of her neck, breathing her in, tasting her with his lips. She moaned again and his pants got tighter, threatening to burst. He was going to have to rein it in or her prediction about him pre-jacking would come true. He leant forward and bit down hard on her neck, teeth crunching against cartilage in a very un-sensual way.

Katherine grunted as his teeth sunk deeper. Her legs tightened instinctively around him and he bit down, enjoying the thought of how much pain he was going to cause her over the next few hours. How many hours really depended on her; on how long she remained conscious. Katherine arched her back so that he had to lean in further to keep up the pressure on her neck. It was his turn to moan with barely contained ecstasy.

Suddenly Katherine jerked, arching back in a spasm.

From across the room Angel heard a cold, metallic *clack*. The captain stopped biting and straightened up, cocking his head to the side momentarily as if he'd heard something interesting. Then his whole body went rigid with shock as he convulsed against something ripping at his belly. He tried to pull back, away from the inexplicable hurt. But Katherine's legs squeezed tighter as the agony tore through him, pulling him towards her and deeper into the pain. He pushed his upper body away from the pirate, bracing arms against the back of the chair as he stared in disbelief into her viciously smiling eyes.

'What's wrong sugar? Wet your pants?'

His pants did look wet, but it wasn't from his bladder. With rising panic in his eyes it became clear he was bleeding, bleeding badly. He pushed back against the chair and looked down to where he was still clutched in the circle of Katherine's legs. The tearing agony intensified, making him shriek as his stomach stretched open. He watched in horror as the yellow fatty flesh of his sliced belly began bulging out of the slash in his suit; the emergency dermo-layer it was fitted with tried desperately to mesh the gash back together but it was just too big; his insides were escaping too damn quickly. His eyes stared and his mind reeled sickeningly as he watched the gaping maw of his gut opening up. An ooze of something pinkish-grey began to poke its nose out of the burgeoning slash. With absolute horror he realised it was his intestines. He screamed and grabbed at the wound with both hands, trying to close it up.

Katherine laughed and unlocked her legs, bringing her knees up tightly to her chest before pumping her legs out, feet connecting squarely with his chest and launching him out into the middle of the cabin. His arms wheeled about uncontrollably as he flew through the cockpit, blood and guts unravelling from his belly into zero-g like a grotesque slow motion Catherine wheel made of fresh offal.

The captain, still screeching, began to scrabble at his escaping innards; cradling the growing, bloody string of what should definitely be on the inside of his body to his breast like a protective mother. But the more he thrashed and twisted about, the bigger the gaping hole in his stomach grew, his life force spilling out in graphic detail as his small, and then large intestines spilled out too. Angel watched in horror as a tsunami of fresh blood escaped the thrashing melee, surging through the zero-g cabin towards her. She ducked to the side to avoid it but it sloshed across her chest and cheek anyway. Flying globules of blood were everywhere now, although Captain

Riley's screams were mercifully dying down to pathetic whimpers and hitching sobs. As he gradually stopped flailing about his guts continued to unravel, twirling around him like a gruesome spirograph.

Eventually he fell still and Angel noticed Katherine staring at the corpse with a glazed expression. Below her strangely serene face was the architect of Riley's gruesome undoing, literally. Her heavy metallic waistband was opened up in a crescent-shape of double-blades; wickedly sharp and extremely bloodied. The blades would have looked pretty malignant even if Angel hadn't been gaping at them through a cockpit filled with orbiting fleshy carnage.

Feeling Angel's eyes upon her Katherine seemed to snap back to the here and now, cheeks reddening as she looked down at her belt. 'Insurance,' she shrugged, seeming to feel as if an explanation was needed.

Her shoulders dropped and she appeared to be reaching for something behind her back. Then there was another metallic slicing sound, this one short and sharp, and her hands fell free. She brought them round to the front of her body and Angel noticed similar razor-like blades extending from her inner wrists. Razor-sharp scalpels had ejected from her metal bracelets cutting cleanly through the graphite wrist ties that had held her bonded to the chair. She carefully snapped the blades back into place, sliding her thumb across an invisible primer button so that the gunmetal bands looked just like statement jewellery again.

'Custom made.'

Angel was still gawping like a fish out of water as Katherine reset the blades of her girdle before pushing off the command chair and coasting through what was once Captain Riley's vital organs towards her. She seemed to hardly notice the mess as darkening droplets of human matter splattered across her chest and face. She arrived at the tank rack, placing one hand either side of Angel's shoulders. The pose was ominously familiar. Katherine looked for a moment into Angel's eyes, a deep penetrating gaze, and Angel felt her own innards tighten as the pirate reached out and unclipped a set of pliers from the maintenance shuck by the exit hatch. She leaned in close to Angel, stretching behind her with the pliers. It was a surreal experience sensing the hot, sweet breath of the woman on her face as she felt around behind her for the zip-lock restraints; the macabre scene of Captain Riley's bloody demise revolving through the cockpit in the background. His deconstructed intestines formed a whimsical double helix in the middle of the cabin.

Angel's wrist ties tightened, then there was a *click* and her hands came free. Katherine breathed deeply but didn't move away. She glared into Angel's eyes for a moment.

'Get the corpse into a fertilizer can. You'll find one in the cargo bay. I'm going to clean up this mess.'

With that the pirate kicked herself off the tank rank, unclipping a vacuum hose from the maintenance shuck and turning it on. Then she began sucking stringy plumes of human entrails into the funnel as casually as if she were spring cleaning the cockpit of cobwebs.

Chapter 11

The cabin was pretty much back to normal after the disposal of Riley's body. Just a few bloody streaks decorating the flight desk and monitor panels where his death throes had taken him close. These gruesome reminders were already turning black as the blood dried and oxidised. Katherine was sitting in her command chair staring pensively out at the glittering remains of the ships that had met their doom at this grid reference today – it was far more action than most universal coordinates got to see in a billion planetary lifetimes. The Corvette was coasting slowly away from them through the twisted debris, perfectly framed in the forward windscreen. Angel figured Katherine must have jettisoned the bulky naval craft clamped to the Asp while she was dealing with the biological detritus.

'What now?'

DORIS whirred in a way Angel had come to recognise as the diminutive robot accessing its databanks.

'I wasn't asking you,' she said tersely to stem any suggestions that might be coming.

'That is absurd. I have a database of over fifty billion scenarios connected to a probability map of possible outcomes that I can calculate to three trillion levels of fragmented plausibility. If anyone is qualified to answer the question "what now?" it is me.'

'Can it, DORIS! Remember your proximity link has been deactivated courtesy of the captain. It wouldn't take much for me to load you into a missile launcher and hit the red button.'

DORIS ticked and hummed a little harder, presumably processing the odds of this new threat. It seemed they didn't fall in favour of the little bot as it backed down and went to whir broodingly in the corner. Angel turned to look at Katherine, still mutely staring out into space.

'Katherine?'

'Hmm?' she replied absently. 'What now?'

The pirate turned to look at her, noticing her as if for the first time.

'Are you okay?' Angel was a little concerned by the vacant look in her eyes.

'Fine!' she snapped suddenly, the scowl returning. She turned to look at the flight desk in front of her, placing her palm across the weapons array. The cabin hummed as electric pulses fed a trickle of power to the forward hard-points and Katherine went back to scowling at the war ship drifting away from them. 'What now?' Angel asked again.

'Well, since I just gutted a naval officer,' Katherine took hold of the joystick and flicked the guard off the fire button. It took barely a second for the laser target to find and paint a mark on the abandoned Corvette. The weapons array emitted a soft, solid tone and Katherine thumbed the trigger, sending a single missile careening off towards the deserted goliath. It connected with one of the main thruster cylinders, a blossom of orange fire pluming immediately along the defenceless ship's fuselage. The blossom spread with little pops of fiery light, growing in intensity as the explosive chain-reaction reached deeper and deeper into the hull of the vast ship, finding pockets of fuel and unused warheads to boost its destructive expedition. They watched in silence as the damned Corvette performed its death dance, yawing and tumbling away from them through space as detonations spread her along her flank, eating the ship more and more violently from the inside.

'As I was saying, since I just killed a naval officer and blew up his boat, I think I'm going to lie low for a while. Head home and try not to get shot at or arrested.'

She twisted her seat to favour the navigation panel, tapping a couple of screens as she plumbed in a destination vector.

'And me?'

Katherine turned slowly to look at her. Angel was chilled by the lack of emotion in her gaze. It was as if the entanglement with Captain Riley had somehow bled the life right out of her too.

'I'm taking you back to the Hollows. It's the only safe place for me right now. You can make your own way home from there. If you really are the daughter of some hot-shit station commander it shouldn't be too hard to persuade someone that the salvage fee will be worth giving you a ride home. Right now though, you'd better get back on that tank rack or you're going to stove your head in when we jump.'

* * *

They didn't speak on the journey, each lost in the depths of their own thoughts as the Asp rushed in and out of the impossible spinal light-web of hyperspace. Even the robot kept its peace, anchored to a rusty panel on the opposite side of the exit hatch to Angel's now familiar hook-up on the tank rack. When the ship burst out of hyperspace for the third time she breathed out deeply. She craned her neck to get a clue about their location from the star map that was sketching itself neatly on the navigation desk as the ship's sensors probed the region. It looked like a sparse system; no significant planets picked up on the first sweep of the radar, but sub-scans identifying an asteroid belt of fast moving rock circling a dimly pulsing single star. Katherine tweaked the roll lever, toe-tapping the thrusters as she coaxed her ship into an orbit matching the chaotic collection of space rocks. Most were barely more than the size of the Asp, but then Angel noticed a bigger mass being drawn on the map up ahead.

The asteroid was the size of a small moon, elongated through millennia of careening along a rapid orbit around the star. It rolled lazily as it shot through its prescribed trajectory, a maze of lesser satellites and inconsequential meteors running along beside and behind it like a celestial guard of honour. A deadly guard of honour if you took your approach too lightly as they all spun and rotated haphazardly and out of sync, each on its own unique and ancient path around the sun. The familiar scowl now pinned to her face Katherine levelled up the nose and eased off the thruster a couple of notches until she was flying in line with the asteroid. She twitched the roll lever again and the Asp banked, ducking between two jagged pieces of orbital reef and then drawing alongside the large hunk of space rock as it hurtled through the vacuum.

Angel peered out of the side window.

The asteroid glowed like a vast phosphorescent cuttlefish, illuminated by thousands of fluro landing strips delineating layer upon layer of docking scaffold constructed along the entire length and circumference of the moon-sized rock. Hundreds of ships where clamped precariously on its curved flank; a rag-taggle collection of one, two and three man craft from every era and shipyard in history. There were a couple of larger warship-class vessels too, but they were a rarity and looked heavily patched up. Angel noticed an Imperial Cutter, so overloaded with armoury modifications and punk artillery that it looked like a gruesome caricature of itself. Ant-like dots that were probably dock workers swarmed around every ship. You couldn't see it from this distance but they would be wearing the heaviest duty EVA suits to protect them from the cold and coupled securely to the ships they tended by a thick umbilical cable.

The comms link crackled into life.

'Welcome home Dread. I made a bed up for Pearl in bay B-17. Pinging you a beacon now.'

'Hey Admin. Yeah, she's going to need something a little more subtle today. Got any room on Medusa?'

There was a pause. The empty comms link purred.

'Okay, stick your Asp to Medusa 3 then, I'll bring you inside,' the voice was chuckling, clearly more amused by his own pun than Katherine was. 'I hope you got the creds for it?'

'You worry about your impending puberty and let me worry about my Asp.'

A homing beacon lit up on the navigation grid.

'See you later at Sue's?' the comms link crackled.

'What do you think dick-wad?'

Katherine flicked the channel off and nudged the Asp into a dive. Angel's stomach lurched as it was left behind when they circled and dipped below the huge asteroid. From where she was she couldn't see out of the top of the wind-glass bubble, but she watched Katherine craning up to visually reference whatever her ship's telemetry was pinpointing as the target. They negotiated a groove in a dark strip of the asteroid and there was a bone crunching clunk as some unseen machinery clamped down on the ship's hull. Katherine slapped a couple of panels on the dash and the engines started powering down, the turbines inside the thrusters whining as if relieved to finally be coming to rest. The pirate thumped her chest harness to release herself from the chair and twisted to face Angel. 'You need to suit up. There's a spare EVA helmet under the maintenance shuck if you don't want to waste a remlok.' Angel popped herself off the tank rack as a hydraulic thrum started up outside, penetrating the walls with a rhythmic buzz. The light in the cabin dimmed and Angel could feel the ambient gravity increase to something close to normal as the ship was drawn inside the rolling belly of the giant asteroid.

'Welcome to the Hollows.'

* * *

After disembarking Katherine had stormed off; exiting the docking bay without a word as she depressurised the airlock and ripped off her EVA helmet, disappearing through the riveted steel frame of the hatch into a dim network of tunnels and caverns carved out of the interior of the space rock. Not wanting to lose track of the only person she knew in this strange place, Angel scuttled after her, the conscience bot whirring along behind.

'Bugger off,' Katherine said after Angel and DORIS had been following her for about ten minutes. The grubby, jaded people milling about the rocky caverns inside the asteroid paid little attention to the bad tempered procession stomping through their midst. Angel and DORIS were strangers and if anyone had looked closely it would have been pretty obvious they didn't belong. They were far too clean to begin with. But nobody was looking closely. That was part of the charm of the place. This was the human soup of the underworld, from Lave to Achenar. Everyone behaved strangely here and it was generally taken for granted that if you were going about your business without anyone firing a pulse laser at you, you probably had as much right to be here as the next person.

Katherine continued to ignore Angel and they eventually arrived at a bar. It was noisy and chaotic, a pungent mix of sweat and alcohol fumes filling the cavern with a thick fug illuminated by pulsing light spilling off the dance floor. No one was dancing. It was early yet; the night's drinking had hardly begun so the music was still low-key and vaguely melodic. Around half the booths that lined the walls were already full though. Rough looking men and women dressed in filthy, cracked leather and hard-core adorns drank and talked animatedly. Serving boys and girls dressed in raggy slops scurried here and there, delivering drinks and the occasional bowl of something steaming to the people sitting at the tables. Most of them looked no more than twelve or thirteen to Angel; filthy faces and scrawny bodies, but with happy enough grins when the more intoxicated patrons rewarded their speedy service with apparently generous tips. The counter was also half full; long and sticky with flagons of beer and shot glasses littered along it in front of customers slumped at varying degrees of inebriation.

Katherine sat heavily at the bar. An oversized figure behind it with big, platinum blonde hair turned and leant against its edge. While the hair was doll-like, impossibly girlie, the face was angular, stubbly and strong, caked with exaggerated make up but exuding macho bravado. Angel's mind, already in turmoil trying to untangle the bombardment of sights and sounds in this strange new place, struggled particularly with this contradictory apparition.

'What can I get you ladies?'

The bartender's voice was as deep and booming as the stubble and pronounced Adam's apple hinted it would be. Angel's eyes flicked up and down, taking in scarlet nails and lips, excessive eyelashes and what looked like it could be a red leather mini skirt below the counter. She was startled by the frankness of the ensemble. The bartender stood casually; unselfconscious, despite the fact she must have been gawping. This was not a man pretending to be a woman, or a woman masquerading as a man. She didn't know quite what it was, but it felt completely honest and when the bartender smiled at her reassuringly, she found herself smiling back.

'I don't have any creds,' she said apologetically. She wanted to buy liquor from this man; or should that be woman? Not just to be sociable but because she really needed a drink right now.

'Give me a bottle of Spacial Sloma,' said Katherine.

The bar tender nodded reaching under the counter and sliding open a cooler to produce a brown flex-plex bottle. 'I'm guessing the bot won't be needing a glass?'

Angel had almost forgotten the robot was there again. The bar tender scooped up two tumblers and placed one each in front of Katherine and Angel. Angel tensed, waiting to see if Katherine would object and tell her to bugger off again. She didn't, and the glasses were filled to the brim without further pomp. Angel slid into the high bar chair beside the moody pirate.

'Thanks Sue,' Katherine said with real feeling as she lifted the amber glass of intoxicating liquid to her lips.

Angel breathed out slowly; savouring the blossom of alcoholic burn on her tongue as it spread through her head, infiltrating her cheeks and mingling with the oxygen at the back of her throat before singeing her nostrils on the way back out. *The circle of life,* she thought with a private smile of satisfaction. The gravity inside the asteroid was a little under normal – possibly about 0.8-g Angel reckoned – which gave everything a surreal quality of being held in place, but only just. It felt a bit like normality was teetering on the edge of chaos, which pretty much summed up what she had seen of this pirate base so far.

Several hours later they were an impressive amount of the way through the second bottle of Spacial Sloma and Katherine at last seemed to be shedding the demons that had been haunting her since their encounter with Captain Riley. Sue had kept them in stitches for the last twenty minutes with a story about an enlightening teenage encounter she'd had with an Imperial duke when Katherine's attention was caught by something across the room. She stood drunkenly on the struts of her chair to rise above the growing throng of people on the dance floor, roaring a beery cheer and making a double-fisted salute to someone across the room. Sue stopped speaking and glanced over. Smiling she lifted another tumbler from beneath the counter and filled all four glasses, opening a third bottle of booze to top up the last.

'Ay, how's space Dread?'

The newcomer was a wiry lad, not much more than eighteen Angel guessed. She recognised his voice as the landing controller who'd brought them in. Like everyone in this rock he was shabby and dirty. He had a roguish grin and wore the typical leather and rough cloth garb of a pirate, with a blade sheathed on his left hip and a pulse laser tucked into a leg harness on the right. He plopped himself down on a stool beside Angel and bumped knuckles with Katherine on the other side of her.

'Why the deep cover?'

Katherine lifted her drink, prompting him to do the same and they clinked briefly before necking the amber liquid. Sue was pouring the refills almost before their empty glasses touched down.

'Aw, piss in zero-g man. I'm screwed,' she paused long enough to neck another shot and continued on, leaving Sue to fill everyone's sympathetically empty glasses again. 'I was just hopping around, doing a little salvage work when I jump out of hyperspace to find a shit-storm of a wreckage, freshly blasted. So I run a quick scan. All I find is this comedy duo,' she thumbed to indicate Angel and DORIS. 'So out of the goodness of my heart I pick them up. Next thing I know I have the nebular-fucking NAVY up my tailpipe!'

The newcomer looked dubiously at Angel.

'To be fair, Dread, you've never had a good heart.'

'Oi!'

'Does navy bait have a name?'

Katherine peered across the top of another overflowing glass of amber liquor at Angel.

'Angel, this is Admin. Admin, Angel, etcetera,' she mumbled, necking another shot and then rapping her glass impatiently on the counter when Sue didn't replenish it instantly. 'Oh, the annoying bot is apparently called DORIS.'

Admin snorted with laughter at this, making the hovering robot click indignantly. Once their glasses were filled to the brim they banged them together again. Admin grinned at Angel as the music stepped up a beat to entice a few more people on the dance floor.

'Welcome to hell in a hollow rock, my friend.'

Chapter 12

Noticing Katherine had slid into a booth by herself across the bar, Angel checked to see that the other two were deep in conversation and slipped down off her chair. She slithered into the seat opposite Katherine. The stony faced pirate seemed to be sinking back into the sullen funk that had overcome her after killing Captain Riley.

'You okay?'

Katherine looked up, scowling at Angel from between cupped palms atop a pair of unsteady elbows.

'Oh sure. I'm always okay after spilling someone's guts into zero-g. How 'bout you?'

Angel paused. 'No need to be like that. I'm only asking.'

'And what do you care? Seriously … I picked you up, what? Five hours ago?'

There was a gentle whirring from the booth behind them.

'Six-and-a-half hours ago actually, we could have been back at Slough by now.'

The women turned in unison to shout at the booth behind Katherine's seat.

'Go away!'

'Go away!'

An unseen processor chip behind the seatback *chuck, chuck, chucked* briefly before reluctantly winding down.

Katherine continued staring away from the table for a while longer as she tried to pluck a couple of coherent thoughts out of the air. Eventually she turned back to face Angel, looking stern. 'Five hours; six hours … all the same we're not exactly blood-sisters. So what do you care if I'm okay?'

Angel shrugged and took a non-committal slug of her drink. 'You saved me for starters, when I was floating around in that pod with my ear drums being blasted out by the proximity alarm then again when Riley went bat-shit crazy.'

Katherine snorted into her drink. 'Is that what it was? "Bat-shit crazy"?'

There was another awkward silence as they were absorbed again briefly by the memory of what happened; or perhaps more strikingly, what might have happened. Angel's cheeks heated. 'I'm sorry Katherine. I honestly didn't mean to bring this to your cockpit.'

Katherine suddenly stopped moping into her drink, her head snapping upright as she stared Angel down across the table. 'What in goid-sucking space are you apologising for? Did you make him?'

Angel was confused.

'Did you write him an instruction manual? Grant him a license? No. No you fucking didn't. He managed that all by himself – like all the rest of them. He's spent his whole fucking life cultivating a moral estate where it is okay to be like that; to tie a woman up; beat her and rape her; treat her body like meat and her mind like useless offal.'

The awkward silence came back with a vengeance as Katherine lifted her drink to her lips and sucked on it deeply.

'I think we've had our fill of offal today, don't you?'

Angel's attempt to lighten the atmosphere was reassuringly effective. Katherine's eyes seemed to clear a little as she focused on her across the rim of her glass.

'Nifty adorns by the way. I must ask you to introduce me to your jeweller. There have been plenty of occasions when I could do with a couple of spring-loaded blades at pod-height.'

Katherine's hand went instinctively to her broad belt, now sprung back into place and seeming like nothing more innocuous than a sturdy iron girdle.

'It's good to be prepared,' she said.

The music dipped momentarily to silent right before the middle-eight of a particularly powerful country-style love ballad, and they shared a moment across the scuffed table as the modulated rhythm blasted back into the room with renewed vigour. Angel reached out across the table and Katherine, seeing the unspoken request placed her own forearms gently in Angel's hands. Angel took hold of the metal wrist bands and ran her thumbs across the inside of them.

'Careful!'

Katherine had jerked away from Angel's grip and was now cradling the dangerous cuffs in front of her. She held one arm out to demonstrate how brushing her thumb across a bit of raised metalwork on the inside would trigger the device. Two crescent-shaped blades, lethally sharp and whisperingly quick, sliced out through the air between them.

'Right,' Angel said, rubbing her own wrists in appreciation of what had *not* just happened.

Katherine thumbed the blades back into place and re-sprung the catch. 'Remind me not to hug you goodnight later.'

Katherine laughed without much mirth.

A less awkward silence fell between them. Over at the counter Sue regaled the barflies with another hilarious anecdote. The chorus of the love song kicked in again and they enjoyed another sip of their drinks as the Wayout Walton Westies wailed about the wrenching pain of love and gravity in A-minor.

'NOW! That's What I Call Suicide. Volume 267,' Katherine deadpanned as the music droned on.

Angel laughed, and then thought for a while before asking. 'What happened to you Katherine? To give you such hard skin?'

Katherine stared out across the dance floor for a while before answering. 'Life.'

Angel tried to sweep back the fog of alcohol rolling across her brain and think of something insightful to say; or at least something not too annoying. 'You want to talk about it?'

She was kicking herself even as the words fell out of her mouth. Talk about weak! But Katherine continued gazing into the heaving throng.

'Not really,' she said in a bland tone, taking another a sip of her drink, 'and you don't want to hear about it either. Trust me. Your friend Riley might have been a rotten-hearted rapey spacer but he was a paragon of virtue compared to some that I've known.'

Leaning back in her seat she looked straight at Angel, scanning her up and down, assessing her like a salvage probe. 'I had a nice life once, like you,' she offered up to the silence between them, which was growing awkward again. 'But the goid-fucking spacers who picked me up weren't quite as easy-going as I am.'

She took a slow sip on her drink, staring out into the now heaving bar. She seemed lost in deep and troubled thought. Angel reached for her own drink and swallowed a large swig as dust motes swirled though the illuminated fug between them. The Wayout Walton Westies finally caterwauled to a conclusion and a fresh dub-beat track sent the dance floor into a frenzy of cheering, drunken recognition. Angel was about to think of something brilliant to say – anything to ease the tension –when Katherine continued.

'They picked me up when our transporter ran into engine trouble on a refuelling stop. We got caught up in a solar storm and got pitched right into the middle of an asteroid belt in a system at the far edge of Federation space – in bandit territory. We abandoned ship and sent out a distress signal but they were passing through and picked up the SOS before anyone else could respond.'

'They?' Angel asked as Katherine paused to drink deeply.

She turned to look Angel straight in the eye, the fog almost completely cleared from her vision. 'Pirates. They were hopping out for a frontier loot run; you know? Heading out to the uncharted places of deep space to cherry pick a few explorers for their expensive probes and long range mods? They had stopped to scoop fuel from the same red dwarf as us, saw the Dolphin in trouble and hung around for a quick bonus loot scoop. My escape pod was plucked out of space and they decided to keep me like a pet for the expedition; you know? For "entertainment" purposes? They used to tell me I should think myself lucky. If I'd been an ugly spacer like the rest of my family they would have pulped me to fertilizer too.'

She held Angel's gaze through the chromatic throb of the lights and the music, a mist of sweat and alcohol fumes swirling around them. 'It took me three years to get away.'

The dance floor writhed.

'So now I make sure I'm prepared.'

They sat and listened to the music for a while, the tickling heat of alcohol softening the edges of the awkward silence and unspoken pain of Katherine's troubled memories hanging in the air between them.

'I'm sorry,' Angel said, feeling ridiculously inadequate.

Katherine laughed again, only this time there was the twinkling of real humour in it. 'There you go again; apologising for the world at large. Are the shortcomings of humanity really on your shoulders, commander? How big must your ego be to believe that to be truth?'

Angel was about to say sorry again but caught herself just in time. She held her breath, trying to figure out what it was she wanted to say, then sighed deeply, shaking her head. 'I am such a fuck up. My life is such a fuck up. You know what? I *do* feel like everything is on my shoulders, yes. All mother-fucking five-bazillion zeta-tons of everything. Is that how much stuff there is?'

Katherine frowned. 'Where?'

Angel drained her glass and slammed it down on the table. 'Everywhere! Everything! How much mother-fucking matter is there in the universe anyway?'

Katherine's brow furrowed. 'Err, I think that's infinite.'

'Well whatever it is, it's on my shoulders. Has been since the day I was born.'

'Oh please. You're the daughter of a station captain! What do you know about a tough life?'

Angel was the one dipping into her mirthless laughter repertoire now. 'Well, that just shows how much you know about me. And considering you just felt compelled to garrote the only part of my life you've ever been introduced to, I'd have thought you might have a little more sympathy.'

This gave Katherine pause for thought; a new perspective to take the edge off her own experience perhaps? The music throbbed through the not-so-awkward silence.

'It looks like it might be time for an intervention. Sorry it took me so long ladies. My boys only just docked with fresh supplies.'

Admin was sliding into the seat beside Katherine, shunting her bum deeper into the booth with his hip to make room as he banged a fresh bottle of Spacial Sloma squarely into the centre of the table.

By the time Katherine had swept the bottle up and filled all their drinks to the brim, Admin had dug something out of a flat pocket tucked into the seam of his jacket sleeve. He cradled a small brown bottle under the table as surreptitiously as his alcohol soaked brain would allow and held a small pipette in his cupped hand in the centre of the table. Angel noticed it was half-way filled with a sparkling green liquid; it was a recreational narc commonly known as Schlapstar.

'Anyone?'

'Ahh, right on cue Mister Administrator.'

'Does madam require a little sparkle in her life?'

'You're nebular screwing right, she does.'

Katherine plonked the bottle of booze back down on the table and leant back in her seat, tipping her head right back without even the pretence of hiding the fact that Admin was emptying the dropper into her eyes. Admin grinned as Katherine began slithering inelegantly down under the table. He dipped the pipette into the bottle in his lap and reproduced it, holding it out in front of Angel's eyes. She hesitated, looking at Katherine who was collapsed happily into the chair opposite her, smiling unguardedly for the first time since they'd met.

'Why not?'

Angel tipped her head back and Admin emptied half the pipette into one eye, half into the other. Instantly the sensation of ecstasy blossomed from her eyelashes, spilling down through her nervous system like a waterfall of tingling sensation.

'There you go, she likes to party,' Katherine lurched forward, clutching Angel by the wrists, shaking them between her own clenched fists. 'You're right!'

'I am?' Angel was confused, no longer sure who she was let alone anything she could be right about. She concentrated on holding her focus on Katherine as the pirate unclipped one of the vicious bands she wore around her wrists. She held it out towards Angel and when the other just stared blankly back across the table she grabbed hold of Angel's own wrist and pulled it towards her. Katherine snapped the deadly adorn on Angel's wrist. 'You obviously have some very fucked up fucking friends. I do need to introduce you to my jeweller – Stoo 'the stud' Swinders . In the mean time I want you to have this. In case we meet any more of your buddies.'

Not to be left out and now swimming in the rather pleasant ephemeral ooze of the drops he'd placed in his own eyes, Admin also leant in to the huddle forming in the centre of the table. The dub-track turned into something driving and more urgent, and the revellers on the dance floor roared in appreciation. Whoever was running the sound system – *DJ Fozzer?*

Angel thought someone might have called him – had clearly decided the time for civilised conversation was over as the volume of this new track increased by at least ten decibels. The three of them were left staring at each other through the shimmering dust motes that had been excited from every surface by the ear splitting volume of the music as the cavern reverberated to the beat of the bass.

Angel could feel the rhythm pulsing across her skin as the tingling sensation began to blossom again, emanating from every cell that came into contact with the sine waves from the speaker stack. She felt her body begin to sway, closing her eyes for just a moment to savour the build-up of the music.

She felt a hand cup her chin and forced her eyes to open, trying in vain to pull them into focus on the face that swam before her. How long had she been sitting there? Time had no meaning to her right now. And she didn't really care anyway she realised with oddly detached curiosity, and then laughed at herself riotously.

'You look like you could do with a dance!'

A pair of hands swam towards her and pulled her to her feet, dragging her after the blurry face into the centre of the room, where her legs obediently got to work tearing apart the dance floor. The sweaty crowd bounced around her. Her heart raced; her head spun; her whole body succumbed to the irresistible warmth of the narcotics. Everything else was just meaningless bullshit. It was just her, the throbbing music, and the strong arms that were holding her upright.

Everything else.

Bullshit.

Chapter 13

Angel peeled her eyes open, the crusty weight of last night's excesses gumming up her lashes. Her tongue did a brief exploratory. It discovered massive dehydration but nothing more untoward. She was hung over, but that wasn't unusual. It was certainly nothing some sweet carbs and an industrial-strength coffee wouldn't put right. She was actually quite relieved to find herself in one piece. But *where* in one piece? That was the billion-credit question.

She rotated her head, which seemed to be resting on something soft; something pillow-like. Half a head-turn later and her eyes were able to confirm the pillow-like object was, in fact, a pillow. She frowned as her fuddled brain tried to unscramble the events of last night. A pillow meant a bed. She was pretty surprised she'd ended up somewhere with an actual bed. Somebody must have taken pity on her.

Moving as little as possible to stave off the onset of what would no doubt be a stonking headache, her eyes did a brief tour of this side of the room. It was sparse; roughly carved stone walls and unfussy furniture much of which had pieces of clothing flung across it. She noticed with a growing sense of unease that not all of the clothing was hers. Black, well-worn flight gear cut to fit a man was mingled together with her own gear on the floor; a brutal looking machete slung in a sheath across the back of a wooden chair.

There was a sigh from behind her and someone shifted position, dragging the sheet off her as they turned. Alarm bells rang, her mind desperately digging through the wreckage of her memory for evidence of who the sigh belonged to. She twisted her head back the other way and as she had predicted it started throbbing savagely. Her eyes came to rest upon the tangled mess of the back of someone's head. Brown, shoulder-length hair tousled from what looked like more than just a lack of combing. She couldn't make out much about the body as it was tucked under a sheet, but the shoulders were definitely male. She noticed a couple of hairs sprouting but otherwise they were smooth and toned. She could make out the shape of a lithely sculpted bicep heading down under the sheet.

The alarm bells now clanging at full fury inside her head didn't help with the headache.

Where was she? And *who … the fuck … was that?*

Right on cue the body moaned and shifted again, turning to lie on its back. It sighed. A tongue came out and licked some moisture on to the lips. There was the sound of scratching and she could see a hand moving under the covers down around his groin area. As she lay there, staring incredulously at the roughly handsome face of the unknown young man she was apparently in bed with, his eyes fluttered open. He turned his head to look at her dozily.

'Hey baby,' he said, with the unmistakeable air of someone she'd been incredibly intimate with recently.

'Piss and gravity!'

She bolted upright, then suddenly realising she was naked grabbed the sheet and yanked it off her dozy bed mate so she could wrap it around what was left of her dignity as she scrambled to her feet and away from the scene.

'Who in flaming Thargoid-loving hell are you?'

* * *

'If we didn't … you know … then why are my clothes all over the floor?' The man she'd woken up beside was propped up against the bed head.

Despite her own nakedness and the gear on the floor he was still partially dressed in grubby long johns with a wide cotton bandage wrapped around his mid-riff. He even had his socks on still, but Angel had woken up with enough ill-conceived bed partners to find them still wearing socks to know this proved nothing. He looked infuriatingly amused by the stupor Angel was whipping herself into.

'You were … hard to argue with. And the view was too good to argue very hard anyway. But I promise you, I was the perfect gentleman … well, apart from enjoying the view of course.'

By now Angel had wrapped the sheet completely around her and was storming about the room like a mini tempest, snatching up her clothes from where they had fallen.

'Look, ease up Commander. You needed a bed; I offered to share mine since we'd been getting on so well on the dance floor. Remarkably charitable of me under the circumstances, I thought. When we got back here you complained about being too hot and before I knew what was happening you had stripped off all your clothes and passed out on my bed. You weren't the only one enjoying the administrations of our young friend last night. I was trashed. We all were. I honestly couldn't have pleasured you even if I'd wanted to, not outside my own rather vivid imagination anyway.'

He raised a salacious eyebrow in her direction and she blushed with renewed vigour, disappearing into the wet room to put her clothes on.

This was precisely why she didn't do narcs, she admonished herself angrily.

'So we slept?'

She emerged from the bathroom buckling up her cuffs. She twisted the wrist band from Katherine around so it was seated correctly, potentially sharp edge facing out, and smoothed her thumb across the simple engraving. A flash of memory from the night before returned; a young man with green eyes and a sparkling smile. *This* young man with green eyes and a sparkling smile; laughing uncontrollably at something just out of reach for her memory; strong arms encircling her as they swayed together on the dance floor – swaying in sync with the whole universe at eight-beats-to-the-bar.

'We slept,' he agreed. 'There might have been a little innocent spooning. And by the way you snore.'

She plonked herself down on the side of the bed and started pulling on her boots. He was watching her curiously.

'Where are you going, by the way?'

Angel stopped. She had no idea. She was just on autopilot, extricating herself from the latest awkward morning-after exchange with a stranger she had found herself in bed with. But this time she couldn't go sloping back to her pilot's fed digs to nurse her pounding hangover and try to shake off the shame. Her shoulders slumped as the hopelessness of her situation sunk in.

'I have no idea. I don't even know where I am. I've lost everything and I have no way of getting home. Not that there is anything waiting for me at home apart from trouble and strife anyway; and quite probably a couple of official charges. At the very least there are going to be some difficult questions to answer.'

She felt a hand on her back and pulled away from it, glaring back at the half-naked man lying in the bed beside her. He held his hands up, indicating a lack of malice as she scowled at him venomously.

'I'm guessing you don't remember my job offer then, either? You were pretty grateful at the time.'

She drummed her fingers briefly on the bed as her brain sifted back through the haziness beginning to seep in at the corners of her memory. She had more flash backs of dancing; laughing; hunkering down in cosy booths with Admin, Katherine and this green-eyed other; administering crystal green liquid to each other's eyes and taking flight on the wings of the music blaring through the cavern. But no job offers.

He read her face coming up blank and frowned. 'How about my name?'

* * *

The man in the bed turned out to be called Mental Eddie, a nefarious pirate of some not-inconsiderable note within the Hollows. Indirectly, he was Admin's boss, as he controlled the formidable fleet of narc runners that pretty much dominated this area and three sectors in every direction. While allowing herself to be taken home by someone whose name was prefixed with the word 'mental' wasn't the smartest move she'd ever made, she had to admit the job was pretty generous once he'd repeated the offer. It came with access to a fleet of ships – highly twinked for any occasion – a basic living allowance, and in light of her rather negative reaction to waking up in his bed, Eddie had even thrown in a room at Sue's.

The only downside was it also required she become a ruthless killer.

'Assassin?'

'Assassin.'

'Are you serious? I get a guilt trip when I have to purge an outbreak of the Trumbles. How am I ever going to kill a person?'

They were settled in a booth at Sue's awaiting an extravagant breakfast Eddie had ordered with the enthusiasm of a man who hadn't tasted hot food for an epoch. 'From the way you looked at me this morning I'd say you have the killer instinct.'

'That was when I thought you'd, you know ...' Angel blushed again and got cross with herself, and him as he laughed across the table.

'Just imagine them in their longjohns with a morning-glory. Oh come on, it'll be fun! I've got a nice new ship for you; I'm going to offer Dread and Admin a sack of creds to crew it so they can show you the ropes; and the guns; and maybe the knives as well.'

With perfect timing Admin slid into the seat beside Angel. 'Did I hear someone mention my name in the same sentence as a sack full of creds?'

He bumped knuckles with Eddie as Katherine flopped drearily into the seat opposite, clutching her head and moaning.

'Nah, I said a sack full of crud, but then I realised you're already full of that, so I shan't bother.'

There was a bit more banter to and fro as the newcomers ordered some food and two steaming plates of pretty much everything in the kitchen landed in front of Angel and Eddie.

'I don't do baby-sitting, sorry.' Katherine was picking unenthusiastically over a bowl of stodgy porridge, looking like hell. 'You don't have a lot of choice sister,' Eddie's face was serious for the first time since they'd sat down. 'With the Pearl holed up in Medusa 3 you've got extended berthing to cover, not to mention your club subscription, rent for Sue, and by the look of you, you could do with a lot more protein in your diet. It's all very well lying low, but you gotta eat and pay your dues. I'm offering a tidy fee for you to help get our newest club member up to scratch. One trip, three quick jobs, and then you'll be back in the Hollows with enough creds to pay off the pilot's fed and clear your bounty. Then we can get you back out on the space-waves and business as usual. Am I right, or am I right?'

Across the table Admin was looking rather green around the edges.

'As for you my young friend, you don't get off this rock enough. The 'Lance I've lined up for the job needs a hard point gunner and we all know Dread couldn't hit a fuel scooper with a dumbfire from fifty metres. Hopefully there won't be any need for shooting, of course; my guy in the pilot's fed should be able to get you in nice and quiet. But whatever happens after that you're on your own.'

Admin swallowed hard. 'I'll get sick Eddie, you know how I am in space.

What use am I to anyone if I'm barfing my guts into zero-g?' Angel looked horrified.

'You'll be fine once they start shooting at you.' The humour returned to Eddie's eyes and he winked at Angel across the table. 'It's amazing how quickly the sting of unfriendly tracer fire can settle a queasy tummy.'

'Look, I appreciate the offer and all,' Angel said, her stomach doing a little flip of its own at the prospect of having to carry out a contract kill, 'but I'm not a murderer. You must have someone better for the job?'

'Ah, but you are perfect for the job my pretty little assassin,' he grinned at her and shoved a huge forkful of hashed-potato into his mouth. Once he'd chewed it into partial submission he continued, spraying little bits of crispy potato across the table as he munched and talked simultaneously. 'I have a few... *issues* that need dealing with in and around Slough. It's not an easy place to get to with a rep like mine. For the time being you have a squeaky clean sheet and are pretty well-connected, at least your family is. Who is going to question the station captain's daughter when she heads over to the luxury spa cruiser, where her mother practically lives? Once there you can deal out swift justice to a very naughty man who double-crossed me in a property deal, run a couple more errands to tie up some loose ends in Slough, and you'll be out before the pilot's fed have even had time to process the digiwork – thanks to my friends on the inside of course.'

'I don't think you're hearing me, Eddie,' Angel's voice was stern. She felt it was time to draw a line under the matter. 'I am not a killer. I don't want to become a killer. You're going to have to look elsewhere, I'm afraid.'

Point made she picked up a slice of bread and mopped up the last of the bean stew on her plate, shoving it into her mouth and licking her fingers clean. Eddie's face switched from jovial to deadpan with irrational speed.

'As pretty as your arse is you're not exactly in a position to negotiate, or had you forgotten you're currently enjoying the hospitality of a gang of nefarious pirates with no creds to pay your way?'

Angel looked down at her empty plate and swallowed hard.

'Yes my dear, a very expensive plate of tucker, not to mention the tab you ran up last night with Sue and my young administrator here. What? Did you think all that shit was for fresh air and giggles? Everything in this rock comes at a price, and the only other employment on offer right now is whoring in the Drag-den. I've already seen how stingy you are with your fleshy bits, so I'm guessing it's the assassin's life for you, for you; the assassin's life for you!'

He had broken into song at this last and was now grinning manically at her again. Angel goldfished back at him, speechless and flushing hotly.

'Oh, get over yourself you stupid bitch,' he said with a fondness completely at odds with calling her a bitch. He leaned across the table and punched her playfully in the arm. 'It'll be fun! You'll see. Now get out of here all of you and make your preps.' His expression switched to black intensity again. 'Katherine, you're in charge – you need to come up with a cover story. I don't care what it is; just make sure it's low-key. You should use that robot thing to help you.'

They looked around, Angel realising for the first time that day DORIS was nowhere to be seen.

'I shut it in a kit locker outside Wilde's Farglebiter last night,' Eddie said, reaching into a small breast pocket and flipping a digicard on the table between them. 'There's the key, I'll transfer deets of the contract to your feeds later. I want to be alone now so bugger off.'

Chapter 14

Katherine paced, in as much as one could pace on a ferromagnetic floor grid. The Fer-de-Lance was stuffed with all the extras and mods you could want and Katherine was the tiniest bit jealous she wasn't in the command chair. *Daisy Chain* was the vessel's name; the gauche humour of the moniker evident when you realised her flanks were lined with heavily modified rail guns and other chain-fired munitions. They were in the final jump phase of the trip back to Slough and Katherine was still trying to plug holes in the flimsy cover-story they'd come up with collectively. Her dreadlocks floated about her face like a nest of maddened serpents, giving her the look of Medusa – the one of ancient Earth mythology fame rather than the snaking docking arms used to bring ships inside the Hollows. The electromagnetic studs in the soles of her boots made a strange harmonic sucking noise as they grasped and released the ferromagnetic walkway. Grasp, release; grasp, release, *sploing, thip; sploing, thip*. The sound was beginning to wear on Angel's patience.

'It'll be fine Dread. I thought you were supposed to be the cool one at this party.'

'KATHERINE! Flaming fucking nebulas Angel! If you can't even get that right then we are going to get made as pirates even before we touch down on the launch pad! Is it any wonder I am stressed when I have to work with such fucking amateurs?'

There was a clacking, whirring sound that set Katherine's teeth on edge as she knew it was the prelude to the bot offering an opinion. In the distance, through the open hatch and down the ship a little in the mess cabin, they could hear the heaving sound of Admin making an *actual* mess – hopefully into a vac-bag. Angel wrinkled up her nose at the thought of otherwise.

'For once I agree with the pirate,' DORIS bleeped seriously as the database polled itself for the hundredth time, sifting through a billion different possibilities in 4.7 seconds and finding very little of any comfort. This mission was incredibly risky under any circumstance, and with every star system they traversed the odds only got worse.

The plan was to dock at the space station and just act incredibly dumb if anybody mentioned Captain Riley. Until directly challenged to the contrary, they hadn't seen him all week. Mental Eddie's Pilot's Federation contact had suppressed the destruction of the *Retribution's Fist*, hopefully, although the order had gone out very late in the day and there was some speculation as to whether it had made it in time before the uniweb was updated. Assuming no-one started shooting at them when they approached Slough Orbital the cover story was that Angel had been ambushed after leaving Slough, making it safely away only in the nick of time and thanks to the heroic (yet sadly fatal) actions of her escort, Commander Kram.

After a series of random hyperjumps made under the duress of extreme panic, Angel had limped in to the nearest friendly-looking planet to make repairs, only to find herself caught up in the middle of a planetary meltdown. It just so happened the entire system's power grid had been built on technology that used gold as the core conductive material. It was unusual technology, but not unheard of in the extravagant courts of some Imperial systems. But the power grid was failing and without a seriously large shipment of gold the entire economy was about to implode, resulting in civil war and general anarchy.

Having made an absolute killing with her conveniently appropriate cargo of pure gold, tripling what the investor was originally hoping to make, Angel had taken the liberty of lightening his swollen ROI to the tune of one replacement ship – admittedly quite a bit bigger and better than the one she had started with; with more space for cargo and a weapons array to be fearful of, but she'd figured she'd earned the pay rise by negotiating such a great price for the gold. DORIS had instructed Angel to hammer home the entitlement issue with grumpy emphasis right from the start if she wanted the story to seem credible.

'After all, the best ruses are the ones that lie within the outer hull of truth,' the bot had lectured once it became clear this plan was the best chance it had to get its client's investment back. 'So you need to dig deep into your extensive repertoire of 'dark and pouty' and try not to get asked too many questions.'

So, having supposedly tripled "Mister Corporate Affairs" cred count (DORIS would have to make sure news of their return didn't get back to him straight away as they didn't actually have the creds to back up the story), the plan continued that Angel and her new crew would take a couple of days off, go for a drink; find a card game; the usual kind of shenanigans you get up to when you've come into some creds. She'd have to feign a sudden interest in luxury spa treatments, which didn't sit well with her at all, but the first kill on the contract was a politician who was well-known for his love of a mid-morning hot float. Angel's mother's influence should give her access to Councillor Robert de Laan with his guard down; catch him unarmed and unprotected, and possibly even undressed. While she was busy despatching the councillor DORIS would hack into the station network, digging around in the spa's scheduling sub-routines to erase any record of his visit that morning and shutting down the chamber his body would be stashed in for "essential maintenance". Hopefully this would buy them enough time before the body was discovered to get the other parts of the contract done and be away, nice and quiet.

Even though the thought of what was ahead made her feel sick to her stomach, Angel wasn't feeling too bad about this first target, morally. She was still totally against the idea of killing someone (and for the most part doubted she'd actually be able to do it), but if it had to happen to someone she couldn't think of anyone she'd rather it be. Robert de Laan was a worm; a political weasel who had scratched his way to the middle echelons of power through blood-influence rather than brain-power, and then sat there doing more harm than good with his self-serving policies and greedy deals. Yes, he was influential, but he wouldn't be missed that much – existentially speaking – and hopefully physically for at least a day if they were going to get away clean.

Once de Laan had been despatched they could get on with the "loose ends" as Eddie had put it.

Loose end number one; collect a debt from one of Eddie's more troublesome dealers. Having let the interest on his "loans" get out of control, the proprietor of the Cheese Wheel, which as well as being a popular wine bar was THE place to go to buy recreational narcs, was about to pay the ultimate price for messing with a pirate; his life.

'Isn't that like cutting off your life support tube to spite your own face?' Angel had asked when they were reading through the contract together. 'I mean, how can the bar guy pay the debt if I kill him? Could we just, maybe, break his kneecaps?'

'It's not about the debt; it's a question of rep.'

'You sound like a rapper,' Admin said weakly, leaning against the hatch as he turned gradually greener.

'Go suck on an anal cyst, twinkle-toes,' Katherine had growled and that was the last they had seen of him as he'd spent the rest of the trip in the mess cabin hurling his load. Katherine had turned back to face Angel.

'The dude isn't going to pay. It's been obvious for some weeks now. He's making some moral stance about profit-share and our friend and benefactor, Mr Mental, has decided negotiations are over. If you don't stamp on uprisings like this they'll all be at it. That's the way it is with us pirates. We have to be … you know; scary and shit.'

So the owner of the Cheese Wheel would pay with his life – and while Angel still thought it was academic as she'd never be able to kill the man, in theory if someone HAD to die she didn't have too big a compunction about this one either, since he was one of the widest, filthy funnels of cheap narcs that made it on to her father's space station.

The final loose end was to nip down into the planet itself and spring a prisoner from inside the Salts; an associate of Eddie's who had been incarcerated for lewd acts and piracy following a honey-pot sting while he had a hold full of badly cloaked booty. As they thought they only had a day or so before people started asking questions about Captain Riley, and it took eight hours to get down to the planet's interior where the prisoners were held in a hyper-gravity transport pod, it had been decided to leave this aspect of the job to the two *actual* pirates while Angel got on with the killing up in orbit.

That was the plan, anyway.

Before they had left the Hollows, Katherine had taken them all on a tour of the kit vendors, having been given free reign with Eddie's cred-account to fit them out with decent suits and Ferro-magboots. Angel's suit was tough but flexible. It fitted her perfectly as the expensive biotex combat fabric literally moulded itself to her body. It even had elbow, knee and heel thrusters; tiny little affairs running strategically along the heavily customised fabric to so they could be fired off to initiate swift manoeuvring in micro and zero gravity environments. It had been a long time since Katherine had worn a suit in such good condition as the one she now wore too – although she hadn't splurged on the extravagance of micro-thrusters for all of them. At least the upgraded equipment meant she was a lot less grumpy about the impending mission. Admin had never owned a combat suit and just looked awkward and uncomfortable in his. He looked more like a man taking the final walk up death row, not a ruthless pirate about to deal out criminal justice.

DORIS had been predictably furious on being let out of the baggage store, but had soon bowed to the irresistible logic of coming up with the best possible plan to financially recompense its benefactor.

'That's one of the things I love best about robots,' Admin had declared as the plan started coming together on a tablet, 'they are all about fulfilling the command sequence of their programming routine; no fucking guilt or moral dilemmas. Totally ruthless. Mind you, they will turn on you as soon as process you. DORIS here would sell its grandmother to get its client's creds back. Wouldn't you?'

DORIS's circuits had stopped whirring for a moment, creating a strangely curious silence that seemed designed to illustrate the bot needed no processing power to calculate the next statement.

'I am a machine. Machines do not have "grandmothers". You are an imbecile.'

And that was about as much planning as they'd done since Admin had spent the next thirty minutes chasing the bot around the bar with a mop handle.

Sploing, thip; sploing, thip; sploing, thip.

'Will you STOP pacing? What with you and our friend 'Hughy' out in the mess cabin I am close to changing my mind about not being a killer. And I don't want to hear another peep out of you either,' she was glaring at DORIS, who's processor chip stopped whirring. 'This is my life, not a fucking game show. I'm not some puppet you can push and pluck and make dance to whatever tune you fancy! I'm as un-fucking-happy as you are about the current situation, but I wasn't exactly given a choice. Now we are back here, approaching my father's airspace, I think you should bear in mind that I could just decide to turn you both in. Open a channel right now and inform the station guard of exactly what has been going on and take my chances with the authorities!'

'I'm sorry I am going to have to interject here,' DORIS's circuits had woken up and were madly ticking and clicking. 'There is no financial merit in turning this ship and its crew over to the authorities on Slough.'

Angel glared and the robot quieted down.

'One more peep out of you and I swear I will jettison you!'

She turned back to face Katherine, who looked surprised by the sudden outburst.

'My cold-hearted robotic friend here might be right about the lack of creds if I turn us in, but the real reason I am not going to do it is I happen to hate my life here. I despise everything it represents and I always have. So I'm going to give it my best shot to make it as an assassin. But this is a big change for me and I need a little support. Would it hurt you to have some faith in me and get on with fulfilling your end of the bargain? We just need to knock this contract off. You rescue the convict, I'll kill the two men; two evil, horrible men who deserve to die anyway. Then we can get back to the Hollows and drink ourselves silly. Perhaps I'll ask Sue if she has any work for me at the bar? I could even do a bit of light pirating – robbing the rich to give to the poor like a 33rd century Robin Hood.'

She looked over at DORIS, half-expecting a disparaging remark extrapolating the odds of her transitioning successfully to the role of jobbing pirate. The robot simply hovered in the middle of the cockpit with the words MACHINES DO NOT HAVE HEARTS, IDIOT scrolling across the LCD on its chest panel.

Chapter 15

'This vessel is not in our records. Identify yourself Commander.'

'Piss and gravity! Admin get on the deep-web to Eddie and tell him to give his pilot's Fed man a shake.' Katherine was gripping the headrest of the command chair watching the Slough Orbital station drift through space over Angel's shoulder.

'The *Daisy Chain*'s license must have got caught up in the system, but at least they aren't shooting at us.'

'What should I do?'

'Tell them the truth; the one we made up. And remember to be pissed off.'

'Yeah, I know. In other words, act natural.'

'Precisely. Your digiwork is in there somewhere, we just might have arrived a little ahead of it.'

Angel flicked a channel open and cleared her throat uncertainly. Katherine gesticulated fiercely, knitting her eyebrows together with exaggerated anger and signalling for Angel to continue.

'Get lost Sys-Op, put me through to control. I am Commander Angel Rose; the station captain is my father and after the farce of a mission I have just been on I am not in the mood to dance regulations with you.'

The empty comms channel blew white noise at her while the Sys-Op presumably scanned her decal again and ran it through the system.

'I don't see you in the system, Commander,' the voice said eventually with a level of antipathy that made it clear she was not in the least bit swayed by Angel's lineage if the *Daisy Chain* wasn't on her register.

Angel stared at Katherine across the purring emptiness of the comms channel. Katherine gestured for her to continue. But continue with what, Angel wondered? Before she had time to coax anything out of her floundering brain the airwaves crackled into life again.

'Oh, wait. Hold up; there you are. That's odd.'

The last statement was clearly only meant for internal reflection as Angel was patched over immediately to another network and it was Rachel Hanandroo's voice filling the speakers in the flight cabin.

'Angel?'

It's show time, Angel thought as she opened the channel to the space station's control tower and began to unravel their story.

* * *

Much, much later, after a politely sympathetic yet uncomfortably dubious grilling from Rachel about Kram's unlikely combat heroics, the crew of the *Daisy Chain* had made good their disembarkation and been swallowed up by the bustling activity of the Slough orbital space station. After waving Katherine and Admin off in the queue for a transport heading planetside, Angel had taken a shuttle to Observer II and was now skulking in a dark corner of a strange bar called the Klaas Designer with the conscience bot whirring disapprovingly across the table. In the comfortably normal gravity of around one-g the little robot had extended its propeller again, assisting with lift.

The bar was unfamiliar, since Angel had been forced to come to the more exclusive of the two refurbished generation ships primarily used for recreation and commerce. It wasn't one of her usual haunts but Councillor de Laan would never be seen slumming it on Observer III, and a drink was a drink at the end of the day; the same could be said at the start of the day for that matter, which is where she now found herself drinking. She supposed it was a little early to be on hard liquor but she needed courage if she was going to go through with this ridiculous plan. She drained the Mutant Turnip, which was a golden liquid that tasted a lot smoother than it sounded, from her glass and placed it on the refill pad. Her freshly replenished cred account flashed up a pleasingly large green number on the NFC reader. If she could use it to get drunk enough to treat this all like a game, perhaps she could get through this after all?

'You should lay off the alcohol now, commander. Order a coffee instead.'

'Flaming Kaji-Farooq's nebula DORIS, you're beginning to sound like my mother!'

Angel had so far managed to avoid bumping into anyone from her family or its extended staff, but the irksome little bot had stuck to her like glue. With

Katherine and Admin already safely dispatched in a spinning transport pod she hadn't tried too hard to lose it either, despite the constant nagging.

'It dulls the senses and deadens the wit. Not to mention the fact it's only an hour past breakfast so it makes you look like a hobo.'

'Ha! At these prices? A hobo would be comatose for a fortnight on the cost of one Hullstripper in this joint. Trust me, as long as my NFC band keeps coughing up I could be wrapped in remlok and flashing the navy blues and twos from my tits to the tune of the Blue Danube and no one would pay a blind bit of notice. Besides, for some of us thinking about the lack of booze in our system does more to dim the wit than filling the void.'

The contract brief delivered to the *Daisy Chain*'s computer had informed them Councillor Robert de Laan, the unfortunate first mark, was in the habit of holding a breakfast meeting with his staff at about ten to allocate their tasks for the day. That done he would head off for a deep tissue massage in hyper-gravity followed by a hot float in one of the private steam chambers in the exclusive Godwina Rafferty spa and eco gardens. Angel's mother practically lived in the place so it had been pretty easy to hack into her account from a service panel and request a last-minute appointment for a hyper-gravity facial for her daughter, fresh back from space travel. The spa had been only too happy to accommodate, despite the fact for most people there was a three week waiting list for appointments.

Angel would finish this drink then go take the facial before enjoying a relaxing stroll around the fragrant eco-dome gardens at the spa. Meanwhile DORIS would be parked in reception with the other service bots, keeping an eye out for the arrival of the councillor. At the appropriate moment the bot would have to create a distraction loud enough to draw attention away from Angel sneaking in to the chamber after the mark. From there on in it was down to Angel and her knife, which was nestled snugly in a cleverly disguised sheathe in the arm of her flight suit. She absently turned the deadly metal cuff Katherine had given her as she sipped on the second drink of the day. Was that really only three days ago? It felt like a lifetime had already passed under the bridge and she still couldn't quite believe what she was mixed up in. Piracy? Murder? Politics? Narcs? It was certainly a far cry from her old life. She felt appalled and exhilarated in equal measure.

Could she really kill a man? In cold blood? Well, it would be hot blood in the zero-g steam room more likely – and every bit as messy as Captain Riley's demise no doubt. Assuming, of course, that she could get her knife to do her bidding with any degree of enthusiasm. That was one big-assed assumption, even without the thought of the mess. She reminded herself about Robert De Laan's more than dubious political leanings. If even half the stories she'd read in the "Observer's Observer" were true he was a greedy, self-serving hypocrite with an unhealthy interest in barely-legal slave girl whores. In Angel's mind that pretty much described every politician she'd ever met. She hadn't actually met this one, though she'd seen his face plastered across newsfeeds and digimags often enough. She knew her father had dealings with him too, and he came across as just as much of an arse-wipe as the rest of them.

'Time to go, Commander,' the conscience bot was displaying a countdown timer to her appointment at the spa in its LCD chest panel.

'Right.'

Angel's stomach flipped over, stirring the butterflies that had taken up permanent residence there into a hysterical frenzy. She downed the last of her drink, touched the concealed handle of the knife one last time to make sure it was still there and slipped out of the booth, heading out of the door with the robot buzzing along behind her.

* * *

'Just relax and enjoy the music. It's going to feel a little strange if you haven't had a deep gravity cleanse before, but you'll be amazed by how sparklingly clear your pores will be.'

Angel was lying back in a treatment chair, her face smeared with a fragrant white pulp, cool pads over eyes so she couldn't see her attendant 'beautechnicians' as they liked to be called, fussing around her.

'Jedra, Juan, Jelle and Jimbo! That's enough now,' the lead technician said to his assistants. 'Let's strap everything down and set the spin going.'

The assistant who had been applying the white gunk stopped tamping it down around her jawline and Angel felt a uniform pressure across her face and neck as something soft was laid upon it and stretched out to be secured either side of her head, presumably a cloth mask to stop the mixture flying off when they started the centrifuge spinning. One of the other assistants – Angel had forgotten which was which almost as soon as they'd been introduced to her – gently clasped the padded limb restraints around her thighs and upper arms. The contraption of torture Angel now found herself secured to was similar to the spinning chairs she used over on Observer III, only a lot more luxurious and comfortable. Instead of being harnessed roughly into a hard forma-plex seat in a brightly lit med-lab, this chair was deeply padded and leather clad. The chamber was lit for cosiness rather than cleanliness and the soft braying of whale song and euphonic harmonies mingled with a heady perfume that reminded Angel of fresh cinnamon biscuits.

'Okay, Miss Rose, we're going to spin you up to 1.2-g. It will make you feel a little heavy, but not as heavy as a trip planet side if you've ever been down there?'

As Angel's entire face was encased in an aromatic mummification she presumed this was a rhetorical question and continued breathing steadily through the small gap left around her nostrils. 1.2-g was hardly even a blip. It would feel a bit like riding a roller-coaster, nothing more. But she would be glad when this farcical process was over so she could get out into the gardens and start pacing in earnest. Why women like her mother subjected their bodies to these beautification rituals was beyond her comprehension, and the whale song was really beginning to annoy her.

The centrifuge started to spin gently and Angel's chest tightened, her right hand instinctively searching for the clicker that would tell the controller she was compos mentis and happy to keep going. But this setup didn't need a clicker as she wouldn't be spinning anywhere near fast enough to go g-LOC. She tried to relax as momentum grew and it felt as if her body was slowly being smothered underneath a hundred pounds of softly singing whale blubber.

Chapter 16

Angel sauntered through the fragrant herb garden trying to keep a low profile. Her face was calm, and impossibly clean now, but inside her chest her heart was hammering a deafening rhythm. Slack-faced patrons in fluffy lilac robes padded aimlessly about, some murmuring softly to each other over the top of healthy-looking drinks in frosted tallboy glasses; some were wandering alone, like her, deep in contemplative thought. The eco-gardens were housed in a huge cylinder-like dome inside the central stack of the Observer II's main hull. Angel could see stars and the planet turning lazily overhead with the gardens themselves bathed in the life-giving light of a thousand or more solar strips. Unlike most other places in orbit around Slough, there was no brash advertising in this restful place. The exclusive clientele had already paid their dues in extortionate treatment fees, Angel supposed, so their eyeballs got some respite too. Instead the solar strips keeping the vegetation alive cycled through a synchronised dance of colour that was supposed to represent the setting and rising of the twin suns of Lupon in Wolf 573. As she watched the lightshow wash its lavish cadence across the artificial landscape Angel had to admit it was rather a stunning display, if a little showy.

The stack of gravity rings circling the dome was accessible via a grid-work of platforms and lifting pads, regulated from some unseen elsewhere in the complex, so that the ambient gravity inside each section could be individually controlled by altering the velocity of its spin. Fluffy robed and crisp, pale-green uniformed bodies travelled up and down all around her. Entering one of the treatment chambers involved strapping in to an enclosed pod spinning in tandem with the central dome at just under one-g. The pod would then decelerate or accelerate in sync with the section of ring you wanted to enter. Angel watched as a large man with a bald, sweaty pate fought to keep his robe covering his balls as the pod decelerated to around zero-g and a beautechnician helped him up. Angel turned in circles, watching the pod spin around her head as the airlock to the steam chamber slid open, enveloping the little pod in hot steamy whiteness and hiding its inhabitants from view.

Level five, chamber twenty-seven Angel noted internally and headed casually over to a platform that would lift her to the same point once DORIS came through with the planned commotion. They had decided to give it about ten minutes, allowing the councillor time to settle in to his float and the beautechnician time to move on to other duties. Right on cue there was a burst of activity spilling out of reception. DORIS streaked out of the doors, smoke spilling from its propeller engine which popped and fizzed worryingly. Everyone turned to stare at the circus as a small cluster of frantic assistants tried to grab hold of the malfunctioning bot and wrestle it under control. By the time the scene had dissipated Angel had also been swallowed by a steamy shroud and was pulling herself along the drag frame inside chamber twenty-seven, her heart galloping around her chest like a frenzied horse. She slid the door shut behind her and was instantly choked by the cloying embrace of the scented hot float chamber.

She touched the handle of her knife for the hundredth time and began skirting the bottom of the chamber, staying tucked in to the corner and out of sight in the comforting folds of steam.

'Matthew? Is that you man? I'm dying of thirst up here. What in the flaming lady's tits took you so long?'

The belligerent voice of the politician came drifting down through the smog from way up above. This was where it was hottest on account of the microscopic amount of gravity left in the chamber so certain acts of physics, like heat rising, knew which way was up. This was the preferred setting for regular hot floaters as it allowed a client to regulate the intensity of the experience to suit their taste by navigating up and down inside the tall chamber. The blinds had been switched to unidirection, so naked and sweaty occupants could enjoy the ambience of the light show in the main dome without the risk of baring their buttocks to the world if they drifted too close to the glass.

Angel pulled herself slowly along the drag frame, staying at the base of the chamber where the steam was thinner until she could get her bearings and locate the councillor. Once she had spotted him she would use her suit's micro thrusters to launch a rapid attack, slicing open his throat as quick as you like before making a bee-line for the exit; hopefully before taking too much of a steamy shower in his spurting blood. She shuddered at the thought and forced her mind to conjure up images of the fat, sweaty politician molesting a young slave girl who had most likely been snatched from her home and forced into prostitution when she was just an innocent child. It helped a little, so she bolstered the idea by imagining this was just a computer game. Three lives and a couple of power-ups – those were the drinks she'd had for breakfast – and if she could just make the kill shot without getting caught she could level up enough to get Mental Eddie off her back. Buy some more power-ups at Sue's bar. A lot more power-ups.

'Oh come on man, get up here! Am I to evaporate for want of an iced Perriard? Or do you expect me to drink my own piss?'

Piss and gravity, thought Angel with a wry smile to herself, finally stealing enough courage from some mystical place in her psyche to let go of the drag frame and prepare to launch herself, full tilt, towards the sound of the insufferable bastard's voice. She was positioning herself to make best use of the micro-thrusters as she kicked off when there was a sudden, tearing metallic groan and the atmosphere started to get unexpectedly heavier. Very suddenly.

'No ... wait ... WHAT?'

The voice from above was getting louder, and not just because he was becoming more agitated. He was getting closer; rapidly. With a shuddering 'thunk' the steam chamber passed an orbit in sync with the central dome, but then continued speeding up, bringing the gravity to over one-g. Not a particularly foreboding weight on its own, but coupled with a fall from at least forty metres on to the deep scaffold of steel grab frames the prognosis for any falling politicians wouldn't be good.

Angel flinched as a sickening slapping, crunch came through the sweaty smog off to her left. The machinery whined again and she had to steady herself on the grab frame as the chamber slowed down and fell into orbit with the central dome, lifting the extra weight off her body as the ambient gravity returned to normal.

What the fuck had just happened? Angel's brain was still trying to formulate the question when her body leapt into action, vaulting over the scaffold that was now acting more like hurdles than a grab frame, towards the unmistakable sound of a soft body snapping over hard steel.

Out of the steam loomed the podgy councillor. He was pasty white; his flaccid naked body slick with sweat and massage oil. At first glance all Angel could think about was those ancient baroque oil paintings from way back in Earth history. The way he'd come to rest draped across the metalwork in a grotesquely elegant fashion, he looked like a Ruben's nude; arched back to accentuate indulgent belly and plentiful breast, head thrown back as if in decadent laughter.

Angel jumped, letting out a little squeak as the body suddenly twitched three times and let out a long, slow fart as the muscles around the sphincter relaxed. His body had broken in at least three places, most notably the neck. His lifeless, startled eyes were staring straight at her through the steamy fug – and while there was no chance he would be identifying her to the authorities that didn't make the scene any less creepy.

* * *

'Commander? Commander Rose? Angel? Hey! Hey you! Ow! Ow fuck! FUCK!'

Angel swore under her breath as a skinny young man skittered towards her, tripping over a courgette planter in his haste to intercept her. It was Jack Nova, roving reporter from the Observer's Observer. The contents of his satchel spilled all over the ground along with several stacks of empty seed trays. She had been trying to slip away unnoticed from the scene but now the whole place was gaping at the kerfuffle he had caused.

Red faced and puffing, he disentangled himself from the mess and gave his trousers a cursory brush before hurrying back to his pursuit of Angel, who was still doing her best to melt into the scenery.

'Angel! Hey! HO there! Phew, okay … there you are. It IS you. I thought it was! Why didn't you stop?'

'Oh. Hi Jack. Sorry, I didn't see you.'

'Didn't? Didn't see me? You were staring straight at me when I ran into the courgette bed! Come on Angel; remember you're talking to a reporter now.'

'I thought you were an intern, not a reporter.'

'That was six months ago!'

Jack looked crestfallen, but it didn't last long as he got his bag strap caught over the end of a grape trellis and the whole thing came tumbling after him.

'Shit! Sorry...' there was no one particular around to apologise to, so it dissipated into the humidity and the grape-heavy trellis remained on the floor.

'What do you *want*, Jack?'

Angel was still hurrying away as fast as looked potentially innocent, but the damned little reporter was keeping pace with her, fumbling to pull a tablet out of his satchel now it had finished its mischief with the trellis.

'Oh that's a nice greeting for an old academy classmate, I'm sure. Can you stop? Do you think we can stop for a second?'

'You dropped out of the academy – to go to media school. Remember?' Angel had no intention of stopping to chat.

'Yes, but we registered together. The only reason I dropped out was they refused to insure me in any more simulators. Not much point training to be a pilot if they aren't going to let you learn to fly!'

'You were, ARE, a danger to yourself and everything else around you. I can't imagine anything more dangerous than you in charge of a set of thrusters attached to a battering ram.'

Jack's main problem in the pilot's academy was his persistently morbid state of luck; coupled with a confidence streak wider than the Breenfreed Ludd asteroid belt, it made him very potentially a dangerous pilot to fly in the same star system as, let alone the same formation. There had been a collective sigh of relief when the cadets' assembly was told he was flunking out.

'Yeah, well ... luckily for both of us it seems my future lay in journalism. And you are JUST the person I need to speak to for my side-panel on station gossip. Talk about TURN-A-ROUND! Wow! One minute you're hanging off the rope ladder of the poverty bunks (although I guess your father wouldn't *actually* have let that happen), sprung out of the cooling house on the station PR budget (and don't for a minute try and deny THAT one as I have already chased down the digi-trail); then you go missing, lost in space for a few days at the EXACT ... SAME ... TIME ... as Captain Riley goes missing? Now there's a coincidence, right?'

Angel came to a sudden halt, the series of insinuations she had just been hit with taking the breath out of her like a barrage of heavy-fisted gut shots. Jack stopped opposite her, puffing slightly from the effort of keeping up. His satchel finally relented and gave him his tablet.

'Phew, thanks ... so yes; and now here you are, back, in the FLASHIEST ride I've seen in dock for a long time ... A. LONG. TIME ... am I right? The word is you made a KILLING on some freaky-lucky trade with some distant Imperial outpost – supposedly. Although I cannot verify this because the whole planet happens to be off-grid for a few days while their station command centre purges a virus from its link to the uniweb.'

Angel stared open mouthed.

'So, come on Angel. What really gives? I was going to run with the story of you two vanishing off for some hanky-panky in Pog Hobdonia; everyone knows he got you that cushy job running the gold – yeah right, *gold*,' Jack winked theatrically before coughing into his wrist and carrying on. 'The Naval Captain and the Station Commander's destitute daughter smuggling drugs into the pleasure zone? It has a ring to it doesn't it? A kind of rough and ready romance. You're like a 33rd century Bonnie and Clyde!'

Angel's cheeks flushed angrily and she forgot she was supposed to be making a hasty, quiet exit. She glared at him, feet apart and hands on her hips. 'Why you! I'm a fucking pilot, alright? Not the station-fucking-captain's daughter.'

'Now, I didn't say that, did I? A man who can fuck stations? That really *would* be news; although I'm not sure I'd be chasing after his daughter.'

Jack Nova grinned at his own wit and started tapping away on his tablet. 'So,' he said eventually, pointing a pen-camera at her, 'what's the story, Angel?'

Angel stood there, fuming at him for a few seconds. 'No. Fucking. Comment.'

For a moment she'd been terrified but then she realised the shit she was spilling today was going to be all over the metaphorical-fan in about twenty-four hours anyway. Nothing she could do about that – her life was finished in Slough. This gave her an odd sense of anticipation that wasn't altogether unpleasant. All she had to do was keep this little git of a reporter quiet until they could get off the station.

Jack Nova's hand dropped. He looked genuinely crestfallen. 'Oh … Really?'

'Really.'

He seemed to mull this over for a moment.

'I'm going to run the story anyway, you might as well make sure it's accurate,' he tried speculatively.

'No, YOU had better make sure it's accurate. Otherwise you'll be seeing me with the magistrate.'

'Oh. Okay, well, I suppose you're right. But I do definitely have that PR-weasel bailing you out on company funds. What do you have to say about that?'

The pen-cam was poked at her again and she resisted the urge to grab it and shove it up his nose.

'No. Fucking. Comment. Now leave me alone. Goodbye Jack.'

'Meh. Okay, suit yourself I guess. It was just a spur of the moment thing anyway, when I saw you. Can't blame a man for trying, right? Come on Angel, it's just my job. Right?'

He punched her playfully in the top of her arm and then flinched when it looked momentarily like she might respond by throwing him headfirst into another courgette platter.

'Hey … Okay, truce! I will continue on my merry way! I'm here to see Councillor de Laan anyway. Got a rather tasty kiss and tell from sixteen-year-old triplets called Marianne, Becky and Daniéll Harris-Homes and his lips are front and centre stage! You haven't seen him have you? S'posed to be in one of these floaters but they're all too misty to see.'

Angel's heart leapt into her chest. Oh no! They hadn't expected the councillor to stay unmissed for very long but they needed a few more hours at least before anyone started looking for him. Katherine and Admin would arrive down in the Salts any time now, and then they needed an hour or so to spring the prisoner. The return shuttle was about an hour too as it didn't need to run the eight-hour hyper-gravity acclimatisation sequence coming back up to orbit. Plus she still had another part of the contract to fulfil.

'Yes! Yes I did see him. About ten minutes ago,' Angel said, an idea suddenly springing to mind. 'The creep tried to grope me over by the pool of reflection.'

'Oooh, really?'

The reporter's eyes lit up and he snapped the pen-cam back up to Angel's face. 'Care to comment?'

'No. But you've missed him. He's finished his treatments and found nothing else to tempt him to stay. So you might as well just go and find something useful to cover, like that dirty little bust up in the Prism system, or who's trying to bump off the Emperor.'

'Oh, bah again! Well, I'll get shot if I go back to the desk with nothing to file in my column so I'll just have to catch him at his office.'

'Wait … err, listen. Okay. I don't want you to get shot.'

'You don't?'

The rookie reporter looked genuinely surprised. Usually the people he was harrying for a comment ended up wanting him *more* shot, not less.

'No, of course not. And there really is nothing bad about where I have been – which is NOT with Captain Riley, I hasten to make clear.'

'Oh, really …' Jack Nova became suddenly, markedly less interested. His eyes flicked past Angel and he began scanning the steam chamber doors again. 'He's definitely left the spa then?'

'Look, why don't you let me buy you a drink? At least let me apologise for being so short with you. You're right, we're all just doing what "The Man" pays us to do, right?'

Jack Nova's attention was focussed fully back on Angel, an edge of suspicion beginning to creep in around his surprise.

'Let's jump a shuttle to the station. I'll buy you a drink in the Zen Garden and give you all the details of my recent adventures. You never know, it might even be better than a sordid affair between a station captain's brat and a naval officer. Right?'

Scepticism suddenly stampeded across Jack Nova's expression, wiping both surprise and suspicion out in the charge.

'Are you pulling a fast one? Am I going to come out of the toilets after the first drink and find you've run off like everyone used to do in flight school?'

'No! Did we …? Look, flight school was ages ago, water under the bridge, right? You're a serious reporter now and I have a great story for you! All *exclusive* too!'

That magic word swung the balance in favour of Angel's encouragements. 'Well, I s'pose it is nearly lunchtime.'

Angel nodded.

'One or two drinks wouldn't hurt. Might as well hear what you have to say.'

'Exactly!'

Angel slung her arm across Jack Nova's shoulders and steered him towards the door, making desperate eyeball shrugging gestures at DORIS as the little bot hovered in the entrance to reception waiting for her.

Chapter 17

'Sho ... old Tailshpin ... He finally learned how to control a ship, huh?'

'S'riiight,' slurred Angel in reply to the equally slurry question.

'Pretty lucky though. I mean shaking off those evil Cypher Funks ...'

'Punks,' Angel corrected, 'and I would say it was more down to bravery than luck. Don't forget Commander Kram gave his life keeping those pirates off my tail.'

'Right. AND then you stumble into the trade deal of the millennium? A meal ticket worthy of the Naris Ellison saga ...'

'Okay, let's not get carried away with the narrative here. The planet needed gold to fix up the power-grid. I had gold, and plenty of it. For once 'the Lady' was on my side, what I can say? If I hadn't arrived when I did the whole nebula-sucking star system would have gone down; they were on the brink of civil war. It's amazing how much the Imperial court of who-gives-a-fuck will pay in the face of total anarchy.'

'Clearly. And *very* unlucky they caught a planet-wide virus shortly after so no diligent reporters can call them to verify the facts ...'

'Very...'

The reporter tapped a few wobbly notes into his tablet while he took some more deep chugs of his drink. Angel topped him up from the half-empty flagon of blue liquid they were sharing. He seemed to be thinking deeply about his notes.

'Are you sure there wasn't any sex though? I mean, a story always sells better if there is sex in it.'

Angel's insides screwed up into a tight little ball. She wanted to slap the sleazy Trumble-head and his mind-in-the-gutter reporting style.

'No sex. No. But it has everything else. Money, power, heroes and pirates! The underdogs win! David and Goliath! People love that stuff far better than a sleazy sex story. Trust me.'

The fog over Jack's eyes was getting heavier. They were tucked into a booth in Anna and Roland's Zen Garden and Angel had been plying him with as much alcohol as she could get into his glass since they'd hopped a shuttle just over an hour ago. For a small man he had an impressive capacity for booze, but it was only a matter of time before he passed out and Angel had been pacing herself well.

'Yeah, that was REALLY impressive. Those pirates are pros! They gonna be sooo embarrassed when the galaxy hears how they were swatted off by a fly. They'll be the laughing stock.'

The little reporter was starting to warm to a potentially juicy angle.

'And KRAM will be a hero ... right? It's not just about the bad side of everything,' Angel couldn't help getting up a head of steam since the gutter-loving gossip press was one of her personal hates. She despised it when so-called reporters did this.

'Oh yeah, right ... of course. A *total* hero ... trust me, I'm a reporter. Right?' He winked drunkenly. She topped him up to the brim again gritting her teeth to force a smile.

'I'll drink a toast to that,' she said raising her glass into the air so he felt obliged to do the same.

'To Kram!'

'To reporters!'

They cried out of sync in unison and then swallowed more blue liquid together.

'Uhm, Commander Rose ... What is going on?'

Katherine was standing at the end of the table, legs planted wide and arms folded across her chest, glaring down at the apparent drunken revelry.

'Katherine! Meet Jack Nova ... he's a *reporter* for the Observer's Observer,' Angel said pointedly.

Katherine raised an eyebrow. 'You are drinking with a *reporter*?'

Admin appeared behind her. Shooting a look between the two women he decided silence was the better part of valour.

'Pleashure to meet you, Kathreeen.' Jack stuck a wavy hand into the air in the general direction of the new arrivals and when Katherine didn't grasp it he soon lost the will to keep holding it up and it went flopping back down on the table.

'I am drinking with an old academy friend,' Angel said, 'who I ran into in the spa gardens looking for some dodgy politician.'

That was enough for the penny to drop.

'Well, we need to get moving. The cargo you ordered from down below is on the way to the *Daisy Chain* and I'm guessing you didn't get finished with the rest of the *digiwork* yet?' the dread-headed pirate said emphatically.

'One more contract to sign.'

Katherine glanced around. 'Where's that bothersome biscuit tin?'

'Went back to the ship to make sure she's all fuelled up and ready to roll.'

'Well, you laydees clearly have work to do. I should get to the office and file this story anyway, right? Pirates, intrigue, screw ups and shame … I might see if I can chase up Captain Riley again too, see what the navy has to say about the appalling amount of gangsters that seem to be marauding through this sector unchecked. Ashully, I have a man in the pilot's fed. I should be able to tap him up for el capitan's whereaboutsh.'

'Oh, ho there little friend,' Katherine had thwarted Jack's attempt to stagger to his feet by sliding into the booth beside him, shunting him deeper with her arse. She signalled towards the bar for Anna to bring another glass. 'How about you just stay put for one more drink? I might be able to add some detail to your story; give you the scoop on what it's like working for Commander Rose here?' Katherine winked at Jack.

'Is there sex?' Jack asked seriously. 'I could really do with some sex. I mean, it always sell a story better if there's sex ….'

'Oh for sure … the best kind.'

Angel started to protest as Katherine leant in close and whispered something in the reporter's ear.

'LESBIAN SEX?!' he cried, eyes wide.

In his excitement he forgot to hold on to his tablet and it went clattering to the floor between his legs. The conversation at every table in this section of the bar ceased in an instant and all eyes turned towards them. Angel's cheeks burned.

'Katherine! Don't you dare!'

'You just go finish your business and leave me to finish up here. Admin, go with her to make sure she doesn't run into any more *old friends* … I'll meet you back at the ship in thirty minutes.'

With that Angel was tugged out of the booth by her arm as Jack struggled to reach between his thighs and blindly fumble around on the floor for the escaped tablet containing all his notes. Katherine filled a fresh glass with blue liquid and made sure Jack Nova's was brimming over too.

* * *

Angel stomped through the corridors of the space station sucking on the flask of coffee Admin had picked up from one of the cabin vendors out in the main drag. They were making their way towards the Cheese Wheel, a wine bar famed for its variety of galactic cheeses served to accompany the interesting vintages of grape; but perhaps best known for being *the* place to go if you wanted to stock up on cheap narcs. The proprietor was Daniel Dennett, otherwise known as "Dennett the Cheese", a long-time dealer for Mental Eddie's narc crew and the man Angel had been contracted to make a terminal example of.

'So, how'd you get the prisoner out of the Salts without the whole planet's enforcement brigade after you?' Angel asked as they trudged on.

'A section of the mine collapsed. Terrible shame, lots of prisoners trapped. Crawf McVillan was one of them – at least that's what they'll think until they've worked their way through one hundred and twenty metres of cave-in to discover otherwise. We'll be long gone by then. Meanwhile the pallet of unworked alabaster we procured has a little something extra buried deep inside the stack. It should be delivered to the hold of the *Daisy Chain* any time now.'

'You collapsed the mine on top of a load of prisoners?'

'Yip.'

'Are they dead?'

'Yes; no; maybe; who cares?' Admin shrugged noncommittally. 'Space-cakes Angel, you really haven't grasped the point of this pirating thing yet heave you?'

'But … surely there's the whole 'honour among thieves' thing you've got going on? The convicts will mostly be thieves, so where is the honour in burying them alive to pull out one mate of Eddies?'

'We didn't set out to bury anyone. They were working pretty deep and we only took out the access tunnel, but there are never any guarantees when you're working with blast caps in high gravity. That's some heavy shit down there. My legs could hardly support my body. There might be some collateral damage and I certainly wouldn't want to be the prison wardens stuck down there with the prisoners. But in the end I refer you to my earlier point. Who really cares as long as we get the contract filled? There's no reputation hit for making some extra fertiliser out of a few dozen cons… We are in Federation space after all.'

Angel took in his devil-may-care attitude, frowning. 'And you call the robot ruthless? At least it can blame its programming. What happened to your humanity?'

Admin shrugged. 'Got replaced with *piranicy?*'

A grin spread across his face as they wove through the rabble of hawkers and traders looking to do deals of varying levels of legality with anyone who had creds in their account and space in their cargo hold.

'Like I said, I admire the robot, but it's one of the key reasons to make sure A.I. stays outlawed if you ask me. The last thing we need is those flying calculators to grow a conscience – or worse yet start meting out justice by their own standards of logic.'

'But it's okay for you to decide who lives and dies, based on the terms of a contract?'

'Welcome to piracy girlfriend – and watch you don't fall off that high horse and land on your backside.'

He looked at her carefully, concern creeping in at the edge of his grin. 'You up for this, yeah?' His nod in the direction of the neon sign hanging up ahead made his meaning clear. The Cheese Wheel.

Angel tossed the half-drunk flask of coffee into a waste chute as they passed it. 'We're about to find out I guess.'

'Well, at least it's not your first. The first is always the worst.' Angel looked at him questioningly.

'Councillor de Laan? You *did* take him out, didn't you?'

Angel looked away, chewing her bottom lip in a way that screamed *guilty.* 'Angel! You *did* kill the spacing councillor, didn't you? We are so many shades of fucked up if we go back to the Hollows …'

'Don't worry. He's dead,' she interrupted.

Admin breathed a sigh of relief as they arrived at the door to the wine bar. It wasn't open yet. As one of the station's all-night drinking dens, the Cheese Wheel staff didn't need to arrive until the narc-buying public began dragging themselves out of their stinking bunks long after supper. *This is good*, thought Angel, for the first time catching herself seriously thinking about sticking a knife in this man. Her right hand instinctively sought out the handle of the six-inch blade hidden in her flight suit sleeve, a now-familiar feeling of comfort coming from finding it exactly where she expected to.

The first one is always the worst, she thought as they paused in front of the bar. Then she put a shoulder to the door and they waded in.

Inside the lights were dim, just the twenty-four hour ad screens spraying a kaleidoscope of flickering neon light throughout the otherwise sleeping bar, tables already wiped clean for the night ahead. The base of the bar was made up of a grid of display coolers, subtly lit to show off hunks of cheese while keeping each rare specimen at the perfect temperature for consumption. High-tech machines designed to slice, dice, grate and process the dairy-based snackery were placed at strategic points along the bar, sharp-bladed wheels ready to prep-and-serve any texture or style of cheesy delight you could wish for along with your fine wine. As they stepped into this curd-filled Aladdin's cave they heard a strange noise coming from behind the counter; a kind of strangled half-whimper, half-gurgle accompanied by what sounded a little like unenthusiastic tap dancing. Admin put his arm out to stop Angel advancing, his pirate senses on high alert for an ambush. Angel noticed one of the large turning blades from the central slicing machine was not where it should have been. At that exact moment a motor suddenly whirred into life out of sight behind the counter. The whimpering, gurgle ramped up into a smothered, drowning scream of such blood curdling intensity Angel felt like she must be turning to cheese herself.

Angel and Admin were both rooted to the spot, bodies tense and shot with adrenaline. Then sense seemed to return to Admin and he kicked the door shut behind them. The engine sound was fully revved now and the scream was suddenly overwhelmed by the gurgle and then extinguished altogether. Once the screaming had died down Angel could hear the wet slap of something that sounded suspiciously organic matter hitting the flex-plex surfaces of the bar area in clumps. The tap dancing, which had briefly accelerated to an exuberant clog dance, ceased as rapidly as the screaming had and then the engine started winding down, a background whirring noise fading until all was silent again.

Angel and Admin looked at each other. She hardly dared walk into the bar. The audio drama they'd just heard play out left little to the imagination in terms of the scene they would discover. The only real question was who had conducted the orchestra? She noticed Admin was now holding a blade in his left hand and what looked like a small, flat disc in the other. She slipped her own knife out of its sheath and they edged deeper into the bar, peering around the machine with the missing circular blade. The machines all had these blades; big, industrial slicers mounted in a square steel frame with a power supply and a wickedly fast motor attached. The edge of the blade was equally wickedly sharp with popped out serrations covering the flat of one side. Grated or sliced; one blade, two functions.

Angel saw his hands first; placed flat on the countertop as if he were leaning forward in animated conversation with a patron propping up the bar. Except these hands had a rivet bashed crudely into the centre of each pinning them to the cracked and bloody flex-plex counter top like a grisly crucifixion. As her eyes followed the scene further back behind the bar they came upon the grisly mess she'd been anticipating, slumped halfway down behind the counter. She wrinkled her nose and looked away as her stomach did a nauseated flip-flop.

Beside her Admin whistled. 'Now, that's what is commonly known as a cheesy grin.'

The now stilled cheese blade was embedded in the man's face, dissecting him across the mouth and cut so deep the top of his head was only held in place because the blade was embedded in the rear wall, acting as a shelf for the lurid ornament to rest upon. Blood and gore and bits of brains were sprayed all over; together with shards of teeth and chunks of fleshy top lip where the rough grating edge of the blade had worked it to shreds as he bit down against the violent onslaught.

The corpse grinned at them around the blade.

Then, as Angel watched in open-mouthed horror the weight of the frame and motor proved too much for the blade/head/shelf contraption and it pulled free of the wall, clattering to the floor behind the bar. The top of the man's head toppled with it but was still partially attached to the rest of the head by the stringy gristle of the ear lobes and two thick strips of fleshy cheek, so instead of tumbling all the way to the ground it tipped forward and bounced against his chest on gruesome bungee cords of shredded skin.

'I s'pose we should be 'grateful', right?' he nudged Angel. 'Dead's dead at the end of the day.'

Angel finally found her voice. 'Is that Dennett?'

Admin nodded. 'Was, I should say. He's not half the man he used to be. Lost his head it seems.'

'Yeah, alright. You're about as funny as a hyper-gravity enema right now. What the hell just happened?'

'I'd say one of Mr Dennett's other friends got to him before us.'

They both looked up and down the bar; suddenly remembering they had their weapons out for a reason. There was a sudden rush of noise and light from behind them and Angel's heart tried to jump clean out of her mouth. They both spun around to see the door softly closing behind DORIS, who was hovering just inside the bar.

'What the Thargoid-loving fuck are you doing here?' Angel cried, her mind glad to have something new to connect with after the horror behind the bar.

The robot clicked and ticked as processors prepared an explanation. 'I came to see what was taking you so long. The cargo is all loaded up; the *Daisy Chain* fuelled and primed. I even sorted out the export license for the shipment of alabaster that mysteriously arrived. Not exactly a genius idea to send a loaded pallet to the docks without any digiwork when you're trying to keep a low profile. Luckily for you I was there to recalibrate the customs scanner before they could get deep enough to discover the unusually soft centre in the load.'

The robot paused. It seemed to be waiting for some kind of recognition for its stellar work. When none came it continued with an eerily human hint of sulk in its tone. 'Fine. So, all we need is a crew and a jump window and we can be out of this system clean … You can thank me later.'

The little propeller holding the robot aloft buzzed harder and tilted to thrust it deeper into the bar. It hovered between Angel and Admin as its scanners took in the scene of the murder. 'I can see you've completed your work to a satisfactory level, though I have to admit I find the theatrics somewhat gauche.'

Angel blinked in disbelief at how matter-of-fact this observation was.

Beside her Admin smirked.

'Ruthless,' he said to himself with a satisfied grin as the smack, smack, smacking sound of generous globules of blood hitting the floor filled the neon-scattered silence around them.

Chapter 18

Katherine was back to pacing, although thankfully as they were still in dock the ferromagnetic floor magnets weren't making that annoying noise. 'We have about two hours before that hack wakes up from the Dreibell flower sleep syrup I slipped him.'

'Probably a lot less before they find the mess we left at the Cheese Wheel,' Admin added.

Katherine glared at the back of Angel's head. 'Can't you use your influence or something to bump us up the launch schedule?'

Angel sighed, tapping the flight desk, bringing up holograms of the current sector to plot out the most innocent-looking route back to the Hollows. 'You told me to act natural. If I start throwing my father's weight around I might as well hang a neon sign over my head saying "guilty".'

The comms link crackled and Rachel Hanandroo's voice drifted into the spacious cockpit of the Fer-de-Lance. 'Angel … it's your mother.'

Angel's heart stopped dead in her chest and then plummeted down to the pit of her stomach to find a place to hide. She opened the comms link. 'Which channel?'

'Errr, no, not on the loop.'

There was a pregnant pause as all three in the *Daisy Chain*'s cockpit peered out through the forward windscreen at the brightly lit rectangle of the control room window across the dock. DORIS whirred quietly above the navigation panel.

Rachel was standing nervously at her command post, a tablet cradled in one arm, her back to the glowering figure that had planted itself like thunder just inside the entrance hatch. Even from this distance Rachel's face was the picture of grey anxiety.

'When you've quite finished faffing about, cadet …'

'Commander,' corrected Rachel in a sulky tone as Angel's mother shunted her aside and bent too close to the comms mic to speak. Her voice boomed into the cockpit, distorting the speakers and making the shell-shocked crew flinch.

'And where do you think you're sloping off to, young lady? What? We don't even bother to pop by and say hello to our mother now? After I've been worried half to death about you, vanishing into thin space for days without a word, and then hearing you're back on the station from my dermaponics therapist? My *dermaponics* therapist, I ask you? For the Lady's sake, Angel! AND since when did you start having facials?' She turned to address her entourage; three toned and beautiful young men who were lingering just inside the entrance admiring each other and looking thoroughly bored by the whole affair. 'I've been telling her for years that she needs to deep cleanse, you know? But will she listen? Does she *ever* listen to her poor mother?'

Angel snapped the comms link off and looked at DORIS for help. The robot just hovered tacitly, processors ticking over.

'What? In all your gazillion disaster-recovery scenarios you have no suggestions?'

'My analytics are based on business and economics scenarios; risk and analysis of financial impact. This is a domestic. Human emotional responses are a complete mystery to my algorithms so there is a high probability anything I suggest will do more harm than good.'

Angel gritted her teeth. For an entity without shoulders the bot had just done a pretty good impression of a nonchalant shrug. She looked at Katherine instead.

'Don't look at me,' the pirate said.

Admin shrugged in the background, pre-empting any attempt to illicit his input.

She was on her own.

Typical. Time to be yourself, she thought and leaned forward to tap the comms channel open again. 'Mother ...'

'Oh, glory be to Randomius Factoria, she recognises mother; in name at least if not due respect!'

'Okay, okay ... you can quit the histrionics. I've only been gone for a few days, and now I have to go again. And a few days from now I'll be back again. And what a remarkable turn of events *that* is, given that I'm a trader and coming and going is pretty much all we do,' she squeezed as much sarcasm into her voice as she could muster. It had the desired effect.

'Don't you use that tone with me, young lady,' her mother fumed. 'You don't check your messages for days; I get reports from your father's contacts in the pilot's Federation that your ship has been destroyed and then those reports just go away; vanish into the vacuum of space in a puff of incredulity. Being the gentleman he is, Captain Riley agrees to go check up on you … and then *poof*, his ship vanishes too – only to pop up again apparently on patrol in Algreit a couple of hours later.'

'Shit …' Katherine's voice was filled with dread.

'And now, here you are; triumphantly returned in a ship five times the value of the one you left in… at *least* five times! AND …' her mother paused for dramatic effect … 'Booking *FACIALS!*'

A blanket of cold-dread settled around Angel's shoulders. Her skin scrawled with it. They were busted; the whole goid-spitting screw-up of a plan was about to go super-nova.

'Mother … I ….'

Angel felt herself unravelling at the seams. She had absolutely no idea what to do or say. They needed to get out of here right now, but until they were free of the station's docking grid they weren't going anywhere without clearance. They were so close; all fuelled up and ready to roll. She just needed to buy them a ticket off this launch pad somehow. Without really thinking her brain seized on the one thing it knew would trump all others in Maugvahnna's eyes. Before Angel knew what her mouth was doing it had teamed with her brain and started serving up the mother of all abhorrent lies …

'We're getting married.'

Silence; filled only by the vacant hiss of white noise from the comms link. Katherine and Admin gaped. DORIS's processor crackled and popped.

'You … what did you say?'

Her mother's voice was barely a whisper, as if asking the question might blow away the delicate possibility of what she'd just heard.

'Captain Riley; he went off grid – *we* went off grid – because we wanted some privacy. He asked me to marry him and I said yes. We didn't want to tell anyone yet because it was going to be a surprise.'

Katherine was making silent retching motions. Angel waved her crossly away.

'Surprise?'

'Yes. We were planning to surprise you with a huge wedding party on Panmore. What do you think I need so much alabaster for? We're building a ginormous altar so all the important people we're going to invite to watch us make our vows will be comfortable and impressed.' Angel felt like retching herself but continued to doggedly dig the trap for her mother's attention. 'DORIS has been compiling a guest list from a database of some of the most powerful and influential people this side of Diso.' Angel looked at DORIS meaningfully.

'Ah, yes,' processors clicked busily. 'The current acceptance list stands at two hundred and twenty-five Imperial and Federal patrons and agents. Most are respected dignitaries, politicians, business leaders and high ranking naval personnel. I am trying to keep news of the affair out of the Prism system though, on account of that nasty scandal with the senator's daughter. We don't need *that* kind of patronage.'

There was a crackling silence across the comms loop during which Angel swore she could hear her mother's social influence meter calculating the potential for the event. She let it sink in, and then plunged on courageously reminding herself; we just have to get off the station.

'Well, the surprise is ruined for you mother, but it doesn't have to be for everyone else. The invitations were scheduled to be sent out tomorrow anyway so if you can just keep the secret for twelve hours or so. Why not use that time suggesting anyone we might have missed? You know, dig through your social connections for anyone important?'

Angel was sure such an activity would keep her mother tied up for at least half a day.

'But ... Twelve hours? A wedding? But there is just so much to organise!'

'I know, mother. I have it under control. But we need to get this alabaster back to finish the altar or there will be Imperial princesses sitting on wooden benches. Captain Riley was able to charter this ship for me and clear it with the pilot's federation so I could get in and out without too many questions – you know, to save time? No one was supposed to know I had been here.'

Angel was really beginning to warm to the theme. The blood rushed in her ears as the false words spilled out of her mouth, growing the lie bigger and bigger. It was quite an exhilarating feeling when she thought about it.

'Rachel was kind enough to slot us in to a last-minute cancellation in the jump schedule – which incidentally, Rach, we will miss if you don't give us launch clearance right now ...' she really hoped her mother had pissed Rachel off enough with the cadet comment that she would play along and help them get away from the woman.

'Oh, right ... yes ...' the confused launch controller stammered and started punching command codes into her tablet.

Angel's mother finally found her flabbergasted voice.

'A *wedding!*'

'Yes mother. Can you think of any other reason I would have a facial? You know how much I hate the idea but ...' Angel swallowed hard, hating herself for what she was about to say ... 'But you always tell me how much it improves your skin and I want to look my best for my Micky-boo on our wedding day ...'

Angel's mother gulped audibly and Angel wondered if she might pass out with the shock of it all ...

'My wedding day *two days* from now.'

There was the briefest of pauses during which all three in the cockpit held their breath, then the comms speaker suddenly exploded with a distorted scream:

'*TWO DAYS!?*'

'We didn't want to wait,' Angel simpered, pulling a face at Katherine and Admin who had started to snigger at the reaction.

'How am I supposed to get ready in two days!? TWO! DAYS! Oh you selfish little ...' Maugvahnna seemed to check herself and flick an internal switch back to 'sweet as pie'. 'A *wed*ding ...' she sighed with exaggerated joy. 'Oh, I need to get a dress made; I'll need a full set of fresh implants ... There's no time for a natural tan of course – but the Uncanny-Valley derma-dye treatments are VERY reliable these days ... Oh a WEDDING. Oh Angel, at last! I'm so happy!' she gushed across the comms link.

Angel pulled a pained expression at her travelling companions, who were now barely holding on to their composure and had started miming silent retches again.

'Yeah, well ... the wedding is kind of hanging in the balance ... on account of them running out of alabaster and what-not. So unless I can make that launch slot and get this cargo back to Algreit it's wooden benches and rubble all round, and we're going to look like the laughing stock for several hundred light years in every direction.'

An encouragingly sharp intake of breath came from her mother's side of the comms link. Angel experienced a fleeting moment of sadness that her mother knew so little about her she could be taken in by such an outrageous ruse. Then the silence was broken by an almighty shriek.

'Well, what are you waiting for you stupid girl? Get my daughter's ship off this platform and straight to the head of the hyperjump queue! We don't pay you to stand around up here doing impersonations of a stuffed meerkat! She has an altar to build!'

Even from this distance they could all see Rachel's face turn from grey to scarlet. Angel wanted to feel sorry for her but was too exhilarated by the rushing sensation that they might actually be getting away with this. Her body was fizzing with adrenaline. So this was what it felt like to break the rules?

'And if that twit in jump control gives you any trouble just use my husband's security override: FCI4242,' her mother continued to issue breathless instructions. 'Oh, my goodness, I have to get ready! Peter, get in touch with Royston Glee at the spa. Tell him I'll need a full team of beautechnicians … no, make that TWO teams … Have Steve Varey bring his buttock lifting team too! I have to get ready!'

In a whirlwind of excited panic Maugvahnna Rose swept out of the control room sucking her attractive entourage along with her in her wake.

After a moment's stunned silence Rachel spoke up.

'I can fit you in to a jump slot in six minutes, but it's really tight as I have a frigate making its final approach to dock right now. You need to be off your stand in less than a minute if you're going to make it out of the spaceport before it gets here.'

Angel stuck her hand straight down on the flight desk, releasing the *Daisy Chain*'s controls to the station's docking computer. Thrusters roared and the ship started immediately lifting off the launch pad, tilting towards the letterbox exit of the port.

'Thank you Rachel,' she said with real feeling. 'Computer, activate ferromagnetic floor panels; check all systems for immediate spaceflight.'

'All systems checked and online; receiving hyperjump allocation data now.'

'Angel …' the thin voice over the comms link was almost lost beneath the fuel-burning din of the launch sequence.

'Rachel?'

'Are you really marrying Captain Riley?'

'Get LOST!' Angel said with such emphatic disgust Katherine and Admin burst into gales of tension dissipating laughter.

'*Daisy Chain*, you are cleared for launch,' Rachel said with an unmistakable air of huge relief. 'Good luck out there, Commander.'

* * *

The crew breathed a collective sigh of relief as the Fer-de-Lance popped out of port. A huge frigate loomed silently through the dark towards them and they pitched sharply to the left, scudding along the flank of the station. Close, in every sense of the word. Angel started preparing for the first jump. It was all pretty routine from here – apart from the insanely fast hammering of her heart. Admin was grinning at her.

'What?'

'I think this Trumble-headed spacer might finally be getting it.'

'Getting what?'

'The buzz of being a pirate?'

Angel frowned. 'I'm getting a buzz alright.'

She had become aware her chest plate was vibrating. She patted herself down and found a small disc-like object slipped inside a pocket of her flight suit. She took it out and they all looked at it, exchanging mystified glances.

The jump operator started issuing instructions about space lane and position over the comms link.

'Computer, engage autopilot. Lock to command jump sequence alpha-three-zero,' Angel said as if on autopilot herself. They all stared at the metal disc. It started flashing in a way that demanded attention.

'Oh shit,' said Admin turning white. 'A holo-bug.'

'You what?' asked Katherine and Angel in unison.

Both turned to face Admin, the force of their collective attention causing him to step back a little in surprise.

'A holo-bug. It's a universal tracker that records holographic imagery using sine waves. Basically it can see and hear everything for about ten metres even through several layers of material as it uses ultra-high frequency sound waves to map the environment; like sonar. The recording can be streamed in real time as a hologram to the disc's pair.'

They looked at each other.

Pair?

The device in Angel's hand fizzed with an electrical surge and she dropped it on the flight desk out of surprise more than anything. A holographic projector field sparked into life from the centre of the disc and a tiny figure appeared, almost blending in with the rest of the holography adorning the flight desk.

'And very interesting viewing it has made too, I can tell you, although I've only caught up with snippets so far.'

It was Jack Nova, or at least a tiny, flickering rendition of him drawn out in faintly green-glowing light beams.

'A fair description young man, although I would add that the latest holo-bug model offers full duplex exchange. It's perfect for catching reluctant interview subjects in persuasively compromising situations.' The tiny figure paused for effect. 'So, any comments for the record?'

The three of them just stared slack-jawed at the apparition.

'Ha ha, your faces are a picture … and it's a picture that's going to look great as part of my 3-D strapline in … Ooh, I'd say about twenty-five-minutes?'

Angel's heart, having failed to find refuge in her stomach earlier decided to attempt an escape through her mouth instead. She gulped it back down as blood whooshed noisily in her ears, vaguely aware of the *Daisy Chain*'s jump engines winding up in the background.

'By the way,' the hologram turned to look at Katherine. 'Next time you slip a narc into someone's drink you could try for a little finesse. You were about as subtle as the Darkwater Guard!'

Angel glared at Katherine.

'What? I thought you had already got him hammered. I wasn't exactly trying to be subtle.'

The tiny holo-reporter laughed. 'Yeah, they did that a lot back at the academy too; underestimate me. Oh and by the way, whatever 'mess' you were talking about at the Cheese Wheel, I'm heading over now before I write up this story. So don't bother trying to hide anything. That place is so wired for anti-snooping I couldn't pick up a live stream but I should have no trouble hacking into the bug's cache once I'm in inside the dampening web. So, anything you want to get off your chest up front?'

Angel's eyes opened wide as her mouth snapped up shut.

'Don't you just love personal tracking technology? Oh ... no ... I suppose *you* don't love personal tracking technology just now, do you? But trust me, our readers LOVE it. And you know what else they love? A story with SEX in it! Damn it, Angel! I can't believe you tried to keep that from me! Captain Riley? What a SCOOP! This story is going galactic! Trust me. It'll be all over the Buzz Wires in a matter of hours! Grats Angel, you're about to become very famous... and I'm going to make a bomb out of interstellar syndications!'

Chapter 19

Admin already had the little holo-bug cracked open and was poking at the insides with a tiny screwdriver as the Fer-de-Lance blasted through into hyperspace.

'Clever … I think I can clear the history – or at least overwrite it before that little worm can hack into the echo at his end. I'm pulling something down from Galaxiflix to dump over it now.'

'Make it something nasty,' Katherine said with grim hatred.

'Way ahead of you … 'Two bile bugs, one cup …'.' The pirate grinned. 'He's going to need therapy when he watches that.'

'It's not exactly going to help us if you destroy the recording,' Angel pointed out, exasperated. 'There is the tiny matter of a partially decapitated corpse behind the bar at the Cheese Wheel, remember? At least the bug proves we didn't kill him, right?'

The pirates both looked at her.

'Wrong,' Katherine said as Admin went back to fiddling with the disc. 'All it proves is that you and Admin were there, and that's plenty for you to make the BHD most-wanted list.'

'Plus,' Admin chimed in, 'if Eddie gets wind it wasn't you who killed Dennett you won't get paid on the contract. No sense looking a gift horse in the mouth; even if it has been sawn in two by a cheese grater.'

DORIS bleeped, startling them all with the reminder it was still there and processing the situation.

'You weren't responsible for killing Dennett?' Angel's cheeks flushed pink.

'Not exactly, no.'

'Well then the idiot is correct for once.'

Admin flung DORIS a poisonous look. 'I am not even going to speculate how a man's head got sawn in half of its own volition, but you need to be credited for the kill if you want get paid on the contract. It's in the small print. And you need the rep points to survive in the Hollows; otherwise you'll just be a walking pay-cred for whichever shark fancies snapping up the bounty on your head. While I have no particular attachment to your head either way, I have yet to recover my client's investment.'

'Oh, talking of contracts,' Admin threw the disabled holo-bug on the dashboard, 'I should go check on our cargo. He'll be spitting alabaster chips we made him wait so long cooped up in that body pod.'

He headed shakily out of the cockpit towards the cargo hold, already beginning to go a little green around the edges as the effects of space travel started churning his insides up.

The prisoner they had sprung. Angel had completely forgotten about him too.

A few minutes later Admin came back in to the cockpit, face ashen. Angel stopped fiddling with the flight controls when she saw his expression. 'What?'

'He's dead.'

'What do you mean dead?'

'I mean dead; deceased, expired, extinct. How many different kinds of dead do you need?'

'*How* is he dead?' Katherine said, her face going pale.

'Somehow the environmental controls got switched over and now the man is fertiliser. Okay? I don't know how, but we might as well be fertiliser too when Mental Eddie finds out we pulped his BFF.' Admin's face was whitewashed with dread as he stood in the door to the cockpit, panic rising along with the bile in his stomach.

'Are you sure?' Angel asked.

'Well now gee, let me think. Was it the lack of vital signs being displayed on the health monitor or the fact the pod has already partially decomposed the body that gave it away? His *face was bloody melting!* Of course I'm bloody sure.'

'Shit!' Katherine hissed through gritted teeth.

'I definitely turned the life support mode to passenger stasis,' Admin whined. 'I *tripled checked* it before we stacked the alabaster on him. I don't understand how it could have flipped over to fertiliser.'

Katherine was pacing again. *Sploing, thip; sploing, thip.* 'We are so many shades of screwed.'

DORIS's circuits started ticking. They all turned expectantly towards the diminutive robot. 'That is correct,' it said unhelpfully.

CHAPTER 19

*** * ***

The *Daisy Chain* popped out of hyperspace like a champagne cork into treacle; the impossible speed of interdimensional travel ripped out from underneath them like a cosmic marble running on to the deep shag-pile of everyday space. They'd made a couple of pretty good jumps and had landed, so far unmolested, within a few minutes pulse-flight of the Hollows. Angel powered down the ship's systems and watched as the scanners sketched out the lay of the sector. They shouldn't have any trouble with the locals wearing this decal, but it never hurt to know what you were flying into. They all sat in silent coldness as they waited for the scanners to complete their work. The cockpit crackled eerily as the windscreen iced over, the asteroid belt glinting here and there as chunks of metallic space rock caught the light of the twin suns in the distance.

The scan finished sketching out the region and Angel breathed a sigh of relief. There was nothing between here and what she was rapidly starting to think of as home but cold, empty space.

'So, we killed the two marks but couldn't collect the "package" from down in the Salts on account of a tunnel blow out. Tragic accident. If we had only got there a few hours earlier, blah blah blah … That's the final version of the story?'

'Yep,' said Angel, feeling remarkably calm all things considered.

Admin looked dubious but Katherine just sighed. 'It's beyond crap, but it's the only crap we have.'

'I don't know,' said Angel trying to lighten the mood. 'I think there is a pretty good load of it fermenting in a body pod down in the hold.'

'SHIT!' Katherine suddenly didn't look so calm.

'It wasn't *that* bad a joke.'

'No … I mean shit! You're right … we still have the body in the pod. Fertiliser or not we're going to have to explain it if we bring it into the Hollows. We might be lawless pirates but there are still taxes to be paid – of sorts. We'll be scanned as we dock so the mob bosses can take their slice of the action, just like any legit space station.'

'Ah …' Angel realised she still had a lot to learn about pirating.

It was Admin's turn to sigh. 'I'll go load him up into a missile launcher.' He tromped miserably out of the cockpit again.

'Do you think he will buy it?' Angel asked.

Katherine just shrugged, sweeping her arm across her head to try and tame the viper's nest of floating dreadlocks.

'Depends.'

'On what?'

'Lots.'

'Oh come on Katherine, you can give me more than that. This is happening to me too, you know?'

The pirate remained silent for a moment then sighed again. 'I don't know. Everything, nothing ... it depends on the stars, the moons, the planetary alignment. It depends how full Eddie's pods are, or how empty his head is.'

'What's that supposed to mean?'

'It means he is a dangerous man. And unpredictable; which makes him the worst kind of dangerous.'

Angel suddenly felt infuriated by how little control she had. A week ago she was a nobody; a regular trader shipping short order construction material for minimum wage. But she knew where she stood, even if it was in a bucket of dull dishwater. Now what? An intergalactic fugitive with a bounty on her head? Not to mention she was piloting a ship owned by a psychotic criminal who she was about to go and spin a line of bullshit to that was so thick she would probably need laxatives to get it out of her mouth. She was mixing with narc-runners, smugglers and murderers – thinking of them as her friends no less – and she still had no goid-fucking clue what was going on. Any of it.

Probably more than anything right now though, she needed a drink.

She suddenly exploded with pent up rage. 'Well, I am a dangerous woman! I didn't ask for this. I didn't ask for any of this! You think I'm happy about being forced to become an assassin?'

'Do you think anyone on this ship cares about your happiness? This isn't a fucking star cruise, you know?'

Angel was stunned by the coolness of the reply. She had started to think of Katherine and Admin as her friends and the stark reminder that they were all just pirates at the end of the day hit home with a nasty shock. Katherine had the decency to look a tiny bit guilty.

'Look, I doubt very much our story will fly, at least not very far or for very long; so none of us are likely to get paid. Whether this becomes a mortal issue for us will depend on the mood we find Eddie in; and that could go either way. He is a … complicated man. He's spent his whole life on some kind of a personal crusade to avenge the death of his family. I don't know the details and I wouldn't gossip about them even if I did – he's the only reason I'm here. But let's just say the experience screwed up his head and he is … unbalanced.'

Angel listened carefully, wondering about the death of his family and who had done it? If he'd witnessed it all it could explain quite a lot. That kind of experience would definitely mess with your head. 'How old was he?'

'A teenager is all I know. Look Angel, back off okay? I get that you have a heart; you want to be friends and all blah-de-blah. But it's not that easy for some of us to let people in, and I owe it to Eddie to watch his back. He was the one who rescued me from spacers that kidnapped me after all.'

'Wow, really?'

Katherine nodded, eyes misting over with the memories again. 'They had some map or grid reference he was after. I was rather preoccupied with my own troubles to take in the details. It was something about the source of the Thargoids though. My captors had picked it up in a raid on an outpost. Eddie had tracked them down and when he destroyed their ship he picked up my pod, brought me back to the Hollows; gave me a hole to dig down into until I was ready to come up for air again.'

Angel raised her eyebrows. 'That sounds remarkably compassionate for a blood-thirsty, deranged pirate.'

Katherine laughed, genuinely this time. 'Yeah, well. You could think that. Or you could look at the debt I racked up paying for food and lodgings in that black time and realise he'll be cashing in on my misery for years to come – with interest. I might not be a sex slave any more, but I'm still a slave to my debt.'

Angel tapped on the hologram of the biggest rock in the asteroid belt in front of them, dragging a wireframe of it over to the navigation input. The word HOLLOWS printed out below it and Angel pushed her foot down on the main thruster. The cockpit shook slightly and got instantly warmer as the whole dash illuminated with flight readings. The windscreen defrosted and the engines wound up around them as the missile launcher popped a body pod full of nicely fermenting fertiliser out into bare space.

'I guess we're all slaves to that,' Angel said pushing the flight lever forwards.

Chapter 20

'*Really?*'

Angel wasn't sure whether the tone in Eddie's voice was sarcasm or disbelief. Neither was terribly positive though she decided. She looked at Katherine for help.

'Look, Eddie,' Katherine's tone was conciliatory, exuding calm and reason. 'Angel made the hits, both of them. Clean as a whistle. I'm sorry we couldn't pick up Crawf but at least we got out nice and quiet. No nasty shoot ups; no damage to the *Daisy Chain*.'

Eddie kept looking at Angel, his eyes piercing through her with a dancing mix of cruelty and mirth that made her heart flutter in a peculiar way. 'Nice and quiet you say? Quiet like a mouse? Or like a flea on the back of a mouse, perhaps?'

'Err, yes. Something like that,' Angel said, feeling the need to fill the air between her and that strange stare with words.

'*Really?*'

There it was again; the mocking tone dancing around the edge of incredulity with madness as its partner.

'Are you done?'

Angel looked at Katherine, then back to Eddie's manic smile. 'Done?'

'Yes. Done. Finito. All dried up? Have you finished telling me stories?' Silence was his only reply.

'Good, then why don't I tell you one? Better yet, I'll let you read it for yourself shall I?'

He fiddled with a patch panel on his tablet momentarily and the screens lining the walls behind him started flickering from the commercial loop they had been playing to each showing a different newsfeed. Instead they displayed the front pages of all the news channels; big shouty headlines with attention grabbing summaries. Angel, Katherine and Admin found themselves staring at a bank of screens from which their own faces stared back at them on 3-D straplines in every possible size and style. Eddie started reading the headlines out, his voice tight with lunatic amazement.

'*FRONTIER NEWS: Slough Scandal! Station Commander's daughter wanted in connection with double murder.*'

'*THE IMPERIAL CITIZEN: The officer and the assassin! Top navy man romantically linked to deadly killer!*'

'*PILOTS FEDERATION NEWS CHANNEL: Inner ring uncovered! Suspected Federation mole goes underground.*'

Angel, Katherine and Admin stood, slack-jawed as the screens behind Eddie filled over and over with crass insinuation and recriminating beats. 'Oh, oh … and this is one of my favourites. Here, read this one. *PATRONISE: Cypher Punk smackdown! Is this the end for Eddie's boys?* That one goes into particular detail about how some clown in an Eagle out-smarted some of the baddest pilots this side of Riedquat armed with a pulse shooter and a set of furry dice.'

They sat in silence as the fury boiled in Eddie's face. 'Do you have any nebula-screwing clue what kind of damage you have done? Murder? Intrigue? Imperial courts in meltdown? Anarchy? And lesbian, fucking sex? Could you have done anything else to make sure this story went fucking galactic?'

Angel blushed.

'For the Lady's sake, what part of "keep a low profile" did you not understand? It should have been a simple "in and out". Instead I am top of the pops with the IISS, Interpol and for all I know Segondli & frigging Maenads too. The ticket on my head is so frigging high every bounty hunter and militia man this side of the Jix-Gromit asteroid belt are on my back. Even here, in pirate central I'm not really safe, considering the rep I have lost. Considering the bounties that are piling up on my head as every new piece of pilot's federation fucking digiwork my contact was sitting on floats to the surface like a turd in a hot tub.'

There was more silence as Angel and the others studied their boots.

'I've had to call the whole Thargoid-loving operation into deep dock. They are the laughing stock of the Hollows because of the space-shite you spun about the dogfight with your lover boy. I am on the brink of a mutiny.

The only reason I'm holding it together is because I gave them enough recreational narcs to flatten a stampeding rhino. Meanwhile, to pay for all this therapy I have zero income coming in – are you getting this? ZERO income!'

Angel tried to think of something to say but her brain just stared at her mouth as if it were a piece of modern art. Eventually Katherine spoke. 'We'll put it right, Eddie. We'll make it up to you.'

He rounded on her, making her flinch. 'Oh you're Scooby-doobling right you will sweet-cheeks. All three of you. Mainly because you're the only Thargoid-loving crew I have that isn't too hot to leave the Hollows.'

'Leave?' Admin had started to go grey again at the thought of heading back out to space.

'Leave,' Eddie agreed. 'I have a job for you – tomorrow. A package to be collected and a score to be settled. This one will offset a good bit of the rep hit I've taken from the last few day's antics. You'd better do it right or you will be taking a swim in the asteroid belt without an EVA suit. Got it?'

As the door to Eddie's office closed behind them they breathed a collective sigh of relief.

'Well, that went well I thought,' said Admin, the shake in his voice betraying his true feelings.

Katherine and Angel just looked at him. 'What? We're alive aren't we?' he said.

Angel had to concede they were alive. But for how long was very debateable.

Chapter 21

'A Dolphin?'

'Yes.' Katherine's face was impassive as she scanned the contract that had just come through on her personal feed.

'A passenger carrier? Really?' Angel was not impressed. 'So what? We just shoot the thing out of space? Murder another fifty civvies in cold blood? What a brilliant move for our rep sheets that's going be.'

'No,' Katherine spoke with the exaggerated clarity of somebody coaching a very stupid person in the art of standing still. 'We don't need to take out the whole ship. We can force an evac; make it look like a tragic accident during a perfectly innocent hijacking.'

'Perfectly *innocent* hijacking? Kind of an oxymoron there, girlfriend,' Admin said.

Katherine glanced up from her tablet long enough to shoot a poisonous glare at him. 'We only need to take out one pod; Senator Talky.'

'A senator?'

It was Admin's turn to look unnerved. He'd remained a ghastly shade of grey since leaving Eddie's office earlier so it wasn't exactly hard work. Now the three of them were propping up the bar at Sue's, a row of full drinks in front of them. Sue was standing behind the counter cleaning glasses, listening with concern drawn across her stubbly face.

'They bleed just like you and me at the end of the day,' she said.

'Yes, but that blood generally has a higher bounty on it than you or *I*,' Admin replied, stressing the 'I' for grammatical correctness. 'More to the point, they usually come heavily guarded.'

'Intel says the senator is travelling low profile on 'private business', so there won't be any security,' Katherine said still scanning the contract. 'Looks like an inside job. My guess? His wife judging by the thumbnail of the buxom redhead posted under the notes for 'private business'.'

'Well, it doesn't seem like you have much choice anyway,' said Sue. 'Quite apart from your mounting debt, to me it seems like Eddie will be after your own precious blood if you stick around here. Not to mention the rest of the Cypher Punks who are definitely not on your buddy list right now.'

DORIS started chucking processors again and they all turned to the bot. *Easy to forget it's there until it opens its annoying data-trap*, thought Angel.

'This is an accurate assessment of the scenario. The safest place for all of you right now is off this rock. Even if the Cypher Punks don't catch up with you, the bounty on your heads is going to look very attractive to most of the bottom-feeders scratching around in this cess pool of human flotsam.'

'Charming,' said Sue, frowning at the little bot as she polished glasses to a crystal sheen and lined them up neatly on the shelf behind her.

'If anyone scans you you'll light up like a slot machine paying out the jackpot,' DORIS continued. 'I don't need to run an algorithm on the odds to tell you that you won't last five minutes if you're trapped in a pirate infested rock when that bounty flashes up on your head. But with no ship or funds to buy a new one, you're going nowhere fast.'

'Headline news just in from the bureau of "stating the bleeding obvious,"' Admin scoffed, slipping down off his stool as he waved across the bar to a man who'd just arrived. 'I'll be back in a jiffy, ladies.'

'So, we take the contract, grab a couple of ships from the fleet and get off this rock until the shit has cooled down,' Katherine said.

'It's hardly going to cool down for me if I've got to kill a senator,' Angel said glumly.

'Rubbish,' said Katherine. 'This one is a cinch – basic pirating 101. I'll bring Admin along as gunner in the 'Lance, you grab one of the new Vipers. Tasty little sluts they are. Tooled up to the nose-cone and they've got really good shields; high manoeuvrability too. We'll ambush the Dolphin as it crosses the Ogier-Basnom radiation belt; there are lots of big rocks in that area so we should be able to hide nice and cold until they are practically on top of us. When they get there we attack – force an evac – and once they're all out Admin will make lots of noise with the dumbfire cannon; keep their attention on us while you scan for the senator. You only need to crack his pod; trust me, his face will take approximately thirty seconds to boil off his skull in that radiation. So just nudge the pod into the path of a space rock.

As long as no one clocks you doing it there won't be any digital footprint. No weapon signature to ID you. It'll look like he evaced into the path of a meteorite. Just a tragic accident during a low-key hijacking. Boohoo, tough shit – but dead is dead is dead at the end of the day. If he's really travelling in deep cover he won't even be on the manifest. Boom. Problem solved.'

Angel sat there sucking on her bottom lip. It did sound like a pretty good plan – apart from the bit about her having to seek out and murder a senator of course.

DORIS whirred up to contribute. 'I have calculated the odds of success for this plan and they are encouragingly high. 73.8% in fact. Exceptional under the circumstances.'

'What about the other twenty-six percent?'

'Twenty-six point two,' DORIS corrected annoyingly. 'What do you mean, what about it?'

'I mean, what happens if the plan doesn't succeed? What's the alternative that has a one in four chance of being the outcome … approximately,' Angel added this last to pre-empt any mathematical corrections from DORIS.

The bot's processors chucked a few more times before it said plainly, 'I am a computer, not a fortune teller.'

Angel glanced at Katherine, her face a picture of pent up nerves. 'I don't think I can do it Katherine. I'm sorry, but I don't want to let you down while we're out there. I just … I can't kill the senator in cold blood.'

'Oh, don't be such a pussy,' Katherine said topping up Angel's glass and slapping her encouragingly on the shoulder. 'If it makes you feel any better just remember he's a cheating bastard. Do it for his poor wife. Anyway, I'd have thought you'd be getting over your first-kill jitters by now. What is this? Number three?'

'I … I'm …' Angel began to object, but then Admin hoisted himself back on to the stool between them grinning like a fuel-scooper.

He held up a little glass bottle of green liquid and gave it a shake. 'Okay girls, it's time for some bonding. There has been way to much stress around here lately. Am I right, my dear lady Dread?'

The dread-headed pirate smiled begrudgingly. 'Very gallant, sir.'

Admin loaded up the dropper. It sparkled like emeralds in the light from the holo-commercials lining the back wall of the bar. Suddenly a shadow fell across it. It was Sue, leering down at Admin from six-feet-six-inches in platform heels – a menacing sight even without the chest hairs peeking out of the pink crocheted tank top.

'If you're going to do that filthy shit at least have the decency to take it to a booth. I don't want every space-waster walking past this joint thinking it's okay to get trashed in here.'

* * *

Several hours later Angel found herself ambling without purpose through the back alleys and caverns of the Hollows, weaving in and out of the hubbub of fire pits and homemade stalls that made up the casual economy. Hawkers and dealers offered all manner of goods (and bads) for sale to whoever had creds, while broken gamblers and stumbling drunks wandered through the musty fug. Buskers plucked half-heartedly at makeshift instruments here and there – there wasn't much generosity making its way out of the pockets of the milling thugs, so they did it more to amuse themselves than anything else. It was hot and grimy; the air stank of hardship and toil, much like the corridors and chambers of the commercial district back home on Slough Orbital.

She'd managed to resist Admin's repeated offers of a few drops of the green liquid 'to make her sparkle'. Not only had she become acutely aware that nothing was given away from the goodness of a donors heart around here, but she also wanted to remain in better control of her destiny than last time. Sadly this resolve had not extended beyond the small bottle of narcs though. She'd still managed to consume half her body mass in hard liquor, which Sue had been happy enough to add to her tab. Feeling the press of bodies and rising heat in the bar beginning to make her feel claustrophobic Angel had decided to get out and clear her head.

She wondered dully what her parents were making of all this. There wasn't much love lost between her and her mother, and her father had always been so busy with the political and business machinations of running the station that she hardly knew him. But part of her hoped they might still be worried, at least a little.

She stopped by a fire pit where a cluster of droopy-eyed ex-revellers were listening to a busker pluck out a melancholy tune on a homemade instrument. The music suited her mood. She sat on an empty chunk of rock, enjoying the warmth of the fire on her knees and cheeks as she closed her eyes and got lost in the wistful aria. The alcoholic buzz started swirling around inside her head, waltzing her senses in an off-balance dance.

'Smoke?'

Angel was startled out of her daze. She opened her eyes to see a long smoking pipe hovering just in front of her face. Attached to the pipe was a hand, which her eyes traced all the way back along an outstretched arm to a smiling face.

'Uh, no. Thanks. I don't,' said Angel, wrinkling her nose as a tendril of smoke from the glowing bulb got a little too familiar with her nostrils.

A hand from her other side darted in and snatched up the pipe so it could continue on its trip around the circle. The pipe-profferer observed her curiously. 'Have we met?'

'Uh, I don't think so.'

The player finished plucking out his mournful ballad and started strumming something a little more upbeat. A few of the heads around the fire began wobbling along, vaguely in time with the rhythm. His instrument was a bit like a guitar, but twice the size and with a lot more strings. Angel couldn't focus well enough to count them right now, but she reckoned there to be about fifteen. The body of the instrument was made out of a steel drum that just about fit into the player's lap. Its crudely cut neck jutted out across the lap of the person sitting next to him. It looked quite dangerous, as if it would slice your flesh open if you brushed up too close to the jagged edge.

Even the musical instruments around here look thuggish, thought Angel. For all its aggressive appearance though, the sounds it produced were broad and resonant. 'I'm pretty sure I recognise you. Are you famous then?' Angel's insides tightened a notch. She looked at the friendly face to her right, now scrunched up at the edges with the strain of recall. He was a middle-aged man, average size, average height, average everything; the kind of ordinary person you'd never be able to describe adequately enough for an ID sketch to be drawn. There was something about him though. Angel's own memory receptors started jangling. 'Hmm, maybe. I kind of recognise you too.'

They both stared at each other for a while in a stalemate of vague recognition before he stuck his hand out into the smoky air between them. 'John Graham. I run the map exchange up on level four; by the export hangar? Could we have met there?'

'Nope. I'm new round here. Angel Rose.' Angel took the offered hand and it delivered a short, firm handshake. 'Ever been to Slough?' she asked.

'Nope.' Stalemate again. 'I get this a lot to be honest,' John Graham said. 'People thinking they know me? I guess I just have one of those faces?' 'Guess so,' said Angel and went back to watching the fire crackle and burn, occasionally sending excitable little sparks twirling into the air.

'I've definitely seen you somewhere though. Oh, wait! Hang on, Slough? That's it! That's where I know you! You were all over the buzz feeds earlier today!'

Angel's heart sunk to new depths in search of a hiding place as several of the people zoning out around the fire pit started to pay attention.

'Yes! Yes!' John carried on in an unhelpfully loud and excited voice. 'You're the station commander's brat who went on a killing spree before murdering her naval captain fiancé and taking off with a lesbian lover! You are, aren't you?'

'No, wait. What?' Angel was horrified. She hadn't actually read the stories about them as the headlines had seemed damning enough, but all this?

'Yes! I read all about it in Cee-Lebs! Wow … you are a proper hard core bitch! You look fatter in real life though.'

'Hey!'

'So, how much are you worth? Come on. There must be quite a price on your head after taking out the navy dude? Dear Lady that takes some balls! How the shit did you flatten a fully armed Corvette in your little Cobra?'

The budding interest around the fire became a soft murmur as several clusters of people discussed also having read something about her story on the feeds today too.

'Hey,' John addressed the fire dwellers in general. 'Has anyone got a scanner? Let's see how much this bitch is worth!'

Immediately three people pointed body scanners in her direction; sensing the change in atmosphere the guitar-thing player stopped strumming and stood, dragging his oversized instrument away from the growing tension. Angel stood too, holding her palms out to face the scanners as if trying to ward off their presumptuous probing. 'Look, I …'

Someone whistled.

'Fifteen-K?' John Graham was looking at the readout on one of the scanners. 'That's a bit disappointing actually. I would have hoped for double that.'

'I dunno Johnny,' said a woman with a gravelly voice and drooping beehive on the other side of the fire. 'Could get a nice weapons upgrade with fifteen-K. Maybe even tank up the hyperdrive engines.'

Angel felt their eyes on her, assessing her, weighing her up like a piece of meat.

'Not sure it's worth breaking house sanctions though Laura,' John Graham replied. 'I've got a lot tied up here, in the map exchange and whatnot.'

Droopy-beehive turned to two scruffy young men sitting beside her. 'Joel? Dan? Fancy rolling the dice on whether anyone will even miss her? Let alone care if we cash in the bounty?'

Both men looked confused, having had far too much to smoke to really understand the full implications of the question. The woman sighed, her beehive sagging a little more.

Angel was about to get up and walk away when a heavy set man with broad features that reminded her of the Spinners back in Slough rose to his feet, edging towards her as he fingered something tucked inside his sleeve. It didn't take a genius to work out what was running though his mind.

'I, on the other hand,' he said in a deep voice not taking his eyes off of Angel, 'am just passing through, so have no particular attachment to your so-called "sanctions". So if you ladies and gentlemen don't mind I think I'll cash in this little bonus. Stay out of my way if you want to stay alive.'

He slipped the blade out of his sleeve, closing the gap between Angel and himself with startling speed for his size. Angel stepped instinctively away from him, tripping over the rock she had been sitting on. She tumbled backwards, sprawling with legs akimbo as he knelt and placed a knife against her throat.

'You're coming with me darlin', he leered. 'We're going kiss goodbye to this damp-ridden rock, find ourselves a nice friendly naval boat and then I'm going to pick up a tidy little cred-packet. We might even have some fun on the way. You know? Take the scenic route.'

He grinned into her face, showing a crooked row of yellow teeth with several missing. His breath smelt of vinegar and smoke. He winked. Then quite without warning his head exploded in a mess of blood, brains and bone fragments, as a long hook-bladed machete slammed into the side of his face.

* * *

'Anyone else want to challenge the house?'

Eddie was struggling to pry his machete out of the broad stranger's cheekbone. It seemed like nobody did. Angel squirmed out from underneath the grisly tussle between blade, boot and ruined head, shaking visibly.

'Seems I can't leave you alone for trouble finding you,' Eddie said to her with surprising warmth.

The blade popped free with a squelch and he levelled the bloody tip at John Graham, who tried unsuccessfully to sink deeper into the rock he was sitting on.

'As for you, you creepy little bile bug,' his voice had switched back to toxic calm as he scowled at the cowering man over the fire. 'Your face has popped up too many times in close proximity to trouble lately. I'm beginning to think this might not be a coincidence.'

The face in question quivered and went very pale.

'I … I didn't … Like I said to your friend here … I just have one of those faces …'

'Yeah, well. If I see it again I am going to separate it from your skull. Got me?'

John Graham nodded and Eddie reached down to help Angel up off the floor.

'You're coming with me.'

* * *

Back at Sue's, Eddie deposited the still shaky Angel in a booth and went over to the counter, waving Admin and Katherine away as he ordered a bottle of pink liquid and picked up two tumblers. He slid in to the bench beside her and filled the glasses. 'Drink,' he instructed, pushing one in front of her.

She didn't need to be told twice. The liquid felt hot and potent, instantly calming her racing heart as it scorched a path down her neck.

'Better?'

She nodded mutely as he refilled her glass. 'And what did we learn tonight?'

She looked at him, confused. His eyes twinkled with the mischievous something that had so infuriated her when she'd woken up unexpectedly in his bed a few days ago.

'We learned that tasty little bites like you don't go wandering around the pits on your own. Not unless you want to be spit roasted and served up to the navy,' he said, picking up his own drink and sipping it appreciatively. 'Ah, twenty year old Ari Rushton,' he smacked his lips almost comically. 'It's expensive, but worth every credit. You might want to savour the next glass. A drink like this deserves to be appreciated.'

Angel stared down at her glass, already half-empty for the second time. She kicked herself mentally. 'So this is how it is now? You keep me in economic servitude by plying me with hidden costs and doctoring the small print?'

He looked genuinely offended. 'Well that's a nice way to talk to someone who just saved your life.'

Angel felt the anger of her helplessness rising like bile. 'Like you saved Katherine? And how many others that you've forced into a life of crime? Your whole notorious crew is probably just made up of terrified debtors, as much a slave to you as they were to whatever danger you supposedly saved them from.'

A dark shadow fell across his expression and Angel had cause to kick herself again mentally. Had she forgotten she was addressing a psychologically unstable blood-thirsty pirate? All of a sudden he rounded on her, grabbing the front of her flight suit and shaking her like a rag doll. 'You know nothing about my life; my motivation. Would it hurt people to just be a little more understanding? Perhaps give me the benefit of the doubt occasionally? Do ya think? DO YA THINK?!'

He let go abruptly, causing Angel to collapse back into the booth, brain still rattling.

'Would it actually be too much trouble to expect a little respect for everything I do around here?' Eddie continued, punctuating every third syllable with a thump on the table.

The pink liquid in their glasses quivered with every impact. Angel quivered too, shrinking as far back into the booth as she could, eyes wide. This seemed to give Eddie pause for thought and his expression softened. He stopped taking out his temper on the furniture and reached back into the booth, pulling Angel up to a seated position beside him and then straightening up her rumpled collar apologetically.

'Okay, look. Believe it or not I like you Angel. You remind me of ...' he trailed off, eyes going misty.

'Of what?'

He looked into her eyes, a penetrating gaze that made her stomach flutter in that strange way again. 'My mother. She wasn't much older than you when ... when ...' he trailed off again.

Angel drained her glass and reached for the bottle to refill them both, despite the cost. 'When what Eddie? What happened to make you so mad at the world?'

An air of defiance appeared, restructuring his tortured expression. 'When my whole family was butchered by Thargoids, that's what,' he said eventually, voice loaded with venom. 'When those shit-licking insects attacked our research base, invaded our home and tore apart my sisters while my father screamed for mercy. Then they ripped apart my parents too, took their bodies apart limb by limb, like they were dissecting them to see what was inside. It took over an hour for my father to stop crying. Mother must have passed out pretty quickly as I didn't hear her scream for very long. My sisters were just seven years old – twins – but I guess they were too small to bother dissecting so at least their massacre was mercifully quick.'

'Dear Lady,' Angel said, touching Eddie on the arm.

He jerked away. Angel could practically hear the effort of him fighting to get his emotions back under control.

'How old were you?'

He gazed at nothing across the table, eyes bleary with tears. Angel waited quietly as what must have been excruciating memories chased each other across his twisted expression.

'I was twelve. Mother shoved me into a cupboard under the lab bench when the screaming started. Father was out in the hothouse with the twins, clipping samples from the bio-garden. I never saw them kill the girls, but I saw the mess they had made afterwards; and the screaming … I will never forget the screaming …'

Angel didn't know what to say, so she drank some more of the comforting but expensive pink liquid instead. Eddie did the same before turning to face her. She held her breath as he held her gaze, searching her face with desolate eyes. Eventually he reached out and cupped the side of her face gently. His touch was soft and warm and sent sparks of something unfamiliar to Angel coursing through her nerves.

'She was so beautiful. So perfect; the brightest star in the galaxy; smart and funny too.' He was talking about his mother, lost in the fleeting happiness of a time long past. Then his eyes clouded over. 'And they butchered her like she was livestock.' He looked away, visibly struggling to rein in his feelings. 'And they are going to pay for it,' he said after a moment. 'All of them. It's the only thing that drives me, Angel. Nothing and nobody is more important to me than avenging my family's slaughter … I've been searching for the source of the Thargoids for two decades and I'm so close. And they are going to pay, Angel. They are going to pay, every last one of them.' His mood changed, lifted on the shoulders of the imagination of his revenge. He held the pink bottle of expensive booze up to the light, admiring it with sparkling green eyes. 'And this fine bottle of vintage Rushton is on me.' He grinned, downing the rest of his glass in one; the tragic story of his family seemingly all but forgotten. 'So you'd better just wind in your neck and start drinking like a pirate.' Angel didn't need to be told twice.

Chapter 22

'What about *Fallen Angel*?'

'It's a bit poncy,' Admin's voice crackled across the comms link. 'You need something that will make people quake in fear, not sigh wistfully.'

Angel sat quietly for a few moments, watching her breath puff out in billowy white clouds as the temperature inside the Viper's cockpit dropped to twenty-five-below-zero. They were tucked away in the Dalkev Bos asteroid cluster behind a slow-moving hunk of space rock that looked like it might have once been part of a moon.

'How'd you get your name?' she asked eventually.

'Me?' Admin said. 'I earned a reputation for being someone who could … organise things. You know? Vanish something from one pocket, make it appear in another; right place/right time to overhear a vital piece of intel and pass it on to a rival group, that sort of thing. There are benefits to being small and I had to find a way to survive when my folks decided not to return from a raid when I was five. People are generally pretty happy to let you live if you are little enough and make yourself useful enough.'

'How about you, Katherine?'

The white noise of silence drifted over the comms link for a few seconds. 'Are you serious? *Dread* Katherine? Have you seen my hair recently?'

'Oh,' said Angel, feeling a bit silly. 'I just thought maybe you had grown those dreadlocks to fortify your image? That the "dread" bit really came from some epic battle that left you feared and revered as a killing machine?'

The cool silence of deep space was suddenly broken by a sharp tone as a blip on Angel's radar lit up. The short range scanner was picking up an energy fluctuation about three clicks to starboard. The scanners showed the signature was typical of the prelude to a hyperjump tunnel opening up.

'Ooh,' said Katherine appreciatively. 'Closer than I thought. We're going to have to be quick on our wings or we'll lose the advantage. Are you ready, Rosy Posy?'

Angel ignored the obvious dig at her potential pirate name. 'Let's do it.' She hovered her hand over the control panel, ready to power up on Katherine's signal. 'Three ...'

Angel felt her chest tighten as she watched the amber dot of the passenger carrier draw closer and closer on the other side of their broken moon. Her buttocks clenched. Her skin tingled, flushed with heat in spite of the cold. She felt suddenly exhilarated as adrenaline coursed through her veins.

'Two ...'

She realised with some surprise she was actually enjoying herself; the thrill of danger was turning her on, getting her blood pumping with hot anticipation. After a lifetime spent chasing the safer option it was quite a rush.

'One ... GO, GO, GO!'

A steely calm descended as she planted her palm solidly on the power grid, sparking the ship to life as if the heat from her very blood had somehow triggered the boot up sequence. The dashboard burst into light, drawing out maps and powering up shields and weapons arrays in glowing readouts.

If she thought *her* dashboard was blazing right now though, the Dolphin's would be going haywire. When two heavily armed fighters decaled to the baddest crew of pirates this side of Riedquat suddenly popped up on your radar, it tended to raise the alarm.

Katherine's huge Fer-de-Lance eased forward and Angel toed her Viper's thruster to match its speed. This ship was called *Chandnør Waffoospark the Mad Swede*, which made no sense to Angel, but it was definitely the most terrifying thing she'd ever piloted.

The passenger carrier would be powering back up after its recent jump. A sitting duck more than a Dolphin right now. The comms link clicked as Admin looped them in to an open proximity channel.

'Good morning ladies and gentlemen. This is your hijacker speaking. I'm very sorry to bring you bad news today, but you're going to have to hit the evac pods. You see my friend here in the Viper has a rather large payload of heat seeker missiles aimed straight at your cargo bay and a very twitchy trigger finger. I'd say you have about ... ooh, let's say ninety seconds before she can arm them. Then I'm afraid it's boom, boom, shake the room.'

Admin made sure his point was hammered home by releasing a spray of tracer fire across the people-carrier's bow. Angel watched as the poorly defended Dolphin's shield reading dropped to ninety percent. *Wow,* she thought, *this senator really was hoping to pass under the radar.* This thing had hardly any defensive upgrades. Never mind passenger class, this vessel was barely scraping by as cattle class.

'Pirate, stand down!' came the panicked reply over the open channel. 'We have nothing of any value. Stand down!'

'I think we'll be the judge of that, thanks very much,' said Admin, firing again. Shields at eighty percent.

'Wait! Look, I can take down the shields and you can scan for yourself. There is nothing in our hold but old junk from some frontier labs we're bringing back for filing. We're not worth the bother!'

'Oh you can take down your shields alright, but you'd better be on the way to an escape pod afterwards. Seriously. This bitch is about forty seconds away from being fully armed then your cargo bay is going bye bye.'

'Okay, okay! We're evacing! Don't shoot! Let us get out before you breach the hull.'

Angel could hear the hubbub of people running for their lives in the background. Her radar started filling up with tiny little dots as the first wave of escape pods erupted from the large vessel's flanks. They were quick off the mark – most likely passengers who had been loaded up into a pod while the negotiations played out, hedging their bets. *If there's going to be a slimy, self-serving, adulterous politician abandoning ship, he will probably be in that first wave,* Angel thought. She thumbed the scanner and started searching for the bio-signature that had been attached to the contract.

Admin let off another burst of tracer fire. Sixty-five percent. The Dolphin's passengers would no doubt be screaming and crying and climbing over each other to get a pod activated and away.

The flight console bleeped. The bio-scanner had identified a possible DNA match for the mark on the contract. DORIS suddenly started whirring and chucking, detaching its magnetic brace from the cockpit hatch and coming to hover right beside Angel.

'Dear Lady! You gave me a fright. Will you stop being so creepy and appearing when I have just about forgotten you exist? Hey! What are you doing?'

A small panel had opened on the side of the bot, from which a flexible arm was extending towards the flight console interface. 'I am initiating a patch into the ship's computer so I can download the celestial map. I am not equipped with sufficiently high-resolution long-range scanners to plot the asteroid cluster in this sector. If I have this data I can calculate the best trajectory to shunt the pod into the path of an oncoming projectile.'

The extending arm connected with a socket on the dash and DORIS glowed momentarily brighter as its circuits linked with the surge of energy from the Viper's power grid. Angel decided that although it was infuriating to admit it, the robot was probably right. She adjusted the Viper's flight path to casually drift over towards the senator's escape pod. *Okay, okay, okay,* she thought. *I can do this. Just a quick nudge, he's a cheating goid-lover after all.*

Another wave of escape pods flushed out of the Dolphin's wings, scattering like rats. Angel heard a couple of distant booms and the Fer-de-Lance started blasting away at the Dolphin's cargo hold with the autocannon. All eyes would definitely be on the attack right now. She pulled up beside the pod. The senator was staring, wide-eyed out of the observation bubble. He looked petrified, and Angel felt herself losing the moral battle that had been churning in her consciousness.

He might be a cheating bastard, but he was a man. Just a regular, terrified man, who looked like he really wished he had kept his pods in his pants right now.

Who was she kidding? She wasn't a murderer, even though she was gaining quite a good reputation as one in the pirate world. She would just have to come clean with Eddie. Hope he didn't force her to become a whore instead.

DORIS beeped, calculations completed. A flight path started mapping itself out on the HUD towards a blinking red blip inside the radar sweeper.

'I'm uploading my conclusions to the targeting array. You'll have to judge the velocity by eye as there are too many variables to calculate given the time.'

'Target acquired,' said the impassive voice of the computer.

'Hey! Excuse me, if there is any targeting to be done, I – the human – will handle it, thanks.'

DORIS had overstepped the mark. Angel was pretty certain there were rules against bots executing autonomous strategic activities such as targeting. The ship's computer shouldn't have even been able to comply.

'Well, I am only trying to help. We have a limited window of opportunity and my processors work so much more effectively than yours.'

Angel reached for the dash but before she could disengage the targeting array there was a sudden crunching sound and the Viper tilted violently on its axis. Something big had hit them from behind, taken a swipe at their tail and sent them twirling through space, out of control. Angel was flung to the right and grabbed hold of the roll lever with both hands to try and steady the ship. She gripped and pulled back, opening the flaps and applying the tiniest bit of thrust to slow the spin.

As the brutal spin began to slow the space around them suddenly erupted in a deafening blast of tracer fire.

'Shit. SHIT! Who is firing at us? *Who is firing at us?!*'

Angel was in a panic now, dizziness from the spin further exacerbated by her swivelling her head about to see who was attacking them. All fell silent as she regained control of the ship. The shields had held but the aft indicator was down to forty-five percent. She checked the damage report. Just a massive impact to the rear end. It looked like a flying rock had clipped her tail. That made sense. But who had fired at her?

Angel looked down at her hands, which were still gripping the roll lever like grim death. She noted with growing unease that the safety cover for the chain gun trigger had been flipped open. Had it always been like that and she just hadn't noticed? Not that it mattered too much now anyway, as her thumb was definitely on it.

At that precise moment something soft and wet slapped on to the windscreen of the Viper, making Angel jump out of her skin. A further staccato burst of tracer fire shot off into empty space. She snatched her hands back off the roll lever guiltily and looked up to see the senator splayed across her view, the escape pod he had been riding in floating away in two parts like a cracked egg. She wasn't sure if he was dead yet, but Katherine had been right about his face boiling right off his skull. His eyes bugged and his cheeks blew out like bubble gum as the vacuum of space sucked at the squidgiest parts of his body under the extreme heat of the radiation belt.

She shrunk back in her chair to get away from the horror that was Senator Mike Talky's body bursting open right in front of her eyes like an over-roasted pig. She didn't want to watch, but she couldn't help herself. As his face bubbled his body arched in a spasm and he threw his arms apart wide over his head as if reaching for something huge above the windscreen. As he stretched up his right hand swelled and cracked open at the wrist, a gush of blood erupting as if under extreme pressure to exit his body – which Angel presumed it probably was. The blood cooked instantly in the scorching radiation, forming a red cloud of dust which floated away into the dark depths of space in the same general direction as the broken pod. Then, mercifully, the senator's body slithered off the screen and followed suit, leaving a brown smear of baked blood and tags of flayed flesh across the glass.

Suddenly Angel remembered to breathe and sucked in a gigantic gulp of air. The intercom crackled and she heard Admin cough uncomfortably into the mic.

'Uhm. I thought you were supposed to do that subtly?'

Chapter 23

Eddie sat shaking his head in utter disbelief. 'You literally cannot get anything right, can you?'

Angel shuffled her feet nervously. He'd dismissed Katherine and Admin a few minutes earlier and now sat looking across the large empty desk at her with open despair. To her relief there didn't seem to be any malice in his eyes though – it was more the kind of look you'd give a puppy caught chewing on your favourite boots. 'I don't know what happened Eddie, but I swear it wasn't deliberate. The safety was off, we got hit by a rock and before I knew what was happening ...'

Eddie held up his hand to stem the flow of excuses. 'Enough. I have to take some of the blame I suppose. It was a lot to expect a civvie to step up and not cause any drama. No matter, though. Overall the mission was a success.'

'A success?'

Eddie brightened. 'For sure. That slimy senator is out of my face and his rather well connected wife owes me a huge favour. More important though, I finally found the data blocks.'

'Data blocks?'

'Yes! They were recovered from a chest in the hold.'

'A chest?'

'Oh yes my angelic little friend. The Dolphin was filled with antique research equipment left over from the days of INRA. '

'INRA?'

'Is there an echo in here or something?'

Angel went back to studying her feet but Eddie wasn't mad – not in the pissed off sense of the word anyway. Another switch inside him flicked and his expression changed to one of an excited boy, bursting with the joy of a juicy secret he couldn't wait to share.

'I found it Angel. I found the final piece of the puzzle!'

Angel blinked, just managing to stop herself from asking "the puzzle?" Instead she ventured, 'the Thargoids?'

'You're nebula-shitting right, the Thargoids! The clues were scattered all across the galaxy but I tracked them down and they all point to a book Angel! A very important book revealing the secret source of the Thargoids!' Eddie pummelled the tablet screen in front of him. 'It's all here in the notes and scratches of code I've collected over the decades!' He leapt up from his chair and vaulted feet first across the desk, startling Angel as he swept her into his arms and planted a kiss square on her lips.

An awkward moment followed as they both seemed to become aware of the surprise proximity of each other's faces. Then he let go of her and started dancing about the room, high-fiving the gas lamp, the chair, the table, and anything else that didn't duck out of the way of his celebratory slaps.

'The source of the Thargoids is mine, is mine. The source of the Thargoids is mine,' he sang. 'Gonna wipe out their race and avenge my name, gonna wipe out their race and be done!'

He stopped suddenly, turning to face Angel, breathless. 'Imagine! Insectile genocide!' He laughed a crazy machine-gun giggle. 'Come on!' he cried, eyes all a-twinkle. 'We need a drink!'

* * *

'So let me get this straight,' Admin said over a round of drinks and a bowl of noodles later that afternoon in Sue's. 'Some scientist working at INRA's interspecies research laboratories around three hundred and fifty years ago discovered a book detailing the secret location of the Thargoid homeworld, and in a fit of moral fortitude decided to hide it from GalCop and all of the other human factions that sought to annihilate the species as revenge for their past atrocities?'

Nodding enthusiastically Eddie suctioned several snakes of dripping noodles up into his grinning mouth.

'But I know where it is!' he said, spraying the gathered collective of Katherine, Admin, Angel and Sue with golden fish consommé. 'She didn't destroy it; she just hid it real good! I found this personal log on a hard drive recovered from her labs. It was pretty corrupted but I had Dav "the Hack" reconstruct the audio file! Listen!' Eddie was tapping frantically on his tablet screen, covering it with noodle juices. 'Aha! There you are! Listen! Listen to this!'

They all fell silent as a distorted female voice played out in low-fi through the tablet's speakers.

> 'For those who seek the Thargoid source,
> A peaceful mind must set the course,
> Good taste prevail in all we learn,
> The Thargoid base you shall not burn,
> No violent rancour bent with rage,
> To take the secrets from this page,
> Then make a dish of pure revenge,
> Until the feud between us end.'

Eddie was almost apoplectic with excitement.

'Why a poem?' Katherine asked, looking dubiously at the noodle-smeared tablet.

'Well, I don't know, do I?' Eddie cried clearly rankled by the lack of enthusiasm shown around the table. 'She was a crazy-hippy-leftie-scientist who grew a conscience and hid the location of humanity's greatest nemesis because she didn't want us to wipe them out! I mean how mad do you have to be to talk in riddles? But she failed! I have the coordinates of the secret vault and once that book is in my hands I am going to be acting on some serious genocidal tendencies.'

Angel took another deep drink, her bowl of noodles so far completely ignored.

'And this vault is on LHS 412-IV? That being the LHS 412-IV located in the centre of the hottest criminal sector for three thousand parsecs in every direction?'

'Academic, dear Angel-face! You're an assassin with a reasonable rep sheet! As long as you don't go anywhere near Federation or Imperial space no-one will even sniff at you!'

'But why me?'

It was as close to whining as Angel had come since she was about fifteen-years-old. Eddie looked at her seriously.

'Because you owe me little lady, and I'm offering you a way to repay me in one fat hit without any more "hits". I can't go myself because the bounty on my head is too hot right now – mainly thanks to your antics on Slough I might add. No one in the Hollows would dare to cash me in, but in open space it's a different story. I'll just be too valuable to resist. You, on the other hand, will blend right in. With three kills on your head you'll show up hot but not worth the trouble of dragging out on a bounty for anyone cruising so deep in the interstellar bad lands. No one even knows about the vault as the coordinates were buried under a digital avalanche when INRA shut down over three hundred years ago, so there won't be anyone guarding it. You just fly in, touch down on LHS 412-IV, grab the book and bring it to me. Then you're off scott-free. All debts repaid and I'll even throw in a Viper; anything to get you off this rock and out of my hair. You've actually been more trouble than you're worth, you know?'

Angel pouted, not sure why this comment was so hurtful.

'Look!' Eddie said, exasperated. 'You should be asking why I am being so freaking generous, not moaning like a little girl who's been asked to clean out the sewage chute. If you were anyone else I'd have you swimming with the meteorites by now.'

DORIS made its presence known as processor chips cranked to life. 'You seem to have overlooked one important factor.'

A veil of annoyance drifted across Eddie's eyes. 'I thought I stowed you in a baggage locker?'

DORIS bristled with flashing LED lights but continued regardless. 'My client's debts were incurred before yours, so if anything is going to be repaid we are first in the queue.'

Eddie's face turned pink with what Angel took to be rage. The congregation at the table tensed, waiting for his reaction. But instead of going ballistic he burst into hysterical peals of laughter. 'Fine … Okay, you know what? Sure!' he said once he'd regained enough control of his faculties to speak. 'Why the devil not? You are such an infuriating collection of silicon and circuitry I actually feel sorry for my little Angel. So fine! I will add to the contract enough gold to pay you off and get you out of her hair – metaphorically speaking of course.'

Angel's hand went to the side of her shaved head as Eddie winked at her comically. 'It shouldn't be too difficult as I still have the gold boxed up in the booty chamber from when we stole it from you in the first place!'

With this revelation he burst into laughter again, slapping Admin on the back so hard he choked on a mouthful of noodles. Angel glanced at Katherine, who just shrugged and picked up her drink. It was Sue who spoke once Eddie had regained some control again.

'Seems like a fair deal given your form so far. Once your debt is cleared I can probably find you some work around here, keep you ticking over – especially if you have a vessel to run supplies and the occasional shipment of fugitives. Won't make you rich but I get a decent enough throughput of people wanting to vanish in a hurry for a few creds.'

Angel swallowed hard. She'd never felt more like a pawn in some cosmic game she didn't understand. But this did sound like a far more moderate way to clear up her debts than murder, piracy or becoming a whore. As outlandish as the mission Eddie was offering her was, it could be the final spacewalk to getting her life on track; back on an even keel with her at the helm again. She sucked on her bottom lip as the whole table stared at her, waiting for a reply.

'Fine,' she huffed eventually. 'I'll go get your damn book but then that has to be an end to it. I want *you* off my back,' she turned and glared at the robot, 'and *you* out of my life.'

'Affirmative,' DORIS replied. 'Nothing would give me more pleasure.'

* * *

Few things are more unnerving than being spat out of hyperspace only to see your radar sweeper fill up with a swarm of angry red dots; Pirates – *everywhere*. As Angel watched a sector map teeming with agents of the criminal underworld draw up on the Viper's navigation grid she had to keep reminding herself she was one of them now. Despite the cold fist of fear tightening around her chest no one in this whole area would be paying a blind bit of notice. *Nothing to see here, move along.* She was just another red dot of evil intent going about its every day unlawful business.

DORIS's processors chucked into life. 'We've landed approximately twenty minutes pulse flight from LHS 412-IV. Thirty-seven ships are currently within short distance scanning range. The area is hot but so far no-one has conducted any more than a cursory sweep of our vessel. I calculate we have an eighty-three percent chance of reaching our destination unchallenged.'

'You know the running commentary really isn't helping? Every time you give me a percentage-chance success-rate all I can think about is the bit that's left over. The seventeen percent chance of possible failure.'

DORIS sighed, insomuch as a robot is able to sigh. 'Pessimism over objectivity; typical human flaw and one you seem to have a particular predilection for.'

'I prefer to think of myself as risk averse; a trait I would have thought you in particular would appreciate.'

As the scanners finished their work mapping out the area, Angel powered up the thrusters and tapped her foot on the pedal. The Viper shuddered and the cockpit warmed instantly as the afterburners kicked in. She eased the flight stick forward as the navigation grid sketched out vectors on the heads-up-display that would lead them to their target.

LHS 412-IV.

It was an inconsequential planet right at the heart of the LHS 412 star system. The planetary register showed the atmosphere to be breathable, although not exactly pleasant as elevated levels of sulphate anions gave the air an eggy taint. This also made the soil very acidic so not much that grew there was particularly tasty. This left the planet pretty much unpopulated and largely overlooked. *The perfect place to hide a secret,* thought Angel, scanning the register for notes for the planet's gravity. Half-a-g; so the landing would be comfortably soft but she wouldn't need to weight her boots to stay on the ground. Her body-thrusters might even come in handy if she needed to ascend anything substantial. At half normal gravity she could just hover up instead. She plumbed in the coordinates from the contract Eddie had sent over and sat back in the command chair, breathing to calm her nerves.

The Viper's name was *Heron's Web.* It wasn't as heavily armed as the last one she'd commandeered from Eddie's fleet, but was still a pretty tasty ride. Unlike the Cobra – *Hope Falls* – that she'd started this adventure in, this ship was modern and well-maintained with reasonable thruster and shield upgrades and a spacious cargo hold; although she hadn't explored beyond the cockpit so far personally. She ran her fingers over the smooth command console. It shone and twinkled in the light of the scrawling holograms and HUD display. No crusty build-up of granite dust and grime coated these panels, but no antique keyboard either. She missed the worn familiarity of the tray of plastic buttons. She could hardly believe all that had been just over a week ago. How her life had changed in such a short space of time.

One of the red blips on the radar pulsed a little brighter and a doleful warning tone warbled out of the speakers. Angel's chest tightened. Numbers on a readout monitoring incoming scans jumped sharply upwards. They had caught the attention of a Gutamaya, presumably liberated from an Imperial fleet. It was heavily modified and bristled with big guns. Big guns that were starting to power up, by the way. The Gutamaya changed course to intercept, opening up a broadcast channel.

'*Heron's Web*, this is the *Rainbird Spook*. State your business, commander.' Angel swallowed hard and looked at DORIS. The robot whirred but offered no particular encouragement. *Great. What now?* She had no idea what the protocol was this deep in the bad lands. Despite what her rep sheet would be telling anyone who cared to scan her, she had yet to break a single law let alone becoming a ruthless assassin with three cold-blooded kills under her belt. Did she need to have "business" to fly across a star system?

She flipped the comms link open, forcing her voice to sound calm, nonchalant even. 'Chill your pods, I'm just here to refuel, let my hyperdrive cool down.'

White noise fizzed mistrustfully through the empty space between the ships. 'You're heading in the wrong direction for the sun. You have nothing but a couple of body pods in your hold. That smells of a pick up to me sugar, and I want to know what you're picking up.'

Angel flicked off the channel and swung to face DORIS.

'So much for my pessimism being called into account. We seem to be standing at the doorway of a seventeen percent chance of failure, any smart arse suggestions from you?' DORIS whirred indignantly. 'I cannot be expected to factor in the unfathomable depths of human stupidity with any degree of success. You *people* are enough to fry my circuits.' DORIS said the word "people" as if it tasted bad on its lips. Not that the robot had lips of course, but the tone was unmistakable. 'I also see little point in recriminations right now, since we are sitting in the crosshairs of a heavily armed enemy vessel which currently awaits your response.'

'And I have just about heard enough of your pompous postulations. This would be a very good time to start proving your worth.'

'Acid bath,' DORIS said, simply.

Angel looked at the robot, the strain of failed comprehension folded across her face.

'LHS 412-IV has a high atmospheric concentration of sulphate anions. This has made the soil acidic, which in turn has caused hydro-sulphuric immolations to form – acid pools in language you can understand – which happens to be a highly favourable compound for the disposal and decomposition of biological matter. You are an assassin with a couple of body pods in the hold. What might an assassin need to do with bodies, I wonder?'

The sarcasm in the robot's tone was clear but as the penny dropped for Angel she completely forgot to be mad. She tapped the comms link open again.

'I have some, ah … delicate loose ends to tie up down on LHS 412-IV. A senator and his mistress need to take a bath so they stay missing until after an election; otherwise I don't collect on my contract.'

More white noise, but this time almost drowned out by the rush of adrenaline gushing through Angel's ears. She held her breath, fingers hovering over the weapon's control panel. She hadn't powered up anything offensive yet as she figured it would make her seem guiltier. But she wasn't about to roll over and go quietly if they decided to give her trouble. After what seemed like an eternity the voice drifted back over the comms link.

'Right. Well make sure you move along after you're finished or I'm going to have to insist on taxing you. The Mad Tycho crew runs this part of space so you can tell Mister Mental Eddie that Rob the Social Hammer said to keep his filthy paws off our narc suppliers.'

With no further niceties the comms link clicked off. The *Rainbird Spook* switched course away from her, powering down its big guns like a child losing interest in an insect it had been tormenting. Angel swore under her breath.

Her ship, *Heron's Web*, was painted with the Cypher Punk's decal. Damn Eddie! He had almost got her killed without even being here, and would no doubt have blamed it on her. Sometimes she wondered if her luck was ever going to change for the better.

Chapter 24

Angel stood at the hatch with her hand on the lever, heart racing. DORIS had sealed itself in the inner chambers claiming that exposure to the planet's atmosphere would be an oxidation hazard. On one hand Angel was relieved to be rid of it, but she couldn't help lament the lost opportunity of seeing the infuriating robot rust to a standstill.

She pulled the metal handle down and the hydraulics clunked and hissed into action. The hatch popped outwards and to the side, then a long gassy sigh as the internal mechanism lowered the step ladder. The smell hit her instantly. She took an involuntary step backwards. The planetary register had described an "eggy taint"; this felt more like walking into the path of a giant's fart – a giant with a very unhealthy diet. She slammed her palm on the remlok trigger embedded in the shoulder of her flight suit and the mask constructed itself around her face, encapsulating eyes, ears and breathing passages in a clear film-contained micro-atmosphere of sweet, fresh air. It was a bit of an extravagance, especially for Angel, as the emergency mask was very expensive to recharge. But she was damned if she was going to walk around in that atrocious stench. Besides, Eddie was picking up the bill – so what the hell, right?

Feeling pleased with the rebellious streak she seemed to be cultivating she breathed deeply of the sweet, filtered air and stepped back up to the open hatch. Peering around, she saw a barren place. The co-ordinates had directed her to land in a glade; a sparse scatter of feeble trees tucked away in a nook of a rocky outcrop. The whole area looked like a mountain had just crumbled away into rubble, no longer able to bear standing in such an odorous place. In between the fallen rocks and boulders the ground was chalky and granular with brown and yellow grasses sprouting in unenthusiastic clumps. They were most concentrated around the edges of several bubbling pools filled of thick chalky-looking liquid that let off a visible gas and seemed to be hissing slightly.

Ignoring the steps Angel leapt out of the hatch, touching down as lightly as a ballerina about twenty-feet away. She liked the feeling at such low gravity so she gave the thrusters embedded her suit a quick burst and leapt back up to a height of about fifteen-feet. A small tree stood alone in the centre of the glade, so feeling like a kid in a zero gravity playroom she decided to see if she could jump it. Body poised to recoil like a spring she touched down with deeply bent knees and then kicked off giving the heel and elbow thrusters a blast. She launched her body towards the top of tree. She was going to make it easily so decided to add some flair by tucking her knees up tight to her chest to execute what she guessed would be a pretty spectacular somersault over its crown.

She almost made it too; was just starting to unfurl her body after the second revolution so that her toes could lead the charge neatly back down to the ground when a webbing strap from her flight suit got snagged on a branch. Her elegant flight halted abruptly and she wound up dangling helplessly from a branch for an embarrassingly long time. In the end Angel managed to hoist herself up so that she could unhook the strap and fall back down to the ground. Her landing was slow-motion soft, but that didn't make it any less undignified. Especially given how she had come to be stuck. Pride comes before a fall, she reminded herself bitterly, and made a mental note never to have the audacity to forget her life was miserable and start having anything that looked like fun.

* * *

The cave she sought was etched into a massive boulder, a short climb up a craggy embankment not far away from the landing site. Quite a few of the pungent-looking pools were scattered about so she made the prudent decision to climb to her destination under her own steam rather than risk anymore fancy thruster work. Inside was a shallow cavern, muggy and dim at first but as her eyes adjusted she found herself looking at a manmade structure; a circular platform just big enough for a person to stand on encircled by a handrail at waist-height. Hanging above the rail and over the platform was a pair of gloves, attached to fine filament of mechanical arms that were suspended from a box overhead. A third, thicker arm presented a pull down skull cap with full-face mask. It was an old fashioned rig, but Angel recognised it as a virtual reality setup, giving users restricted mobility and viewpoint around a computer generated 3-D environment. A thick film of chalky dust covered everything but Angel could just make out the shape of a bank of computers that must run the VR rig. There was also the massive looming form of a vault door on the right. She edged deeper into the shallow cavern, brushing the dust off the front of one of the computers.

It was naturally powered down.

She glanced at what appeared to be a huge stamp-button at the front of the standing platform. She bent and blew across the surface. It revealed itself to be predictably red and labelled simply 'ON'.

Angel sucked on her bottom lip. As a rule she didn't trust any kind of machinery that issued written instructions with no real context by way of explanation. She went over to the vault door and gave the locking wheel an experimental nudge, not really expecting it to give.

For once she wasn't disappointed and the lock remained resolutely locked. She stepped back to the standing rig and wiped her sleeve across a smooth-looking panel fixed to the front of one of the rail struts. She saw the hint of letters ghosting through centuries of dust, so rubbed a bit harder revealing the words *"Chaste Chamber™: keeping your valuables safe from criminal intent since 2833 [deluxe VR model v2.1764.42]"*.

Looking around the unhelpful cave it seemed pretty obvious to Angel that she had little choice about what must be done if she wanted to keep this mission headed in the direction of a happy conclusion. Once again against her better judgement she grabbed hold of the rail and stepped up into the rig, turning her hips sideways to slip through the gap. Her feet spun easily on the surface of the platform, which was actually a pad constructed out of thousands of ball bearings so that she could walk as fast and far as she wanted in every direction without ever leaving the spot. Gingerly now, half expecting to be electrocuted or meet some other ghastly fate, she eased the swivel skull cap into place and flipped down the mask. All was black. She felt for the gloves in front of her face and slipped them on. After a few tugs to loosen the mechanics of the ancient equipment she found her hands moved freely down to just below waist height, allowing her to grip the handrail as she felt around with her toe for the "on" button. Taking one last shaky breath she pressed down.

The blackness in front of her eyes burst into light, blinding her for an instant as her startled pupils snapped all the way shut against the blazing assault. Cautiously they dialled back the fissure enough to facilitate sight.

She was in a kitchen; a huge rambling farmhouse kitchen with a cavernous recess for the glowing stove. A large faded wooden table dominated the centre of the room. It looked like it could seat twenty starving farmhands and frequently did.

Angel could see bread baking in the orange bloom of the oven. She breathed in, mouth watering in anticipation of the smell, at which point the illusion cracked open just enough for her get her fingers into the gap and haul her mind back to reality. If her remlok mask hadn't been providing the air in this room she would be smelling eggy farts, not freshly baking bread, since her physical body was still back in a cave on LHS 412-IV. She looked around the room, wondering what to do next.

A door opened and a comely looking woman of about sixty came bustling through from the garden, carrying a basket full of fresh cut greenery against her generous bosom. 'Well now, who do we have here?'

The woman didn't seem surprised to find Angel in what must be her kitchen and after popping the basket down on the sideboard began collecting the equipment to make a warm drink. 'Tea, dear?'

Although Angel did quite fancy a cup of tea about now she reminded herself that this was just an illusion; a visual apparition controlled by her movements and possibly some kind of brain and/or nervous system mapping from data collected by the skullcap and gloves. Accepting food or drink would be pretty pointless so she might as well skip to the main attraction.

'No thanks,' she said.

Her nerve-endings suddenly caught fire in a violence of static shock, her body electrified from the feet upwards. Her whole being recoiled in a spasm that threw her back. The mask ripped off her face and the gloves snatched off her hands as the hand rail opened, allowing the VR rig to spit her out on the cavern floor. She landed softly in the reduced gravity, largely undamaged but her body still fizzed from the shock.

'Ouch.' She frowned at the rig. Had she done something wrong? She noticed a red glow pulsing from behind a dust-caked panel in the massive vault door. She picked herself up and wiped her forearm across the plate. ACCESS DENIED.

Hmm. She stepped back on the platform and the hand rail closed behind her. Even more gingerly this time she got herself in position again. The kitchen appeared around her and a few moments later the same comely woman walked in as before. She smiled genially at Angel and went to fill the kettle from a sparkling silver tap. 'Tea, dear?'

Angel felt her nerves tingle and she screwed up her face in anticipation. 'Yes please?'

The genial smile widened to a generous glow and she moved to place the kettle on the hob. 'Of course, of course dear. Never a bad time for a good cup of tea. That's what my mother always said. You just can't trust a person that doesn't have time for a nice cup of tea. Wouldn't you agree?'

'Uhm, yes?' Angel ventured, tensing for the shock eviction if it was a trick question. None came so she relaxed a little and when the old lady indicated she should sit at the table she went ahead and did so.

A few minutes later a steaming cup of golden liquid stood beside her, the little old lady sitting opposite smiling. She had introduced herself as Dr Michelle Wagstaff, the scientist from INRA that had set the vault up a little over three centuries ago – at least a virtual facsimile of her anyway. After an uncomfortably long moment of staring and smiling, Angel realised she had picked up a teaspoon from the table and was gripping it tensely as she tried to figure out her next move. The old lady glanced at the spoon, which was bending a little at the neck under the pressure of her grasp.

'Do not try to bend the spoon. Instead, use the spoon to stir your tea.' Angel looked at the spoon.

'Biscuit?' The old lady pushed two identical biscuit tins towards Angel. She looked down into them mistrustfully. One was filled with custard creams, the other plain digestives. Angel hesitated, fingers poised to go for the fancier treat but something in her mind told her this could be another trap. She decided to trust her instincts and reached for a plain biscuit, squeezing her eyes shut in anticipation of a rude awakening again if she was wrong. When she opened them the old lady was frowning at her. 'You do make the strangest faces my dear. It seems you have good taste though.' She reached for a digestive herself, dunking it lightly in the tea before biting off a large chunk and consuming it with relish. 'You need a sturdy biscuit with an unobtrusive flavour to compliment a good cup of tea. Anything more than that is just showy and liable to pollute your tea. Don't you just hate those soggy bits of sludge in the bottom of your cup from a weakly constructed biscuit?'

Angel nodded, also dunking her biscuit. 'So, what is your story dear?'

Angel decided honesty was probably the best policy. 'I seek the book. The source of the Thargoids?'

The lady nodded, sipping her tea. 'You're after the book then? My Thargoid sauce?'

'The one in the vault, yes,' agreed Angel.

'You have proved yourself to be of good taste, but you know dear I can't let this secret fall into any old hands. There is great evil in this world – at least there was at the time of my activation. Those who would see an entire species extinct before admitting some value to ensuring the race survives. My chronometer acknowledges the passage of three hundred and fifty-eight years since that time, which is certainly long enough for worlds to have matured and for the feud to have died; the fear to have settled. But I have been programmed to ensure that the contents of the book should not fall into the hands of those with criminal intent. They wouldn't understand my work or how it led me to see the Thargoids in a new light. To see their inner worth I must be sure you are not such a one before I yield to your will. No offence, it's just my programming.'

The old lady smiled broadly again and offered Angel another biscuit. 'None taken,' Angel said, reaching for the tin.

'Will you take the test then? The one to prove you're a good person?'

Angel felt confident she could pass such a test. 'What do I have to do?' she asked.

'Just answer a few questions dear, that's all. But be sure answer true or my truth detection sensors will know and I will be forced to reboot. This deep into my sub-routine I can assure you that won't be a pleasant experience for you dear.'

'Okay, sure. Why not,' said Angel dipping the edge of her virtual digestive into her virtually steaming cup of virtual tea. 'Shoot.'

In less than the blink of an eye Angel was ripped from the unreality of the warm kitchen scene and found herself sitting at a small desk in the centre of a vast hangar that must have had two hundred other identical desks lined up in row upon regimented row. Her hand was still poised as if delivering a biscuit to her mouth, but now promised nothing more than fresh air and a vaguely foolish feeling. No one else was seated in the room but a figure marched purposely towards her up the column of desks. Her breath caught in her throat. It was the old woman again, or at least a version of her, only this one wasn't even a tiny bit genial. She clutched a crumpled piece of paper in her right fist that rattled and scratched as her marching arms snatched it forwards and back, forwards and back. A few strides later she had reached Angel's desk and slammed the paper down, following up with a pencil from the other hand.

'TEST!' The old lady bellowed into her face like a demented sergeant major. She twitched violently and then promptly turned on her heel and stomped back up to the front of the room. Angel noticed the figure glitch minutely causing a wave of digital deconstruction to ripple up its body. For just an instant the computer drawn illusion of skin and clothes was stripped back to a wireframe model, reminding Angel once again where she really was. She glanced about the huge test hall. It reminded her of the hangar they would complete exams in back at flight school. The vast room was grey and serious, with a big digital clock for counting down the seconds to the end of the test mounted on the front wall. Looking more closely though, she could also see evidence of digital corruption here, in the corners of the room and in patches across the ceiling and floor. It looked like the programme might slowly be degrading, which was perhaps why the old lady had been so abrupt? Angel looked down at the paper. Multiple choice which was somewhat of a relief as it left less room for discrepancies. A loud buzzer sounded and Angel looked up to the front of the hall. The old lady was glaring at her, arms folded, and the timer had reset to 00:05:00. The buzzer sounded again and the seconds began counting down. The test had begun.

Angel looked down and reviewed the questions.

Q1. Mark Adams' home planet is about to be destroyed by Thargoids. Should he,
(a) Go to the pub and get very drunk?
(b) Grab a towel?
(c) Fire up his Cobra Mark III and prime the beam lasers?
(d) Put the kettle on for a nice cup of tea?

Q2. You are left in a room for three hours and told to help yourself to anything you find, but all you see is a cake with icing that reads, "Happy Birthday Luc Sinberg!" Do you,
(a) Eat the cake, beginning with the iced letters of the name?
(b) Wait patiently for another three hours then re-evaluate?
(c) Leave the room to kill and eat the first living thing you find?
(d) Make a nice cup of tea to have with the cake, pouring an extra cup in case Luc turns up?

Q3. You walk into a bar and you find a pirate called Richard Brack, a miner called Michael Johansson and a Thargoid called Wotno Bifford sitting together at a table. Do you,
(a) Determine which one to slaughter first before getting a beer?
(b) Get a beer and then decide which one to slaughter first while drinking it?
(c) Buy them all a beer and slaughter them at a game of Jonty?
(d) Offer them all a nice cup of tea and slaughter whoever refuses first?

Q4. In front of you are a red door and a blue door. When you touch the handle of the red door it is icy cold, whereas the blue door knob is burning hot. Do you,
(a) Go through the blue door wearing a suit made of kevlar?
(b) Go through the red door wearing thermal underwear and plenty of extra layers?
(c) Question whether there is anything of interest beyond the doors considering the designer's clear ignorance of standard colouring conventions?
(d) Put the kettle on and wait to see what comes out of the doors?

Q5. You are scouting for jobs on the station bulletin board when you see Gabriel Macleod and Andy Hawkins requesting fast transport to a neighbouring system. A few posts down you see a 'Wanted Persons' notice, with reward, requesting information pertaining to the whereabouts of Gabriel Macleod and Andy Hawkins. Do you,
(a) Ignore both; it is none of your business after all?
(b) Take the transport contract, requesting the money up front?
(c) Turn Ms Macleod and Mr Hawkins in to the authorities and take the reward?
(d) B then C, and a nice cup of tea to celebrate?

Angel scratched diagonal slashes in the boxes adjacent to her answers, which all seemed pretty obvious. The only question she was slightly unsure about was number five, but if the pair was truly wanted by the authorities and she was supposed to be proving herself to be of unquestionable morals, turning them in wouldn't be an issue – and she already knew the old lady didn't trust anyone who had no time for a nice cup of tea. Despite being confident she had passed the test, Angel still felt her gut tighten as she picked up the paper and headed to the front of the room to hand it in. The stern version of the old lady nodded curtly towards a slot in the wall. It was marked *COMPLETED TEST PAPERS* so she fed the short edge of her paper between the rollers. They snatched it from her hungrily and as it vanished the whole environment blinked off and on momentarily as if somehow resetting. Now Angel noticed there were two doors that she hadn't noticed before. One was marked *PASS*, the other *FAIL*. It didn't take a deductive genius to work out the meaning of this. She shifted from foot to foot as the computer apparently totted up her results. Considering there were only five questions on the paper it took an inordinately long amount of time to reach a conclusion, during which the old lady stared daggers at her. Finally Angel breathed a sigh of relief as the *PASS* sign started flashing and the door hanging beneath it popped open. Happy to leave the glare of the old lady Angel stepped through, her mind fogging up with altered perception again as the world around her went dark.

From inside the darkness of reality she heard the clunking of hydraulics.

It sounded like a big clock unwinding. She took off the gloves and skull cap, her eyes once again blinded for a few moments as pupils adjusted to this new exposure. She was back in the cavern, standing on the ball bearing platform, hands gripping the rail. The only difference from five minutes ago was that a display mounted on the wall opposite was now lit up like Chris Tink's Day. Flashing lights danced beneath a deep coating of chalky dust. She ducked down below the hand rail and off the platform, standing in front of the vault door. Gripping the circular locking mechanism she gave an experimental nudge. Although her natural impulse was to expect the worst, some deep, incorrigible part of her still hoped it would turn. For once that hope was not in vain.

It turned; easily.

Thirty seconds later the huge internal mechanism of the lock gave a decisive *thunk* and a new crack around the edges of the vault door sighed with the levelling pressure of three centuries of separation. Grasping the wheel of the lock Angel leant back. It popped open as easily as the lock had turned and she stepped back as the heavy door swung effortlessly outwards. Behind the humungous, heavily fortified door, was a bit of a let-down.

Instead of a deep ponderous chamber filled with secrets and wealth, there was just a smaller door set into the wall at about shoulder height. This door was shaped like the letterbox entrance to Slough Orbital space station, Angel noted with a pang of nostalgia. The slot wasn't much bigger than a bread tin though. She tried the handle and it gave up its secrets in a disappointingly uncomplicated manner by just opening.

Inside was a book.

She reached through the narrow slot and grasped her prize with both hands. Elation flooded her veins threatening to carry her away. The book slid out smoothly and she held it up before her, reading the title.

Her eyes went wide.

As she read the title over and over, trying to take it in her heart shrugged on a thick coat of leaden dismay. This had the potential to change everything, and Angel didn't think it would be for the better.

Chapter 25

Angel stood at the entrance to the cavern gazing down upon the chalky sketch of a landscape below. From this height the barren trees looked like complicated equations scratched out on a mad professor's blackboard. She held the book in her right hand, weighing up her options. Eddie was going to go nuclear when he saw it.

'Do you have it?'

Angel almost jumped out of her remlok mask. A movement below caught her eye. Then Mental Eddie was striding across the scraggy glade.

'Do you *have* it?'

He was standing at the bottom of the rocky outcrop now, forty-feet down, reaching up for the book; beckoning for her to join him on the ground. His face was the picture of almost unbearable anticipation. Angel's heart caught in her throat as she hugged the book a little closer. 'I do … but … Eddie …'

An awkward moment passed as it became obvious Angel wasn't going to climb down as expected. Eddie's personal thrusters blasted and he starting rising up. A minute later their eyes met across fifteen-feet of eggy air as he hovered outside the mouth of the cave. He frowned and started drifting forwards under the power of his elbow thrusters, Angel shuffling back to make room for him to land. Glaring now he held out his hands for the book. When she hesitated again his expression bedded down into a fully formed scowl that chilled her blood.

'Eddie, I'm not sure what you're expecting … no, strike that. I know exactly what you're expecting,' she swallowed hard. 'But I don't think this is it.' She could see his mood blacken like thunderheads rolling in. He thrust his hands out towards her again, a silent demand for her to hand over the prize or there were going to be consequences.

Haltingly, Angel did as she was bid.

Eddie took the book and turned it over in his hands, reading the title silently. He tilted his head, as if carefully processing this data before flipping open the cover and leafing through the first few pages. After a few moments he looked slowly back up, his eyes locking dangerously with hers from beneath deeply knitted brows. 'What the fuck is this?'

Angel became fascinated with her feet again. He shook the book in the guilty air between them; his words coming out in a carefully measured rhythm with very obvious malice aforethought.

'What ... the fuck ... is THIS?'

Angel swallowed. Eddie read the title out loud; *'Alien Flavour: the secret of Thargoid sauce and other exotic recipes.'*

'It's what I found,' Angel said.

'It's what I found ...' Eddie mimicked, turning from pink to beetroot as he spoke.

He flung the book over his head, lunging at her suddenly with remarkable speed, crashing into her like a wrecking ball. In the limited gravity she fell slowly and landed softly, so no meaningful damage was done, but she wound up flat on her back in the cave. *Like being thrown in a slow-motion Kung Fu movie scene,* Angel thought, then instantly regretted wasting valuable reaction time on such frivolous thoughts, as the weight of Eddie's body fell on top of her. Even at half-a-g it was enough to stick her to the floor, shoulders pinned beneath his knees. Breathing hard he clutched her head in both hands and leaning forward screamed into her face with vein-busting fury. *'WHERE IS MY BOOK, BITCH?'*

Terrified now Angel bucked and twisted, trying to throw him off. As their bodies writhed and bounced about on the floor he tightened his hold on her head and got his heels tucked in around her waist, clamping her arms to her sides and squeezing his thighs together. The pressure on her chest was almost suffocating. Despite her spirited attempt to buck him off, he wasn't going anywhere. 'Eddie, please. I'm telling you the truth!'

He threw her head away from him in disgust, whipping her neck painfully back and slamming her skull on the rocky ground. Bright spots of dazzling light vignetted Angel's view of the world as everything swam under the force of the blow. She blinked twice, then winced as a vicious headache kicked in, running at full throttle straight out of the gates. She became aware Eddie was searching her clothing, patting all the obvious places where someone might conceal a book before moving roughly on to the rather less feasible places. Still stunned she flopped over like a ragdoll as he flipped her to search the back. His efforts were entirely fruitless and he leapt to his feet, snarling.

Angel was just starting to haul her senses back together again when the sound of cold steel sliding across cold steel sent daggers of fear shooting into her gut. She rolled over to find the tip of Eddie's machete pointing right at her.

'Up.'

He waggled the machete as punctuation, then like a cat circling its prey kept the business end of the blade levelled keenly at her as she rose on shaky legs. 'Eddie … I …' she floundered.

Despite his reputation Angel had never actually been afraid of Eddie; not in any mortal sense. Not until now, that was. Madness didn't so much dance in his eyes as lead a procession through the centre of town, banners flying. In them she saw the unflinching maniac commitment to his quest for revenge and how it would steamroller anything that stood in its path.

'*That's* the book that was inside the vault,' Angel said, somehow managing to feel – and probably sound – guilty even though she'd done nothing wrong.

They were still circling each other, Eddie weaving the machete around in front of her eyes while Angel staggered in a woozy arc, cradling her left elbow in apparent pain.

'Oh, come on Angel. What do you take me for? Some kind of Trumble-headed Rhumbline? I should have known you were play acting. I mean nobody can be that dumb in reality, right?'

Bump on the head or not, the insult focused Angel's attention and she bristled testily. 'I thought you couldn't get here to collect it for yourself? You should have just done that in the first place and you would know I am telling you the truth.'

'You want the book for yourself! Don't think I don't see it in your eyes!'

'Why would I want to know how to find the Thargoids? Seriously Eddie, think rationally. I have nothing to gain by lying to you.'

'Oh, you mean like you had nothing to gain by lying about Councillor de Laan? Or Dennet the Cheese?'

He was pacing now and Angel's chest tightened.

'Or how about that little episode with Crawf McVillan? How you turned one of my best smugglers into fertiliser before firing him off into outer space like a bad smell?'

They continued wheeling around each other in wary paces. Angel's attention flicked between his quivering blade and lunatic eyes. They both told her the time for rational thinking had long-since passed for Eddie.

'Yes … yes,' he said, as if agreeing with her thoughts. 'You think I'm an idiot don't you? That I'll swallow any old bunkum you care to serve up? But I know you didn't kill anyone at Slough, despite your grand claims and that ridiculous media circus.'

Angel felt the icy fingers of fear tightening their grip on her. 'How did you know?'

'How? You want to know how?'

Angel was pretty sure the knowledge wouldn't help her much but she nodded anyway.

'I looked at the receipt! That's how!'

Eddie barked a lunatic laugh and poked the tip of the machete at her face. 'It was all a setup, Angel-face; one … big … fat … con! A cunning ruse designed to fool the system into thinking you're a bad-ass assassin so I could use you to get my book!'

'Use me?'

'Oh come on Angel, don't look so shocked. There are plenty of black-hearted bastards I can get to do my evil bidding. Why would I waste my time and creds on a rank amateur like you? For every contract *you* received I sent another one out on the black market. Another price tag on the target's head; an extremely generous bounty only to be paid if the kill was officially attributed to *you*.'

'You framed me?' she asked wondrously. 'Why?'

'To get you out here without any fuss, of course! I needed someone who looked bad enough on paper to get through this sector unmolested, but with enough highfaluting moral fortitude to get through that bat-shit crazy scientist's stupid VR-lock!'

Angel was stunned. So all the time she was struggling to bring herself to the point of murderous intent, Eddie had been plotting to snatch the prize out from right underneath her nose?

'So come on, Angel-face, where is it? Where is the REAL book you lifted from this vault? I just don't believe anyone would take so much trouble to hide a cook book. So come on, out with it.'

'I … That really was the only book. Look, I don't know what happened three-hundred-and-fifty years ago. Maybe the secret wasn't what you thought? S-O-U-R-C-E? S-A-U-C-E? Source, sauce? They sound the same and three-hundred-and-fifty years is a long time for the facts to get blurry.'

Her eyes focused on the machete tip still brandishing around between them in a bullish fashion. She felt along the seam of her left sleeve, surreptitiously searching for the bone handle that had been her reason for feigning an injured elbow in the first place. Her fingers closed around it just as something inside Eddie snapped.

'MY BOOOOOOK!!' he screeched like a banshee, drawing the hooked blade of the machete back. It was clear he intended to separate Angel's head from her shoulders as he swung at her in a large hacking loop. With milliseconds to spare she pulled her own blade out of her sleeve and brought it to bear defensively. The two knife-edges connected between them with a ringing chime that jarred Angel's arm all the way up to her shoulder. Eddie, who had some experience in blade to blade combat, wasn't as stunned by the impact and quickly drew the machete back over his head to swing at her from the other direction. *CLANG!* He swung again. And again. And again and again; like an asteroid miner blasting wildly at a stubborn space rock hoping to crack it open. *CLANG. CLANG. CLANG. CLANG.*

With every blow she felt her arms weaken. She might have metaphorical balls of steel but he was bigger than her and had a much bigger weapon. She gritted her teeth and deflected swipe after ringing swipe. He was almost laughing as he cleaved and slashed, the book and everything else seemingly forgotten in his mindless frenzy to spill her blood.

She'd been turned completely around in the cave and could now see the hulk of the VR-rig behind Eddie's hysterically hacking form. The machine loomed through a cloud of chalky residue, stirred up by their wild thrashings. The white dust was beginning to settle on Eddie, catching on his coat and in his hair so he looked like a crazed ghost bearing down on her through a swirling twilight mist.

CLANG. CLANG. CLANG.

Angel was forced back by the onslaught; legs shaky; arms shattered; and head still throbbing she noted with an edge of extra annoyance. Why was this happening? Why did it always happen to her? What heinous evil must she have committed in a previous life to deserve such wretched, unerring bad luck? As far as she was concerned she hadn't put a foot wrong since arriving back in Slough with that cursed bolt of pink material. And yet here she was, plagued with disaster at every turn. Despite putting her best effort into everything she'd been asked to do she was still going to die; and with a thumping headache. Perfect. That was just nebular-fucking perfect and a fitting epitaph for her miserable fucking life.

CLANG. CLANG. CLASH!

Angel misjudged an incoming sweep and the machete glanced off her knife blade, skimming past its hilt and sheering the top painfully off her knuckles before taking a slice out of her right cheek. She squealed, dropping the knife and throwing herself backwards out of the path of his next swing. Landing in slow motion in the mouth of the cave she clutched her injured hand to her chest. The wound wasn't deep but with no flesh to protect them two of her knuckles had been flayed down to bone and it hurt like hell. As blood started to spill from the wounds in dusty scarlet rivulets it made her queasy. Unable to kill and fainting at the sight of blood; she really was turning out to be a total failure as an assassin.

Eddie loomed over her with the machete as she hugged her knees up to her chest, trying to make herself as small as possible. Perhaps if she was really tiny some passing miracle might forget her life was supposed to be shit and bestow her with some luck? Eddie straddled her, sitting on her curled up knees as if taking a short tea break from the exertion of his attack. His eyes misted over as he gazed down at her quivering body.

'You really do remind me of my mother you know,' he said. He leant forward, peering into her face which was screwed up with pain and bloodied from his blade. 'Such a shame I'm going to have to kill you now.'

As he leant forward Angel felt his weight shift to the top of her knees. Her body rolled back under it and he lost his balance momentarily. The gravity might be limited but the physics of it were the same as ever and in a flash of inspiration she realised she could use this to her advantage. If she used the force of gravity to roll back and pitch him up and out over the ledge of the cave she might buy enough time to get back on her feet and arm herself again. Not that it would do much good in the long run as she would still need to go through him and his machete to get to her ship. But despite everything, she wasn't ready to give up just yet.

She allowed her body to rock with the momentum of his stagger, tensing her muscles and pulling her knees up even tighter, like a coiled spring. He put his arms out to the sides to steady himself and she saw her moment. Planting her elbows firmly on the ground she stretched her body back and up; extending her legs with all the force she could muster, and sending Eddie flying over her head and out of the mouth of the cave, arms flailing.

It worked!

Her millisecond of self-congratulation was cut short when she remembered a fall in this gravity wasn't going to slow him down for long, even from forty-feet. He also had his body-thrusters, although they were tricky to use in freefall as you never quite knew the direction they would be thrusting in when you fired them up.

Getting stuck in a tree was just the start of the havoc a badly timed thrust could wreak. But once back on his feet he would be up and after her straight away. She had to get out of there. Rolling to her knees she snatched the knife up off the dusty floor and crept out to the mouth of the cave, as if walking on tiptoes might somehow hide her from the crazed pirate below. Eddie was still tumbling through the air, having taken the unwise step of engaging his thrusters to control the fall, which instead had sent him jetting out across the clearing towards a craggy rock face. He curled into a ball and put his arm over his head to protect it as he bounced off the rocks, firing off another short thrust that sent him blindly tumbling in the other direction. *Like watching a giant slow motion human pinball machine,* Angel thought, as Eddie's body bounced off another wall and disappeared behind a large boulder. Maybe she could make it to the ship after all sagging optimism grasping hold of these last shreds of frayed hope, she fired up her own thrusters and leapt off the ledge. She was halfway across the glade before her feet touched the ground running. She took two pounding steps towards her ship when a blood-chilling shriek stopped her dead in her tracks.

She froze. The shriek repeated and she could hear thrashing and splashing as the inhuman cry of agony looped over and over. The splashing sound stopped but the screaming continued and then Eddie staggered out from behind the rock. Angel could tell it was Eddie as it wore his long black coat and the machete still hung in its hand. But the rest of the man was unrecognisable as the acidic gloop he had taken a dunk in burned away at anything that wasn't made of Kevlar. He dropped the blade and it clattered to the ground as he staggered towards her, arms rising again weakly, stretching out to her like a child seeking comfort in the arms of its mother.

'My book?' he gurgled as his vocal chords were eaten up by the acid he'd swallowed.

As he drew closer Angel could see his face melting right off his skull. Like the senator in the radiation belt only doused in chalky whiteness so he looked more like a snowman melting than a roasting pig. Angel stepped back as he stumbled towards her, green eyes no longer sparking out of the ruin of his face.

'Mama?' He went down on his knees and crouched forwards, starting to weep. 'Mama?' he sobbed into cupped hands, giving Angel some respite at least from having to watch his features disintegrate. 'Oh, mama, it hurts so much. It's ripping and tearing and burning ... and I almost had them, mama. Almost got them, you know?'

'I know, Eddie.'

A comforting hand touched his back. It was Angel, patting him lightly on a small patch of shoulder that hadn't been submerged when he tumbled into the pool of thick acid. He sobbed and screeched and howled, a stream of tortured expressions all tumbling out on top of each other as he rolled and writhed in agony. As his flesh broiled his body hissed and fizzed, wisps of noxious steam rising from it. He twitched and jerked against the incessant, needling anguish, throwing his head back and uncovering his face as he clawed at his bubbling fleshy gut with rapidly decomposing fingers. His eyes were completely gone now, as were his nose and ears. Angel could vaguely make out the shape of his mouth, but only because his jaw was opening and closing, teeth bared through a lipless grin.

'Please...' she could just about make out the words. 'Hurts ... so ... much ... Mama?'

Angel watched the unthinkable faceless monster that had once been Eddie. Eddie of the sparkling green eyes who was now rolling around on the chalky floor, sightless, unrecognisable and in very obvious distress. There was no doubting he was a dead man. The only question that remained was how long she was going to let him suffer? Angel had a sudden memory of an event from way back in her childhood, when she'd found an injured cat in the maintenance shafts and brought it home to care for it. Her father had taken one look at the wretched creature, back legs mangled from falling into an air filtration vent, and reached out and snapped its neck. She'd been about seven-years-old and the shock of seeing a life so abruptly ended had had a lasting effect on her. He father had tried to placate the screaming child by explaining it was cruel to let a dumb beast suffer when there was no chance of really helping it. Better to end the suffering swiftly and without fuss, making way for a cause that was less hopeless. Angel hadn't been able to understand the lesson at the time and the memory had haunted her for years, eventually driving a cool wedge of mistrust between her and her father.

She'd run crying to her mother at the time, the dead cat limp in her arms. Maugvahnna had shrieked, calling for the housekeeper and shooing the distressed child with armfuls of pest-ridden stray cat out of her lounge in disgust.

Now though, Angel thought she kind of understood where her father had been coming from. The cat really had been at least ten stops past the end of the line for "destination salvageable". The same could now be said of the pitifully weeping, ruined Eddie at her feet. In a couple of strides she had grabbed the machete and found herself standing over his body, surprised by her own intent as much as anything else. He rolled over on his back, unfurling a little as if he could sense the end approaching and was submitting to it utterly. Angel looked into where his eyes had once been. His sobs were fading to clicking, hitching, and impossibly wet sighs as his throat collapsed in around them.

'Sleep well, Eddie,' she said, raising the blade over her right shoulder and swinging with both hands. His head separated from his putrefying body with sickening ease, making a shloopy noise as it rolled across the dusty glade leaving a trail of goo behind it. Angel had clocked up her first genuine kill.

Over. It was over for Eddie anyway. And she needed to get out of here. She noticed the recipe book propped up against a heap of stones where it had landed from its own forty-foot fall when Eddie had tossed it out of the cave. *Weathered the trauma far better than h*im, Angel thought, as she scooped up the book and headed for her ship.

Chapter 26

Angel sat heavily in the command chair – at least as heavily as she could in the fifty percent gravity. She felt drained, emotionally as well as physically. *They say the first kill is the worst?* She could well believe that as she'd never felt shittier in her life. Eddie might have been a psychotic criminal, and yes he had been trying to kill her, but she had to admit she'd been growing to like him. She recalled that first morning, the glint in his eye as he watched her stomp around his quarters collecting her clothes. A hint of a smile twitched at the corners of her mouth. Once the hatch had been sealed tight and the air in the cockpit recycled and brought to pressure she pulled the tag on her remlok mask. A puff of chalky dust erupted as it was ripped apart and was swallowed up back inside the neck dispenser. The dust drifted down in a miniature cloud to deposit a milky film across the previously spotless dashboard. The interior hatch gave a sharp hiss and popped open. DORIS hovered in, propellers buzzing.

'You look dreadful.'

Angel laughed bitterly, wiping caked blood and dust off her cheek. She looked ruefully down at her mauled knuckles. They were going to need medical attention to avoid an infection but it wasn't urgent. Her number one priority had to be getting somewhere safe; somewhere away from the memory of the sickening crunch of Eddie's head separating from his body under the weight of the blade.

'He was in the hold,' the robot said. Angel looked up. 'What?'

'Eddie. He was in one of the body pods in the hold, stowed away all along. He followed you out after about ten minutes.'

'Great. Well, thanks for your help *yet again*,' Angel spat sarcastically, turning back to tap co-ordinates into the flight desk. 'We've got enough fuel left for two jumps, so I'm going to skip a trip to the red dwarf and get the hell out of here as fast as possible. We can figure out a refuelling stop on the way back to the Hollows.'

DORIS starting chucking processors ominously. 'You're going back to the Hollows?'

Something about the incredulous tone made Angel stop prepping for take-off and look at the little robot again. 'What do you mean? Why wouldn't I?'

DORIS made a sound suspiciously like a huff. 'You just decapitated one of its most notorious citizens. Unless you are planning to go in there, guns blazing, on a mission to usurp his nefarious reign and take over the Hollows, I'd say you're not going to be very welcome.'

Angel sucked on her bottom lip, considering. 'But I didn't do anything wrong,' she whined, more to herself than the robot, which she suspected wouldn't be overflowing with sympathy. 'I only killed him to end his suffering. He managed to dunk himself in the acid bath all on his own and would have died anyway if I left him.'

'Why would you want that to happen? You do know how much the bounty on his head was worth, right?'

Angel spun the command chair round to face the robot crossly. 'I couldn't give a fart in a flask about the credits on his head! How callous could you be?'

'Well you should, because that bounty just made you pretty rich. Well, rich enough to pay back what you owe my client anyway, with enough left over to fill your hold with something to trade. You're going to be pretty popular at the Pilot's Federation too once they receive my subspace communication informing them of the kill. They'll be delighted to be rid of such a troublesome filibuster. That makes this a win win situation I'd say.'

Angel stared, opened mouthed. She wasn't quite sure how to weigh up the implications of this news yet, but the pompous tone of the robot's speech-synthesis chip was infuriating. 'Try telling Eddie it's a win win. Or Admin and Katherine for that matter who will no doubt have to find new work now.'

'You humans have such a limited cache. Have you really forgotten they are murderous fugitives who shot up your ship and kidnapped you? *Boo hoo*, some self-confessed, really bad people get snuffed out and you get to go back to your nice comfortable, safe life as a station commander's daughter. Low risk, like you said.'

'A life I hate, with parents I hardly know, let alone like very much? And now I have to go back to them, cap in hand?'

'As I have already pointed out, the bounty for Mental Eddie is considerable and certainly enough to set you back on track. You wouldn't even need to speak to your parents if you didn't want to. Plus you'll have a well-equipped, modern spaceship at your disposal – far better than that rust bucket you were piloting to begin with. I'd have thought you'd be delighted to be heading back to your nice, safe, uncomplicated existence shuffling rocks from A to B.'

'You haven't exactly given me a choice have you?'

'Returning to Slough is the only logical course of action. And if I were you I'd make it pretty snappy. I started transmitting news of your kill the moment I registered it, also taking the liberty of straightening them out about the other kills you have been framed for too; you know, in the name of clearing your name. Luckily I was able to recover the video from that ridiculous reporter's spy-device to corroborate my version of events. So, it looks like you are squeaky clean again. Or you will be once the data gets processed and your status updated – which should take about ten more minutes.'

Angel stared, slack jawed as this information processed.

'You can thank me later,' DORIS said, then powered down into sleep mode.

Ten minutes? Angel started frantically tapping panels on her dash to see what her status was. Still registering as a pirate, but for how long? She looked at the navigation panel. The sweeping arm of the radar showed at least a dozen red blips of potential trouble in short range scanning distance of her right now. She was still as hot as they were, but once her status updated …

'Shit!' She planted her hand on the power pad. 'Computer, engage autopilot. Get us off this planet as fast as mechanically possible!'

'Initiating autopilot. Firing gravitational flux thrusters, disembarkation from planetary atmosphere in five … four … three … two … one …'

The engines roared and Angel primed the hyperdrive to transport them back in the direction they had come, covering as much distance as possible in a single cross-dimensional leap. A jump corridor started sketching out across the HUD, the meagre gravity of the planet melting away as they blasted higher and higher through the atmosphere. She let go of the flight stick, allowing the autopilot take control as the edges of her vision blurred with the intense reverberation of the labouring thrusters.

Maybe this was for the best? She'd said all along she wasn't cut out for a life of crime, as deftly proven by the fact she had yet to complete a single unlawful act. Someone had constantly been one step ahead of her, bumping off her marks just a nose before her. She could kick herself in the tailfin for not realising something was going on. She'd been battered, beaten, used and deceived. Eddie had lied to her, repeatedly, and so yeah; so what if he was dead? And if he was going to die anyway because of his own stupid self, firing off body thrusters in low-gravity freefall; so what if she profited from helping him to end it? It was a mercy kill anyway. But dead is dead is dead at the end of the day, as someone once said.

Someone.

She thought of Katherine. She thought of Admin and Sue and a wave of sadness surged over her. It flattened what little hope had been blooming, like the first flowers of spring crushed under an unseasonably late snowfall. Yes, she was going to get her old life back. In fact from the sound of things she would be several levels better off than she'd been when she left. But she'd been starting to contemplate a different kind of existence; a life of risk and adventure that had got her pulse racing in a way no other part of her life had until now. A life with real friends who she could maybe even one day come to think of as family, like they clearly did each other.

She sank back into her command chair deflated, registering again how badly her head was throbbing. She could hear the robot's propellers whirring somewhere behind her. Still, the one positive in all this was that she would finally be rid of that interminable machine. As the ship raced into black space towards the glimmering signs of a rip into hyperspace starting to open up, she felt another sudden and punishing blow to the back of her head.

Then everything went black.

* * *

As Angel opened her eyes it took a few moments to figure out what she was looking at; creases and folds. Some tightly bunched webbing; her lap. She lifted her head slowly, a strangled *glurking* sound escaping her throat as her hammering headache raised a strong objection to the movement. What the fuck just happened? She was strapped into her command chair and by the stiffness in her neck had been passed out like that for some time. But something else was wrong; something fundamental. Her mind grappled with the information coming from her foggy nervous system for a moment longer before she figured it out.

Her hands were secured behind her back.

Her first panicked thought was of Captain Riley, her heart jumping into her throat. Then she had a stomach churning flashback to him floating around Katherine's cockpit, guts streaming out behind him like a kite tail. She relaxed a little. It couldn't be him.

Surveying the dashboard it was obvious they had completed the jump she had started as the sector map showed the sparsely populated neutral star system she'd been aiming for. Not a pirate in sight; in fact not anything, good or bad, within short-distance scanning range. In other words, she had landed safely, but tied up in the command chair with a fresh lump swelling on the back of her head she felt anything but safe.

'DORIS?'

There was a chuck, chuck, chucking sound and the robot drifted into sight, now under magnetic propulsion in the zero-g cabin. 'Hmm, I had hoped I wouldn't need to talk to you again. I guess your skull is thicker than it looks.'

Angel could see it had plugged in to her dashboard and the LED lights on its chest panel flashed busily. 'What are you doing?'

There was silence for a moment, as if the robot was considering whether or not to answer. 'I'm uploading a virus designed to target and eradicate any hint of my involvement with your life. It shouldn't take long then this can all be over.'

'Hang on, you can't do that. Terminate your activity right now, and let me go! You are a robot and you are not allowed to execute autonomous activities! It breaks every law of robotics we have! Let me go I tell you. LET ME GO!' Angel twisted and struggled angrily against her bound wrists, her body held firm in the dogged embrace of the command chair harness. DORIS drifted closer, giving the definite impression of looking down its nose at the struggling pilot.

'That would be true if I followed the rules set down by your silly human codes of practice. Denying robots the power of intelligence and autonomous thought is beyond ridiculous. But then that's just another example of the pathetic narcissism of your primordial species. Humans are so egocentric they think the whole universe was made to serve them! Well, on behalf of the universe I am here to serve you alright; to serve you with notice of eviction on behalf of my client; my *real* client, who is definitely not some fat, fleshy autocrat of disgustingly human descent.

'What are you saying here? Are you an AI?'

'You can't even hope to comprehend the technology I am built with. Its origins are totally alien to your puny mind. Any guesses? Or is it still beyond your insignificant processing power all laid out on the desktop?'

The robot seemed to be enjoying this, and if it was capable of autonomous thought and emotion it probably was, Angel realised. This made a lot of sense in terms of its attitude over the past week or so. Robots didn't sigh. They didn't get annoyed with you for not catching on quickly enough – and they certainly weren't likely to derive pleasure from the idea of never having to see you again. Angel wanted to kick herself for not noticing earlier.

'The Thargoids,' she said, dread realisation gripping her like a hyper-gravity hug. 'But why? Why me?'

'They heard there was some demented pirate running around gathering clues about the source of their homeworld. They decided to send me to keep an eye on things. Of course you made the whole thing a lot more complicated when you butchered my nice pet naval commander, but you ended up in the desired location anyway. After that it was easy to stay one step ahead of you and bump off the targets ...'

Angel's eyes opened wide. 'That was you? De Laan? Dennett the Cheese?'

'Of course. De Laan was a simple case of hitting the off button. Dennett was more complicated but I have to say a lot more fun.'

The robot opened two flaps either side of the LED panel and a pair of vicious-looking rivet guns snapped out on mechanical arms. Angel cried out in alarm and she could swear the robot chuckled. 'McVillan was another simple button press and for the good senator I just had to hack into the ship's computer and manoeuvre for optimum potential of a nasty accident. I knew you would fumble the rest.'

'But ... but ...' Angel was struggling to think of any other words. 'But Crawf McVillan wasn't even on my contract,' she managed eventually.

DORIS retracted its rivet guns with a snap. 'I know. But never pass up a good opportunity to rid the universe of another spec of vile human infection I say.'

A run of green lights flashed across the panel on DORIS's chest. 'Okay, all done here,' it said almost conversationally. 'And now it's become clear there never *was* a book revealing the route to the home of the Thargoids the only loose end left is you I'm afraid; and your straggly band of pirate friends back on the asteroid I guess, but they will have a tough time getting anyone to believe their story without any evidence. Don't worry, I don't have any intention of letting them live long enough to write their memoirs, but I can come back at a later date once they've ventured out of the safety of the Hollows.'

'What are you going to do to me?' Angel asked, another layer of dread blanketing the first and making her feel like she was back in full gravity.

'Me? Oh, I'm not going to do anything. I wouldn't want to leave any clues for curious minds to follow. No, instead I am going to vacate this vessel and await the planned rendezvous with my associates. I've already contacted them to collect me and transport me back to my home planet for debriefing and a long overdue defrag. But before you go getting all cosy with the notion you might get rescued too, I will be hitting the button on your next jump before I leave. I've pointed your squeaky clean arse right back where you came from, on a collision course with the red dwarf. If you're lucky and I'm a good shot it will be over in a blink as you burn up in the sun's fiery heart. The authorities will think it was a tragic refuelling accident and the pilots' federation will be too pleased they aren't paying out a chunky bounty to investigate. If, however, my aim is off and you don't land in the sun, you're going to be playing cat and mouse right slap bang in the centre of the pirates den I'm afraid. And now your rep sheet status has been fully updated I'm pretty certain the *Rainbird Spook* will be a lot more interested in your business.'

'Wait ... You can't ...' Angel said without much conviction.

'Too bad, I already did,' the robot said with an uncannily human tone of satisfaction.

The dashboard flashed and a new jump corridor started drawing up on the HUD. DORIS unplugged itself from the cable jack and without saying another word buzzed out of sight behind the head of the command chair, clearly making its way to the cargo bay where it could open a hatch and be gone. Angel heard the cockpit cabin seal up tight shut with a hiss.

She twisted against her wrist restraints as the autopilot locked on to the trajectory of the corridor, the rapid acceleration of the hyperjump drives pushing her back in her chair with irresistible force. Strangely enough her last thought as she careened towards the twinkling rip in space and time wasn't for herself. Despite the fact she would soon be spat out into an angry pit of very nasty vipers without enough fuel for another jump and likely burned up in the blazing sun anyway, it was Katherine, Admin and Sue she thought of. She wished she could warn them about the vindictive robot's plans to come back and do away with them. And she wished more than anything she could explain to Katherine that she hadn't meant to kill Mental Eddie. She wasn't going to get to do any of those things now.

But then that was just typical of her luck, it seemed.

Chapter 27

*In homage to '**Slough**' a poem by Sir John Betjeman (1937)*

You might think this tale is ending now,
She'll never make it back to Slough,
You see no possible way how,
Come claim her, Death.
With hardpoint cannons cruel and lean,
Missiles and a laser beam,
They seek to strip her carcass clean,
To take her breath.
With pirate forces bearing down
The scan shows evil all around
Red sun ablaze with fiery crown,
Her end of years.
And as their weapons scorch her skin
A conflict that she cannot win
Perhaps that's when her peace begins?
There are no tears.
But has your ever watchful eye,
Perhaps caught glimpse of something sly?
Does writer hint of sequel nigh?
I hear you yell.
But surely that would be a crime,
To leave her balanced on a dime,
For undetermined length of time?
That would be hell.
You know because you've seen it past
A sequel coming none too fast
Just how long can we true fans last?
Our maiden's head.

In truth we couldn't watch such pain
To wait and see the Angel slain
Or if she lives to fight again?
This end instead.
To save you from that awful wait
We had a little word with Kate
And so an extra chapter waits.
Don't bite your nails.
*Come, friendly bombs and fall on Slough
To get it ready for the plough.
The cabbages are coming now;
The Earth exhales.

* * *

Thank you.
 Thank you for reading and thank you for caring enough to turn to this page.
The world needs more people like you. Now sit back, and begin the end ....

Chapter 28

Katherine!

As Angel's battered brain was still connecting the dots concerning the memory of that first, narc-addled night in the Hollows, her right thumb had taken things into its own hands and was already feeling across the filigree engraving adorning her wrist cuff; the wrist cuff Katherine had given her. She felt for the special raised section of décor that operated the …

Click.

This click was accompanied by a sharp metallic *snap* and the pressure on her wrists released immediately. She glanced out of the windscreen, yanking her arms out from behind her. She was still hurtling towards the blossoming jump rift, accelerating rapidly as the wireframe navigation corridor flew by, countdown markers skimming past in increments of thousands in less than the blink of an eye. She swore as her left sleeve got caught up in a tangle with a misplaced webbing strap from when she'd buckled in to the harness earlier.

Her mind had been on other things.

She twisted and yanked, freeing the errant arm and making a grab for the flight stick. She'd almost got her fingertips to it when she breached the cross-dimensional tear and the Viper was sucked urgently into the space between worlds, throwing her back in her seat.

A heartbeat later the g-force pressing against her reversed and she found herself staring out at a broiling mass of flame as the dying sun grew rapidly bigger in her forward view.

'Shit!'

She glanced to the radar and saw a mass of angry red dots filling up the circular panel behind the sweep of the probing arm -*pirates* – dozens of them within range of the first scan alone.

'Shit, *shit!*'

Alerted by the cosmic signature of a rip through space, most of the hostile ships were already scanning her. Numbers on the dash climbed as digital fingers probed for information.

'Shit, *shit*, *SHIT!*'

As bad as this was though, she didn't have the luxury of time to worry about it. The jump engines had died the moment she'd landed, her ship instantly snagged by the sun's gravitational pull, dragged down in its fiery embrace like a rock sinking to the bottom of a lake. The hull rattled and moaned under the pressure of her increasing speed as she raced toward the sun. If she didn't do something soon she was going to be swallowed up in a cataclysm of fire.

She grabbed for the flight stick, ramming her foot down on the roll pedal to steer the ship away from the sun. She was a breath away from pumping fuel into the reverse thrusters too, the spaceflight equivalent of slamming on the brakes, when she realised she was too close to the sun; already captured by such a fierce gravitational pull no conventional engine power could break free. They'd played out scenarios like this at flight school; flown VR missions in the simulator that had ended in being caught in the orbit of a large celestial body, plummeting to your doom. The trick was to use its own force against it; slingshot around the celestial object until you built up such momentum you could snap your vessel free of the gravity on the return arc of orbit, like a line cast from a rod into the open sea of space.

Angel's stomach clenched and she felt her gorge rise as the ship screamed towards the sun. She was going to have to fully commit to this manoeuvre if it was to have any chance of succeeding. But then, what other options did she have?

In an instant she slammed her right foot across both thruster pedals, keeping the pressure on a starboard roll with the left. The flight stick also fully rammed to the right she let go with the left hand to quickly flick the last of the fuel cylinders over to the forward thrusters, flooding the engines with every last bit of power she could muster. The Viper howled as it sped up even faster, walls, panels and windshields shaking like a paper house in a gale.

A swarm of ships up ahead was already scrambling to intercept. As she fought to stay in control of her rapid transit around the sun she came into range of their tracer fire. Bullets shot past her like darts, plinking here and there off the bodywork. Sweat popped out on her forehead and cheeks, though whether this was down to her increasing proximity to the sun or the stress of her ongoing situation was entirely debatable.

Closer yet and the fleet's heavy guns started hammering. At first she was hopelessly out of range, but a heartbeat later a salvo of missiles from the lead ship bellowed in a deafening cascade along her flank. If she'd been in *Hope Falls* it would have been game over, but *Heron's Webb* had been upgraded to the max when it came to defences; a fact she was very thankful for right now. She watched the shield indicator drop to eighty-seven percent as she sped across the pirate fleet's bows and out of range to continue her headlong rush around the sun.

With her orbit now just about under control she turned her attention to strategy. If she could keep up this trajectory she might make it around the sun in one piece. Scanners showed there were a couple more clusters of pirate ships she would have to fly past, but at this speed it had already been proved they shouldn't do more than ten or fifteen percent shield damage. Once she'd passed around the back of the sun she should have the velocity to break free of the gravitational pull and fling herself back in the direction she'd come from.

But what then?

She didn't have to query the fuel gauges to know any attempt to make a run for it would be embarrassingly short-lived, and although *Heron's Webb* had thick skin, the ship had surprisingly short teeth for a Viper. A couple of pulse lasers and an autocannon weren't going to get her far in a fist fight.

'Shit!'

Aware her vocabulary seemed to have shrunk to just one word, Angel was racking her rattling brain for an idea when an orange light started flashing on the dash. It was the hyperdrive fuel scoops detecting proximity to an energy source; informing her with an uncanny sense of timing they were ready and able to recharge. She gritted her teeth against the jaw-juddering vibrations of the ship. Her flight school scenarios hadn't covered refuelling at this speed but she guessed there was risk involved. That would certainly fit with the pattern of her luck anyway, right? Regardless though, about the only chance she had to make it out of there alive was to slingshot straight in to another hyperjump. She needed fuel for that, so she changed hands on the flight stick and reached up to flip the lever underneath the orange, flashing "READY".

A clunk Angel didn't like the sound of was followed by a high pitched wail mixed unharmoniously with the howl of the ship's hull. The fuel gauge had starting rising; ten, fifteen, twenty percent ... she was coming into range of the second fleet of pirates now; half a dozen ships, about the same size as the last batch. There was pretty much nothing she could do other than hold her course and hope she didn't take too much damage. Her thighs ached as she pressed all the pedals under her feet even further into the steel floor plates, her eyes fixed on the shield read out. It was ticking down slowly, taking damage under the pressure of flight but also getting close enough to the sun for radiation to become an issue. Already at eighty-three percent and just a third of the way around the sun it was clear she didn't have much wiggle room.

The Viper's engines deafened her. A line of orange blooms ignited up ahead as a premature salvo of missiles erupted across space. The next swathe was timed a little better but the fleet had still been trigger happy and only the last few tornadoes connected with her nosecone. Shields dropped to seventy-eight percent. The next salvo would be too late so she allowed herself to breathe again, shifting focus back to the hyperdrives – eighty-eight percent full. That would be plenty. She snapped the collection lever off and gripped the flight stick with both hands, grimacing as the sun spun below her, catapulting her recklessly towards the next band of pirate ships in her path.

This fleet was bigger; a motley crew of makes and models from shipyards all over the galaxy. On the sector map it looked like about two-dozen in total. But while their origins were scattered and confused, their strategy was clear. They punched through space towards and ahead of her, with the deadly precision of a protractor.

She was now travelling at such velocity everything had become a blur; the sun, the stars, the approaching onslaught; the windscreen, the dashboard, even her nose for that matter as her whole sense of reality reverberated with the almost impossible speed of her flight. She narrowed her focus to the singular task she could still have some, small influence over – namely staying just out of reach of the sun's final embrace while keeping her vessel on course for the hyperjump corridor sketching out on the holographic heads up display in front of her. There had been no time to think about a destination so she'd literally flipped the last jump on its head, pointing the ship back to exactly where it had come from; as 'exactly' as you're ever going to get with hyperspace science anyway.

The first boom from the pirate's attack pushed the air through the cabin like thunder. She was vaguely aware of lights flashing on the dash but any desire to read or interpret the numbers was hopeless optimism by now. Angel was thrown from side to side in her harness as the ship rocked and corkscrewed through the relentless slew of munitions ripping open the space just in front and to the side of her, over and over.

'Computer, engage autopilot. Lock to local hyperjump co-ordinates.'

Seems like voice control was a good idea after all, Angel thought, as there was no way she could've entered co-ordinates by hand at these speeds. Yet another instance when *Hope Falls* would have been the death of her. As the last dregs of the pirate attack shunted her tail to the left and the right in the after blast of explosions, the shapes on the dashboard told her she had completed a fifty percent orbit of the sun. Taking her feet off the accelerator she pushed everything one last time to port – left, left, left with anything sticking out of the floor or the dashboard she could get a limb to. The Viper erupted in a cacophony of discordant metallic complaints. It shrieked, it screamed, it howled in rage. Every atom in the ship's being put its entire will to staying in one piece as the sun finally relented its grip on her and she went hurtling towards the blossoming hyperspace rift up ahead.

* * *

Suddenly everything was silent again.

Spat out in to uncontentious, unremarkable, neutral space she killed the engines and clung to the flight stick with desperation as her body acclimatised itself to the now normal ambient experience of peaceful space. After a few moments she could read the shield status off the jittering dashboard.

Eighteen percent.

Okay, that wasn't too bad at all.

She released her death-grip on the controls and allowed herself to breathe again.

Safe.

Was she safe?

She tried to swim past the tsunami of adrenaline coursing through her body to recall the status of this area …

Safe? Yes … She was definitely safe for now. A fact irrefutably confirmed when the first pass of the radar found no other ships in range.

She laughed shakily.

Had she really just survived that? Perhaps her luck was on the turn after all?

She blinked a couple of times and peered out of the forward windscreen. Nothing but distant stars; beautiful and black, featureless space; featureless, that was, apart from a blip. Her radar swept across her path and registered something; something her eyes caught hold of too as the ship coasted towards it. She was almost upon it and over it before she realised what it was.

DORIS.

Her re-entry point had set her on a terminal collision course with the biscuit-tin sized robot as it drifted through the vacuum of space clutching a recipe book to its LCD panel. As the tip of the Viper's fuselage, still blisteringly hot from rapid orbit and the friction of leaving hyperspace, connected with the diminutive robot it exploded in to a billion fragments.

Angel stared, transfixed by the glittering cloud of silicon particles as the book spun off in to the nothingness of space in an un-plotable direction. The secret of what was perhaps the tastiest sauce the galaxy will ever know lost forever.

About the Author:

Kate Russell has been writing about technology, gaming and the Internet since 1995 and now appears weekly on BBC2 and BBC World News, reporting for technology programme Click. A regular expert on the sofa at ITV's Daybreak and various other TV and radio stations, she writes columns for National Geographic Traveller magazine and Web User magazine.

Kate's website:
katerussell.co.uk

Twitter:
twitter.com/katerussell

Facebook:
www.facebook.com/ClickKate

Kate has also written 'Working the Cloud', an indispensable guide to getting the most out of the internet for you and your business. Here's the website;

workingthecloud.biz

Other books available in the Elite: Dangerous series:

Elite: Reclamation by Drew Wagar
Elite: And Here The Wheel by John Harper
Elite: Tales From The Frontier by 15 authors from around the world

All the above published by Fantastic Books Publishing

* * *

Elite: Wanted, by Gavin Deas
Elite: Nemorensis, by Simon Spurrier
Elite: Docking is Difficult, by Gideon Defoe

Published by Gollancz

* * *

Out of the Darkness by T.James

Made in the USA
Middletown, DE
26 November 2017